*"You're the most courageous man
I've ever known,"*

Jessica said, sliding her hands over his shoulders.

At the word *courageous,* Devon looked up at her. "Don't say that. You don't know—" He bit off the statement and turned away. After a moment he spoke again, more softly this time. "I'm not the man you think I am, Jessica."

Then he turned toward her, searching her eyes. And the dark sensuality in his own eyes made her tremble.

Dear Reader,

Welcome to Silhouette **Special Edition**...welcome to romance. Our New Year's resolution is to continue bringing you romantic, emotional stories you'll be sure to love!

And this month we're sure fulfilling that promise as Marie Ferrarella returns with our THAT SPECIAL WOMAN! title for January, *Husband: Some Assembly Required*. Dr. Shawna Saunders has trouble resisting the irresistible charms of Murphy Pendleton!

THIS TIME, FOREVER, a wonderful new series by Andrea Edwards, begins this month with *A Ring and a Promise*. Jake O'Neill and Kate O'Malley don't believe in destiny, until a legend of ancestral passion pledged with a ring and an unfulfilled promise show them the way.

Also in January, Susan Mallery introduces the first of her two HOMETOWN HEARTBREAKERS. Was sexy Sheriff Travis Haynes the town lady-killer—or a knight in shining armor? Elizabeth Abbott finds out in *The Best Bride*. Diana Whitney brings you *The Adventurer*—the first book in THE BLACKTHORN BROTHERHOOD. Don't miss Devon Monroe's story—and his secret.

The wonders of love in 1995 continue as opposites attract in Elizabeth Lane's *Wild Wings, Wild Heart,* and Beth Henderson's *New Year's Eve* keeps the holiday spirit going.

Hope this New Year shapes up to be the best ever! Enjoy this book and all the books to come!

Sincerely,

Tara Gavin
Senior Editor

Please address questions and book requests to:
Silhouette Reader Service
U.S.: 3010 Walden Ave., P.O. Box 1325, Buffalo, NY 14269
Canadian: P.O. Box 609, Fort Erie, Ont. L2A 5X3

# DIANA WHITNEY

## THE ADVENTURER

*Silhouette®*

SPECIAL EDITION®

Published by Silhouette Books
America's Publisher of Contemporary Romance

If you purchased this book without a cover you should be aware that this book is stolen property. It was reported as "unsold and destroyed" to the publisher, and neither the author nor the publisher has received any payment for this "stripped book."

To my daughter, Holly Hinz Newland, of whom I am very proud. Thank you for being so very supportive. Your dad and I love you a bunch.

 SILHOUETTE BOOKS

ISBN 0-373-09934-7

THE ADVENTURER

Copyright © 1995 by Diana Hinz

All rights reserved. Except for use in any review, the reproduction or utilization of this work in whole or in part in any form by any electronic, mechanical or other means, now known or hereafter invented, including xerography, photocopying and recording, or in any information storage or retrieval system, is forbidden without the written permission of the editorial office, Silhouette Books, 300 East 42nd Street, New York, NY 10017 U.S.A.

All characters in this book have no existence outside the imagination of the author and have no relation whatsoever to anyone bearing the same name or names. They are not even distantly inspired by any individual known or unknown to the author, and all incidents are pure invention.

This edition published by arrangement with Harlequin Enterprises B.V.

® and TM are trademarks of Harlequin Enterprises B.V., used under license. Trademarks indicated with ® are registered in the United States Patent and Trademark Office, the Canadian Trade Marks Office and in other countries.

Printed in U.S.A.

## DIANA WHITNEY

says she loves "fat babies and warm puppies, mountain streams and California sunshine, camping, hiking and gold prospecting. Not to mention strong romantic heroes!" She married her own real-life hero twenty years ago. With his encouragement, she left her long-time career as a municipal finance director and pursued the dream that had haunted her since childhood—writing. To Diana, writing is a joy, the ultimate satisfaction. Reading, too, is her passion, from spine-chilling thrillers to sweeping sagas, but nothing can compare to the magic and wonder of romance.

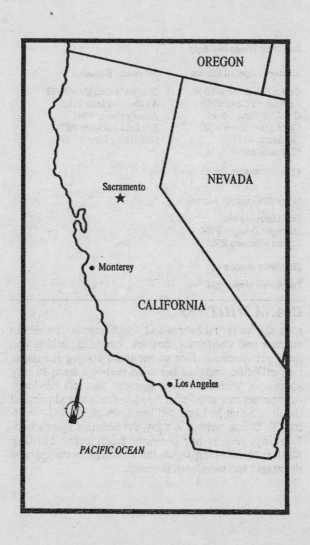

## Prologue

Twelve-year-old Devon Monroe peeked behind the Black-thorn Hall administration building, looking right, left and right again. He didn't see anyone but took another nervous glance before he swallowed hard and gave the signal. His three dorm mates scurried around the corner and took their positions. The smallest boy, ten-year-old Roberto Arroya, hunched at the corner of the redbrick building. He was the sentry.

The other two whipped out spray cans pilfered from a guy who'd been painting handicapped spaces in the parking lot. The fellow would probably be pretty ticked off when he got back from lunch but Devon didn't much care. He and his buddies had important stuff to do.

As the other guys waited for final instructions, Devon's gaze swept the area one last time before he gave the final nod. Plastic lids were popped off and the steady hiss of spritzing paint filled the air.

Devon glanced at his watch, then looked across the weedy lawn to the bushy embankment leading up to the 405 Freeway. He could barely bite back a grin. Blackthorn Hall was supposed to be a juvenile detention facility but it wasn't anything but a lousy POW camp for kids. Pretty soon, everybody driving by was going to read all about it.

"Hey, Dev. How's that?"

"Hmm?" Devon turned his attention back to the powder blue message scrawled on bloodred brick. HELP! OGDEN MARLOW IS A NAZZI. He issued a disgusted snort. "Aw hell, Tommy. That's not how you spell *Nazi*."

"It ain't?" The ponytailed eleven-year-old looked over his shoulder. "What's wrong with it?"

A husky blond boy dropped his paint can. "You dork." Larkin McKay carefully wiped a blue smudge from between his fingers. "There's only s'pose to be one *z*."

As Tommy stepped back to consider the problem, Devon noticed that he looked kind of peaked. Of course, Tommy never looked real good on account of his asthma, whatever that was. All Devon knew about asthma was that it made Tommy breathe funny and he had to suck on some kind of weird plastic tube. Tommy called it an inhaler.

Devon thought the whole thing was pretty disgusting but it wasn't Tommy's fault. He hated being sick all the time. If it hadn't been for this asthma business, Tommy wouldn't even be at Blackthorn Hall. He and his homeboys had been running from the cops when Tommy had had an attack and been caught. So here he was.

Now he slanted a mischievous glance at his buddies and gave the paint can a vigorous shake. "No sweat, man. I got it covered." Tommy took a wheezing breath and sprayed a sloppy line through the extra letter. "There. That oughta make ol' *Hog*man think twice 'bout taking away privileges."

Devon frowned. Just thinking about how mad the chancellor was going to be was enough to give him the willies. "Maybe this wasn't such a good idea, Lark."

Larkin bristled. "You're just mad 'cause it was *my* idea and not yours."

Devon set his jaw and stepped forward, clenching his bony fists. "Yeah? Well, it was a dumb idea, butt-head. If we get caught, we'll spend so much time in the Box that our heads'll be flat."

At the suggestion that they could be relegated to the windowless isolation chamber, Larkin's blue eyes faded to rusty gray. His chin quivered. "We won't get caught."

Devon knew that Larkin was scared but would rather chew worms than admit it. Lark never let anyone know what he was thinking. Devon figured that was because the guy thought it was his fault that his folks got divorced. Devon didn't really know what the big deal was. Divorce stunk but most grown-ups got one sooner or later. At least Larkin had a mother, which was more than Devon could say.

The problem really got bad when Larkin's mom went and got married again. Larkin hated his stepfather and he hated his stepfather's kids, too. Said they were a bunch of boneheaded twits. His mother kept telling him to be nice to them but nobody ever told *them* to be nice to Larkin. So he kept running away. When his folks got sick of looking for him, they said he was *incorrigible*—a big word that meant they didn't want him anymore—then dropped him off at the Hall. Devon thought that was a pretty crappy thing to do. So did Larkin, who now shot a leery glance at the small brown youngster hunched at the corner of the building. "It's still clear, right, Bobby?"

Roberto turned fiery dark eyes on his comrades. At ten, he was the youngest of the group...and the angriest. He was also the brightest. One of the teachers had called him a genius. Bobby took a lot of razzing for that, but Devon figured it must be true because the kid was two grades above everyone else his age. The only reason Bobby was at the Hall was because his mother beat him up whenever she drank too much, and she drank too much all the time. So Bobby had been put in protective custody, which was just another way of saying that nobody wanted him either.

Of all his Blackthorn Brothers, Devon felt closest to Bobby. He smiled as the kid stuck up a defiant thumb, signaling that the administrative campus was still deserted.

Relieved, Larkin managed a strained smile. "See? Cripes, Dev, chill out. You weren't worried 'bout getting caught when you soaped the vice-chancellor's Beemer."

Devon couldn't dispute that, although he'd pulled off last week's prank alone and put only his own skinny bottom on the line. This was different because his friends could get in trouble, too. Tommy, Larkin and Roberto were the closest thing to family Devon had ever had. He'd never known his mom, and his dad didn't give a tinker's damn about anything except making money. Since Crandall Monroe spent most of his time in Europe, he'd turned Devon over to Aunt Emmaline, an obnoxious, selfish old crow who had more ex-husbands than she could count on her fingers.

Emmaline hated Devon almost as much as he hated her. The only reason she'd agreed to take care of him was so she could live in a fancy house and pretend she was someone important. She never missed an opportunity to remind Devon that he was a burden to her and a disappointment to his father.

So he'd found a group of kids who liked him just the way he was. The problem was that they stole cars for fun and they were good at it. Devon wasn't so good. He got caught on his first try.

Once at the Hall, however, Devon had made real friends for the first time in his life and at the moment, he was having second thoughts about the risk those friends had taken with this spray-painted-protest thing. Devon wanted people to know about how mean the administrators were, but it would have been better if he'd done it alone so the younger boys wouldn't be involved.

Unfortunately, he'd been outvoted.

A ragged gasp caught Devon's attention. He looked up just as Tommy dropped the spray can and frantically started digging into the stenciled breast pocket of his uniform. The boy took another wheezing breath and adjusted the mouthpiece of his asthma inhaler. A pink flush crept across his hollow cheeks.

Devon's heart sank. "You having another attack?"

"Nah," Tommy croaked, then emitted a sound like air being sucked through a flat straw. His hands trembled slightly as he squirted the medicated mist into his throat and struggled to inhale. In less than a heartbeat the air slid smoothly into his lungs.

Roberto suddenly leapt up, plastered himself against the cold brick and issued a strained whisper. "They're coming."

With a graphic oath, Tommy dropped the inhaler back into his shirt pocket. Larkin's frantic gaze darted from the wooded embankment beside the freeway to the naked expanse of lawn that stretched between their present location and the sanctuary of their dormitory room.

Devon instantly took charge. "This way," he whispered, then ran toward a concealing cluster of bushes at the base of the embankment. He motioned for the boys to follow.

Roberto sprinted by and dived into the thicket with Larkin right on his tail. Devon crashed through the brush, spun around and hunched down. Peering through the foliage, he was horrified as Tommy tripped. The boy fell face first into the grass just as Ogden Marlow and one of the vice-chancellors rounded the building.

Shouting and swearing, the two men rushed over and hauled the poor kid to his feet. Devon saw terror in Tommy's eyes. From that point on, everything seemed to happen in slow motion. Devon watched helplessly as the two men shook Tommy like he was a rag doll. Then they screamed in his face, yelling questions about who else had been involved. Tommy clamped his lips together and didn't say a word.

Devon was sick with fear. He knew Tommy wouldn't rat on his buddies even though he was going to be punished bigtime. Devon wanted to go out and rescue his friend but if he did, Marlow would see Bobby and Larkin. Confused and panicked, Devon just sat there like a stupid lump while the men grabbed Tommy's skinny arms and hauled him through the gathering crowd.

As Tommy and his captors disappeared around the building, Larkin snagged Devon's wrist. "What are we gonna do now?"

Devon silenced him with a look and pointed to a sullen group of young inmates mulling around the courtyard. Larkin slunk farther back into the concealing brush.

For the next fifteen minutes, the three boys sulked silently, each absorbed with their own thoughts, their own terrors. Devon knew he had to be strong because his friends were counting on him. Tears pricked his eyes. He felt like a coward, cringing in the bushes like a scared rabbit while one of his Brothers was being interrogated. Maybe even tortured.

Every Rambo movie he'd ever seen ran through his mind and his imagination soared with graphic horrors. He wondered if Tommy was being beaten. Or maybe they were dripping water on his forehead, trying to drive him nuts. Worse, maybe they'd stripped off all his clothes and locked him in the Box.

Devon shuddered at the thought. The Box was a cinder block vault so small you couldn't lay down and so cold that you couldn't feel your feet after the first hour. It was dark, damp and filled with the stench of fear. Then the air got thinner and thinner, until you felt like you were being smothered by a clammy hand. That's when your lungs started to ache and your muscles cramped into big old knots. If you were real lucky, you passed out.

Devon hadn't been that lucky.

The thought of another stint in the Box scared Devon to death, but he could take it a lot better than poor Tommy could. Devon decided that as soon as he got Larkin and Roberto back to the dorm room, he'd march into the office and take full responsibility for the vandalism. He'd tell old Hogman that Tommy had tried to stop him. Devon would be put back into the Box but Tommy would be free.

A hushed whisper broke into Devon's thoughts. "Everyone went away," Roberto was saying. "Do you think we can go now?"

Devon studied the deserted courtyard. "Maybe. I'll go out first. Wait for my signal."

The two boys nodded somberly and Devon eased out of the brush. He stood there a moment, then slowly crossed the grass toward the disfigured wall of the administration building. A white glint caught his eye. Devon's heart sank as he scooped up the inhaler. Without the medicine Tommy might get real sick, so Devon knew he had to hurry.

After making sure that the coast was clear, he lifted two fingers into the air. The bushes behind him rustled and Devon led his scared roommates back toward the dormitory.

Forty-five minutes after Tommy had been dragged away, Roberto and Larkin were safely in their room and Devon was careering across the campus, mentally rehearsing his speech and clutching the precious inhaler. He sprinted around the south wing of the administration building and jerked to a stop.

For a moment, he stared stupidly at the ambulance that was parked at the entrance with red lights flashing. Then a pair of white-coated medics wheeled out a gurney. A brown ponytail peeked from beneath the concealing shroud.

Devon's world would never be the same.

## Chapter One

Devon Monroe hefted his stuffed duffel, stepped into the transit and wearily allowed a shoving mass of exiting passengers to sweep him into the pulsing LAX concourse. Beside him, a young woman emitted a delighted shriek and propelled herself into the joint embrace of a smiling, gray-haired couple. Devon's journalistic eye glimpsed a CSU sticker on the woman's haversack and absently deduced that she was probably a college student returning to her parents' home for summer break.

A nervous businessman brushed by, polished heels clicking a direct path toward a cluster of public telephones. Since the plane had landed twenty minutes late, Devon figured the agitated fellow must have cut his schedule too close and, judging by his bulging valise and the perspiration beading his tight brow, was about to botch a career-breaking appointment.

In truth Devon didn't give a tinker's damn about the businessman's problems or the young woman's summer vacation. Snap judgments were a hazard of his profession and a critical eye on his surroundings had kept him alive to report newsworthy events from the world's most volatile locations.

Fourteen hours ago he'd been dodging mortars in the crumbling ruins of a Baltic city emersed in bloody civil war. Now he'd been transported into a place where people were incensed by a malfunctioning traffic light and missing a business appointment was a tragedy exceeded only by the horror of a dinged BMW.

Stepping out of the crushing human stream, Devon sagged against a secluded wall, squeezed his stinging eyes shut and massaged his gritty lids. In a war zone, where staying alive was all that mattered, people at least had their priorities straight.

"Welcome home, Mr. Monroe."

Startled, Devon dropped his hand, lowered his gaze and stared into a pair of vaguely familiar ocean green eyes.

The lovely eyes crinkled with her smile. "You don't remember me."

Swallowing the heartfelt denial that teetered on the tip of his tongue, he settled for a lackadaisical shrug. "Sorry."

Her smile widened to reveal a striking flash of even white teeth. "There's no reason to apologize. Our last meeting was brief, and, if I recall, not particularly memorable." She extended a slim hand. "I'm Jessica Newcomb, your father's executive assistant."

Devon straightened, staring rudely before remembering to accept her proffered hand. "Of course," he murmured, comparing her delicate features with the sophisticated beauty he now recalled.

The meeting she'd mentioned may not have been memorable for her but Devon had never forgotten the elegant blonde who'd measured him coolly then dismissed him without a second glance. He'd been irritated but not surprised, having already assumed that anyone who owned a luxurious Century City condominium, drove an expensive sports car and was always tastefully dressed in the latest designer fashions probably fed on money like a vulture on carrion.

But that was then. Now Devon's gaze slid the length of her, openly measuring her subtle transformation. Her loose, oversize outfit was decidedly out of vogue and her hair was different—shorter, fluffier and a slightly lighter shade. She was also thinner and her exquisite sea foam eyes had lost the insolent sparkle that had both annoyed and intrigued him.

"You've changed," he announced, more curtly than intended.

Her smile faded into a tight line. "You haven't."

There was a brief flash of pain in her eyes, along with a revealing glint of vulnerability that startled him. He considered apologizing for his trademark bluntness but discarded the notion when he noticed her contemptuous appraisal of his rumpled travel fatigues.

Wrinkling her nose, she encompassed his attire with a regal swish of her hand. "Perhaps you'd like to freshen up before going on to the hospital."

He would have killed for a hot shower. "Later, after I've seen my father."

When she hiked one golden brow, he thought she was going to argue the point. He almost hoped that she would. He was tired, cranky, so dirty he itched and hungry enough to eat those pricy kidskin boots she was wearing—in other words, he was spoiling for a good fight.

Unfortunately, Miss Newcomb chose not to accommodate his baser instincts. Instead, she acquiesced with a condescending smile and shifted her gaze to his bloated duffel. "Did you check any luggage?"

"No."

"Very well. The parking garage is this way." She lifted her pert nose as though avoiding an unpleasant odor and glided through the crowded concourse without a backward glance, just as she'd done during their last ill-fated meeting.

The fact that she expected Devon to trot along like an obedient puppy irked the hell out of him. If he hadn't been so damned exhausted, he'd have turned left instead of right, rented himself a car and taken off on his own. But then he wouldn't be able to watch the sway of her lean hips as she swiveled through the bustling swarm.

With a pained sigh, he followed.

Jessica felt rather than heard Devon fall into step behind her. For a moment she'd thought he might brush her off and disappear into the crowd. Part of her had hoped he would; the other part would have been disappointed. For Crandall, of course. Certainly not for herself. Her boss's estranged son was obviously the same unshaven vagabond she remembered—arrogant, brash and irritable.

That judgment was confirmed as they waited for the parking garage elevator. Devon glowered at the luggage carousels and muttered, "I don't need a lousy chauffeur."

"No one needs a lousy chauffeur. Fortunately, I happen to be a very good one."

He regarded her sullenly. "Let's not and say we did, okay?"

She blinked. "Excuse me?"

A jarring bell signaled the elevator's arrival. Sighing, he hefted the duffle and followed her inside. "I'm sure you had no choice about this assignment, so how about I just rent a car and let you go on with your business."

The offer was tempting. Unfortunately, this airport courtesy call concealed a deeper motivation, one Jessica wasn't yet ready to reveal. "It seems rather extravagant to waste money on a rental when there are several vehicles at the house."

His lip curled in an unappealing smirk. "My father would be apoplectic to hear his gated Bel-Aire estate referred to as a common house."

Instantly angry, Jessica dropped the pretense of civility. "You've spent three days with him in five years. How dare you presume to know him?"

Devon's jaw sagged only an instant before his eyes flashed blue fire. "Who the hell do you think you are, lady? You don't know squat about my father and even less about me."

"Your father is a kind and decent man. I've worked with him for—"

"Have you lived with him?" Devon growled. "Do you know what it's like to be the son of a man who doesn't even know you're alive?" Suddenly his eyes widened and he spun around, but not before Jessica recognized the pain he'd inadvertently revealed.

Her anger drained away. "I'm sorry. You're right, of course."

The elevator jerked to a stop. Devon exited before the doors had completely opened. He dropped his duffle, raked his hair, jammed his fists against his slim hips and stared at the oily concrete floor.

Regretting her outburst, Jessica swallowed hard, squared her shoulders and came up beside him. "I was out of line, Mr. Monroe. I apologize."

He fixed her with a narrowed gaze. "Where's the car?"

She sighed, murmured, "This way," and led him down the sloped corridor.

Obviously, this wasn't going to be easy. Despite the fact that she personally found Devon Monroe to be brusque to the point of rudeness with an annoying vocabulary that was blunt, coarse and occasionally crude, she charitably allowed that the judgment might be somewhat biased. After all, they'd only spent a few hours together and that had been two years ago during his last trip to Los Angeles.

For Jessica, that had been quite enough. She remembered how excited Crandall had been, confiding a hope that his son's visit signaled a truce and a willingness to ease the strain that had always marred their relationship.

It hadn't. Devon had hobbled home on crutches, surly as a thwarted billy goat. When he'd left abruptly days before his scheduled departure, Crandall, whose feigned dispassion hadn't fooled Jessica, had once more immersed himself in work.

She still didn't know exactly what had happened between the two men and was mulling over that when a hunter green glint caught her eye. "This is it," she told Devon, gesturing to the twenty-year-old Jaguar that was her pride and joy. Pulling out her car keys, she opened the trunk to receive his duffle.

He eyed the gleaming vehicle with undisguised scorn. "Why am I not surprised?"

Exasperated, she propped a weary hip against the sleek fender and folded her arms. "Do you harbor a seething resentment against imports?"

"Nope." He slung the bulging bag into the roomy trunk and brushed his hands together. "I owned a Hyundai once. Not particularly prestigious but it got me where I wanted to go."

It didn't take a Ph.D. to realize that *prestigious* was the operative word in that statement but Jessica was too tired to care. She unlocked the passenger door without comment, slammed the trunk and was opening the driver door when Devon suddenly leaned over the low-slung roof.

His penetrating gaze reflected worry and a hint of fear. "My father...is he all right?"

Touched by the unexpected display of concern, she was barely able to suppress an urge to reach out to him. Instead, she tightened her grip on the open door. "Crandall is doing very well. The doctors expect to release him in the next day or so."

Devon pursed his lips and frowned. "So soon?"

"As I told you on the telephone, it was a mild heart attack. There doesn't seem to have been any permanent damage."

"This time."

She scrutinized his bland expression and saw no trace of sarcasm. "I think Crandall understands that the attack was a warning to slow down and make some changes in his life."

Devon's upper lip twitched. "He didn't want you to call me, did he?"

Taken aback by the accurate assessment, Jessica responded automatically, without considering that the truth might be hurtful. "No, he didn't. But I thought you'd want to know."

An exquisite sadness clouded Devon's eyes as he studied his distorted reflection in the waxed roof. "Yeah. Thanks." The clipped words were issued with a gentle gratitude that was both startling and touching.

The brooding man was an enigma, yet Jessica suspected that beneath the crust of gruff indifference lurked a tender heart with a capacity to feel both love and pain. She wondered why he expended so much effort to conceal that. Even now his handsome features were chiseled into a dispassionate mask with his stubbled jaw clenched, sculpted lips stretched into a tight, hard line. Only his eyes gave him away, perhaps because he was too exhausted by the grueling trip to maintain the obscure visual shield she remembered.

Suddenly Devon raked his tousled brown hair, took a shuddering breath, then yanked open the car door and folded his six-foot-plus frame into the passenger seat. Taking the cue, Jessica slid in beside him, wincing as a sharp pain reminded her that she'd moved too quickly. She caught her lower lip between her teeth, absently massaging the ribs just below the throbbing scar.

"Are you all right?" Devon asked without turning his head.

She yanked her hand away, wondering if he had an extra set of eyes hidden behind his earlobes. "Ah . . . sure. Fine. Just a muscle cramp."

When he made no further comment, she fastened her shoulder harness and began the arduous routine of coaxing the recalcitrant engine to life. After depressing the clutch, she shifted into neutral, pumped a squirt of fuel into the touchy carburetor and hit the ignition. The Jaguar whined, turned over once and died. After repeating the process three times, the engine coughed to life.

Intensely aware that Devon was staring at her, she allowed the engine to rev until the sound changed from a high-pitched scream to a mellow chug. Then she pasted on a stiff smile and turned to her incredulous passenger. "Buckle up," she said cheerfully.

Devon stared. "Are you aware that some cars actually start as soon as the key is turned?"

"Ralph has always been independent," she replied, affectionately patting the padded dash. "Besides, I've never had any use for wimpy cars that poop along on the freeway and go into shock every time you shift into passing gear."

He cocked his head, listening. "I hate to burst your bubble but it sounds like old Ralph needs a new set of plugs."

"You're absolutely right. That's on my agenda for the weekend. Now if you'll fasten your seat belt, we can be on our way."

Devon stretched his lean legs under the roomy dash and tossed a lazy arm over the tan leather backrest. "I don't like seat belts. Too confining."

"I'm sorry to hear that but Ralph insists that all of his passengers buckle up." Seeing the resistant glint in Devon's irked eyes, she smiled sweetly. "He can be very stubborn."

Devon's hand hovered over the door handle. For a moment, Jessica thought he might simply get out of the car rather than capitulate to the whims of a mere woman; instead, however, he hauled the harness across his broad chest, snapped the buckle, folded his arms and silently glared out the window.

Exhaling slowly, Jessica backed out of the stall and followed the yellow arrows out of the tiered parking garage.

She merged into the heavy airport traffic, inching along Century Boulevard toward the freeway on-ramp. At each red light, she angled a covert glance at her sullen passenger and felt a twinge of sympathy. He really did look exhausted. Fatigue settled beneath his reddened eyes like bruises and the khaki fatigues he wore looked like they hadn't seen a laundry tub in weeks.

After days of trying to track Devon down, she'd finally found him in a hotel on the outskirts of an east European city that she couldn't even pronounce. That had been yesterday morning and from his disheveled appearance, she surmised that he must have left for the airport within minutes of her phone call.

The thought crossed her mind that she might have inadvertently misled him about the seriousness of his father's condition. As she guided the Jag up the freeway on-ramp, she chanced a brief glance at him. "When we spoke yesterday, I hope you didn't get the impression that Crandall was gravely ill."

He idly watched the passing scenery. "No."

"I mean, it wasn't necessary for you to drop everything and rush to his side." Silence. "Of course, I'm glad that you're here. I know Crandall will be pleased to see you."

Devon continued to stare out the window without response.

Obviously communication was not the man's strong suit. Jessica, however, was nothing if not persistent. After she'd merged onto the clogged freeway, she switched subjects and tried again. "I read the series of articles you wrote about peacekeeping troops selling donated relief supplies on the black market. Compelling stuff. I'm glad the Pulitzer committee agreed."

Devon stirred restlessly, seeming uncomfortable with the subject of his success.

"Your father was very proud of you," Jessica murmured, pressing the accelerator to keep pace with the increased speed of surrounding traffic.

"Was he?"

"Of course." She didn't add that he'd also been horrified by the risks his son had taken to infiltrate the murderous gang of international thugs. "Why do you sound surprised?"

"My father has never been particularly pleased by my chosen profession."

Jessica couldn't dispute that. During the years she'd worked at ElectroSonics, Crandall had frequently expressed disappointment about his son's disinterest in the electronic manufacturing facility that had evolved into a multimillion dollar international conglomerate.

In fact, Devon Monroe seemed a deliberate antithesis of his refined, highly educated father. The only similarity between the two men were striking good looks and an uncompromising drive for professional perfection that she feared would be the death of both. Whereas Crandall Monroe internalized his burning zeal to succeed, Devon sought physical danger, bolstering his intrepid reputation with perilous excursions into the world's most treacherous territory.

Jessica knew that Devon's dangerous exploits upset Crandall and believed that constant worry about his son's safety had contributed to the older man's physical problems. During that infamous last visit Devon had shrugged off comments about his father's concern, causing Jessica to fume silently and label her boss's nomadic son as a foolhardy, self-important jerk. Now she was beginning to wonder if the relationship between the Monroe men was more complex than she'd first—

"Look out!" Devon shouted.

Jessica jerked the wheel, muttered under her breath and barely missed the steel stepladder that had bounced from the bed of a utility truck several car-lengths ahead. In the rear-view mirror she saw a compact car squeal sideways and veer into the next lane, forcing a speeding pickup to brake sharply.

Devon snapped off his seat belt and twisted to look at the rear window. "Pull over."

"Wh—?"

*"Pull over!"*

Behind them, tires continued to screech as she yanked the wheel and steered onto the narrow shoulder. Before the car had stopped moving, Devon leapt out and raced back down the freeway. Jessica spun in her seat and was horrified. Since the ladder blocked all of the right lane and part of the next, panicked drivers were swerving in every direction. Brakes squealed. Horns blared. And while speeding vehicles fishtailed across the freeway, Devon ran the line like a suicidal quarterback.

Jessica stared out the rear window, frozen with fear when a vehicle struck the ladder then veered out of control onto the narrow shoulder—straight toward Devon. She whimpered once then held her breath, wondering how on earth she could ever explain to her boss that his only begotten son had been squashed into road kill.

Gears shrieked. Brakes locked. Smoke poured from the car's rear tires. And a millisecond before impact, Devon vaulted to his left and clung to the ivy-covered embankment like a treed cat. The car swerved back into the lane and sped on as though such annoying interruptions were common during a normal L.A. commute.

Devon hopped off the embankment. Jessica started to breathe, a condition that again momentarily ceased as the impetuous fool continued his death-defying quest by dodging the speeding traffic and finally dragging the bent ladder safely out of the lane. With a satisfied nod, he brushed his hands together and loped lazily back toward the parked Jaguar.

He slid into the front seat, eyes shining, cheeks flushed, exhilaration oozing from every pore in his reckless, irresponsible body.

Jessica was livid. Not only had he just scared ten years off her life, the brash fool was grinning as if he'd just scored a touchdown in the Super Bowl. "That was without a doubt the stupidest, most moronic act of idiocy it has ever been my misfortune to witness."

His grin widened. "Don't hold back, Jessie, just tell me what you think."

"I think you're a thrill-seeking cretin with a death wish," she snapped. "And don't call me Jessie."

"You can call me Devie if you want."

"I don't want to call you Devie. In fact, I'd be perfectly happy not to call you anything at all." Infuriated by his smug expression, she clutched the steering wheel to keep from grabbing his ears and shaking some sense into his thick skull. "Now that I've seen you in action, I can understand why your poor father is in the hospital. Worrying about you would give anyone a heart attack."

The maddening grin faded into his clenched jaw. Devon stared outside and spoke without looking at her. "Oddly enough, I don't like seeing people maimed and killed, particularly if I can do something to stop it."

Flexing her fingers around the steering wheel, Jessica tried to sound reasonable. "What you did back there reflected a wanton disregard for your own safety. Your life is just as valuable as anyone else's. How do you think your father would have felt if anything had happened to you?"

A muscle twitched beneath his ear. He stared through the windshield, allowing the silence to drag on before he finally spoke. "Let's go."

Jessica sighed, increasingly aware that the pain in her side was now throbbing into her armpit. As adrenaline drained from her aching body, fear was replaced by sudden exhaustion. Her knees trembled. Her fingers shook. Her neck was too tired to hold her head up.

Placing a wobbly hand on the gear shift, she angled a glance at her grim passenger. "Buckle up."

Devon complied without comment. It was a small victory. She wondered why it felt like a defeat.

"Is this his room?" Devon asked.

"Yes." Jessica touched his elbow as he reached for the knob. "Your father is still a little pale and weak. Don't let that frighten you. The doctors say that if he takes care of himself, he should make a complete recovery."

Under ordinary circumstances, Devon might have covered his concern with a flip comment but her compassion was genuine and didn't deserve to be mocked. "Thanks for the warning."

She rewarded him with a tiny smile. "After I give Crandall his messages, you two can have some private time together."

Devon frowned. "You bring his work to the hospital?"

"It's either that or rip out the phone and tie him to the bed." Her green eyes sparkled. "Besides, he has to relax in order to get well and work is his only relaxation. If Crandall doesn't have his thumb on the company's pulse, his blood pressure soars and he starts making unpleasant suggestions about how the doctors should utilize their medical apparatus."

Devon was not amused. He was all too familiar with his father's obsession with work, a compulsive devotion that had destroyed his own childhood dream of having a normal family. But if Devon had been unhappy, Crandall had not. After all, he had what he wanted—money, power, freedom. Too bad having a son had never been part of his father's wish list.

As Devon followed Jessica into the sterile room, the reason for her warning was startlingly clear. The wan man was lying in a maze of dripping tubes and beeping monitors, his blanketed lap covered by a clutter of loose paper and bound reports.

"You've got company," Jessica said brightly.

Crandall opened his eyes, peered over his rimless reading glasses and looked straight at his son. The first words out of his mouth were, "So you're not dead yet."

Jessica covered her eyes and moaned.

Devon simply shrugged. "Not yet."

The older man scrutinized him sharply. "At least your limbs seem to be intact."

Extending his arms, Devon wiggled his fingers then alternately lifted each leg to assure his father that they worked. "Everything's present and accounted for."

"A temporary condition, I'm sure."

Jessica looked shocked. Devon was merely amused. Over the years, Crandall Monroe had repeatedly attempted to recruit Devon into the family business—voluntarily or otherwise. His father had tried everything from bribery to coercion to blatant manipulation. During Devon's last trip home, Crandall had gone a step too far. After discovering his father's devious scheme, Devon had cut his visit short and abruptly returned to the field. The two men hadn't spoken since.

Now, grumbling and looking somewhat embarrassed, Crandall feigned interest in riffling the papers in his lap. "What brings you back to L.A.?"

Devon leaned casually against the wall. To Crandall, a sick man was a weak man and if there was anything in the world that Crandall Monroe despised it was weakness. So to spare his father the humiliation of acknowledging his illness, Devon skirted the subject entirely. "I had to take some time off—too much accrued vacation." It wasn't exactly a lie, although from the corner of his eye he noticed Jessica's jaw sag. He jammed his hands in his pockets and rocked back on the heels of his worn combat boots. "So, how's it going?"

Crandall took off his glasses. "Fine, thank you."

"Good." Devon nodded and casually glanced around the homey room. "That's good."

"You're looking...well," Crandall said, although his cool gaze inspected Devon's rumpled attire with obvious disapproval.

Jessica seemed bewildered by the strained interaction between father and son. "Devon has only just arrived. He came directly from the airport."

Irritated that she felt a need to defend him, Devon quelled her with a look. "Didn't you say something about messages?"

"Yes, of course." She reached into her smart suede shoulder bag and extracted a clipped stack of pink notes. "I've handled most of these already. Marketing overestimated sales of the interactive diodes this quarter so manufacturing is scrambling to correct production quotas."

Crandall put on his glasses and flipped through the stack. "Have schedule revisions been completed?"

"Not yet. They should be finished by the end of the week."

"See that they are." He dropped the message stack on the table beside his bed. "I'll expect an explanation of how such incompetent projections can be avoided in the future."

"Marketing is already working on it."

"Good." Crandall sank tiredly back against the pillow and gave her a weak smile. "Thank you, Jessica. As usual, you've handled everything brilliantly."

"I learned from the best." Returning his smile, she affectionately patted his waxy hand. "Now you and Devon have a nice visit while I go make a few calls."

After informing Devon that she'd wait for him in the main lobby, Jessica left and a strained silence shrouded the room. Crandall plucked at the bedclothes. Devon shuffled uncomfortably, trying to think of some benign small talk that wouldn't lead to the hostile confrontation that seemed to be inevitable whenever they were together.

Crandall cleared his throat. "How long is this vacation of yours?"

"Hmm? Oh. A few weeks, I guess." He didn't mention that his abrupt departure had so angered his employer that the holiday might turn out to be permanent. Instead he added, "Until I get a new assignment."

"You'll be staying at the house, of course." Crandall's tone broached no argument and none was offered.

Despite misgivings about returning to his father's sprawling estate, it was still the only home Devon had ever known. Except, of course, for his months at Blackthorn Hall. He supposed that shouldn't count, but in many ways the sparse dormitory shared with his friends had been a refuge, a place where he'd felt needed and loved.

"Gunda will be pleased to see you," Crandall said suddenly.

"I've missed her," Devon said, noting but not dwelling on the fact that his father had avoided expressing his own pleasure—or lack thereof—in seeing his son. Instead, Devon turned his thoughts to Gunda Meineke, the dear housekeeper who'd raised him with a mother's love.

Over the years, they'd always kept in touch. He had, in fact, received a letter from Gunda a few weeks ago but she hadn't mentioned Crandall's illness nor had she been the one to call and inform him of his father's heart attack. Devon assumed that Crandall had forbidden her to do so. Of course, he'd also told Jessica not to call but apparently she'd been less intimidated by her employer's bluster. Devon admired that.

A stifled moan caught his attention as Crandall shifted restlessly in bed, thrusting the shaft of papers aside and wincing as he pushed himself into a more comfortable sitting position.

Devon reached out to fluff his father's pillows, only to have his hands slapped away. "I'm not a damned invalid," Crandall growled. Despite the indignant protest, the minute movement caused his breathing to accelerate and small beads of perspiration were dotting his furrowed brow.

Straightening, Devon stepped back, conflicted by feelings he dare not express—worry, fear and secret affection for the man who had constantly rejected him. But now he saw fear in his father's eyes and realized that this powerful, intimidating man was all too human. It was a stunning revelation.

When Crandall turned away, Devon quietly left the room. In the corridor, he sagged against the wall, shaken to the core by the reminder of his father's mortality. He hadn't felt this helpless since the day Tommy Murdock died.

## Chapter Two

Jessica sat in the mauve armchair a few feet from a row of public telephones lining the hospital's plush waiting area. She crossed her ankles, tapped the upholstered armrest with restless fingers and fretted about what had happened between her boss and his estranged son. The strained interaction between the two men hadn't been completely unexpected, of course, but the source of friction had certainly taken her by surprise. She'd never seen Crandall behave so coldly. His behavior had shocked her to the core.

After five years of working with Crandall Monroe, Jessica certainly wasn't blind to his faults. He was indisputably difficult, perfectionistic and frustratingly hard to please. But he was also compassionate and understanding, a man of unquestioned integrity who would never betray the confidence of a friend. Jessica admired him immensely and trusted him completely. Yet he'd acted as if his son's presence had been less important than a visit from the postman.

Jessica was completely baffled by that, and by Devon's faked indifference, as well. Despite his obvious concern and the fact that he'd just traveled halfway around the world to reach his father's side, he'd stood there with a blank expression implying that his sudden appearance was nothing more than coincidence.

There was something odd going on between the two men, something that transcended whatever problems they'd had during Devon's last visit. A guilty twinge served as a reminder that Jessica had held Devon solely responsible for those problems. Now she was beginning to wonder if she'd misjudged him.

Her silent speculation was interrupted as he emerged from the corridor and glanced around the spacious lobby. Before she could react, he spotted her, ambled over and settled wearily in the closest chair.

He wiped his face with his hands. "Did you finish making your telephone calls?"

"Yes. I just had to check in with the office, then let Gunda know that you'd arrived safe and sound." When he didn't respond, Jessica fiddled with the hem of her blocky, hip-length jacket. "I'm supposed to tell you that she's preparing *Rindsrouladen* and *Kartoffel . . .* something."

*"Kartoffelpuffers."*

"Ah. Well, whatever they are, you're having them for dinner."

His eyes warmed, just a little. "They're German potato fritters."

"Umm. Sounds good."

Leaning forward, Devon propped his elbows on his knees and stared at his scuffed boots. "You're welcome to join us. Gunda always makes enough for a small army."

Jessica declined the polite but perfunctory invitation. "Another time, perhaps."

His only response was a thin nod; then his eyes glazed and he was completely lost in thought.

Folding her arms, Jessica leaned back and regarded this enigmatic man, noting how different he was from his paunchy, round-faced father. Other than matching heads full of thick russet hair, the men were so physically different it was difficult to believe they were even related. Crandall was a good four inches shorter than his son, with an orbital face that would have seemed jolly if not for the hard glint in his shrewd, dark eyes.

In contrast, everything about Devon Monroe was sharp, angular, from his chiseled cheekbones to his patrician nose. But the eyes didn't fit. Devon's crystalline blue irises were outlined by a dark cerulean shade and reflected a secret softness that seemed strangely alien in an otherwise foreboding landscape.

She cleared her throat. "Is everything, ah, all right? Between you and your father, that is."

"Hmm?" Devon blinked as though seeing her for the first time. "Oh. Sure."

Somehow she doubted that. "I hope you understand that Crandall has been through a lot the past few days."

He nodded without conviction.

"That doesn't excuse his rudeness, of course." Jessica twisted her fingers together, wishing she didn't feel compelled to defend her boss. "I'm sure he doesn't realize how brusque he sounded."

Devon's lips curved in a sad half smile that made her heart flutter strangely. "Don't worry about my feelings. My father and I understand each other."

She took no comfort from that, nor was she certain she believed it. Having lost her own beloved father, she was dismayed and deeply saddened by the obvious emotional distance between the two men. She was also determined to change it, although at the moment, that task seemed a monumental one.

Still, she had to try. She owed Crandall that, and so much more.

* * *

*"Lieber Gott!"* Gunda exclaimed as Devon stepped into the expansive foyer. "Your bones walk beneath skin!"

Grinning, Devon dropped his duffel onto the polished marble floor. "And you are more beautiful than ever, *Liebchen.*"

"Such a naughty boy." The blocky woman slapped his arm then proudly patted her thick waist. "I am old and I am fat. But you—" She wiggled a reproachful finger. "Does no one feed you?"

"Not like you. Now give me a hug." He swept the laughing woman into his arms and swung her around until she squealed in protest.

"You will break yourself!"

"Not me. I'm macho. Haven't you heard? I run through battlefields with a tank in one hand and a Minicam in the other." Devon lowered her to the floor and kissed her flushed cheek. "I like your new hairstyle."

"Do you?" Blushing madly, Gunda fluffed her freshly layered locks with her fingers. "There is so little left, my head feels like a balloon."

"It makes you look years younger," Devon assured her, although in truth he rather missed the fat braid that had been wound at her nape for as long as he could remember. Despite the alien mob of permed honey brown hair and the fact that her apple-round face had begun to sag at the throat, Devon still considered her to be beautiful.

Gunda had been like a mother to Devon, comforting him when life had turned cruel, offering warmth and love to counter his father's indifference. If not for her, he'd have never known softness, never experienced the solace of a nurturing touch. Seeing her again brought back the memories and the gratitude. He affectionately framed her plump face with his palms. "I've missed you."

Bringing up her thick hands, Gunda grasped his forearms. "Then why do you not write more often? It has been two months."

"I know. I'm sorry." Sighing, he released her and stepped away, knowing that she'd be horrified to learn that up until last week, he'd been interviewing a notorious rebel leader who'd been known to permanently dispatch journalists who'd dared write an unfavorable report. "How's Katrina?"

At the mention of her beloved granddaughter, Gunda lit up like neon. "Last week she asked for water!"

"No kidding? That's great!" Since the autistic seven-year-old had rarely uttered an intelligible word, Devon shared the housekeeper's excitement.

"It's because of you. If you had not found this special school…" The woman's voice broke. She wiped her misty eyes. "Now my Katrina has a chance to live."

"I just made a few phone calls," Devon murmured, embarrassed by the praise. He hoisted his duffel and glanced up the winding staircase.

Gunda followed his gaze. "Of course, you are tired and hungry after your trip. You must rest."

"When will the *Kartoffelpuffers* be ready?"

"Soon," she assured him, then glanced around the foyer as though just realizing that they were alone. "Where is Miss Newcomb? I was hoping that she would stay for dinner."

"She had other plans." At least, Devon assumed that had been the reason for her abrupt departure. After a silent drive from the hospital to the house, Jessica had dropped him off in front of his father's mansion, politely refused a second invitation to sample Gunda's German cuisine, then driven away looking pale and exhausted.

The housekeeper sighed. "Ah. That is too bad."

"Do you know her well?"

"Not well," Gunda confessed. "I do not believe anyone knows Miss Newcomb well."

That didn't surprise Devon. There was something elusive about her, along with a sense of secrecy that was oddly intriguing. "So you find her aloof?"

The woman's blue eyes rounded. "*Ach du lieber!* I find no such thing. Miss Newcomb has always been very friendly and kind, although she doesn't care to speak about herself."

"Maybe she has something to hide."

"Always you seek the worst." Gunda shook her head and gestured impatiently toward the stairs. "Go now. Wash yourself. Change into clothes that do not reek so you can enjoy the fine meal I have prepared."

"Yes, ma'am." Grinning, Devon touched two fingers to his forehead in a sloppy salute. He hoisted his duffel and started toward the stairs.

"*Warte mal,*" Gunda said suddenly. "I nearly forgot. Mr. Arroya read about your father's illness in the newspaper. When he called to offer his good wishes, I mentioned that you would be home soon. He asked that you call him." With that, she strode down the hall like a panzer and disappeared into the kitchen.

Devon clutched the carved banister in a white-knuckled grip. It wasn't a surprise that Bobby had called. They always got together when Devon was in town. This time their reunion would be different. This time he knew what Bobby expected. He just wasn't sure he could go through with it.

Clutching a stuffed key ring, Jessica stepped off the elevator on the sixth floor of her sculptured condominium complex. Her poor feet, victimized by excruciatingly fashionable narrow-toed pumps, screamed in protest. Her muscles ached. She was weary to the bone.

As the mirrored doors swished shut behind her, she quickly scanned the crystal-lit corridor. Since it was deserted, she kicked off her shoes and moaned in relief. Thank God tomorrow was Saturday, a day of loafers and sweatshirts and sloppy blue jeans. Except, of course, for the hours she'd spend in the hospital with Crandall. Then she'd have to reassume the executive persona that she'd so scrupulously nurtured for the past five years.

At the moment, however, she wished that she'd opted for a less-urbane career. Maybe she should have become a veterinarian. She loved animals, after all, and every vet she'd ever seen had been dressed in a comfortable lab coat and baggy slacks. And not one of them had been wearing high heels.

Sighing, she wiggled her swollen toes on the plush velour carpet, scooped up her shoes and limped to her apartment door. Her fingers trembled so it took two tries to fit the key into the slot. Finally the lock clicked and the door swung open.

Once inside her disheveled apartment, Jessica collapsed on a secondhand sofa from a nearby thrift shop and propped her throbbing feet on a coffee table made from a slab of polished granite and molded concrete blocks. God, she was tired. She'd overdone it again. Her ribs throbbed, she was fatigued to the point of nausea and the damnable weakness had overtaken her so quickly that it was frightening. She had to slow down. And she would. Next week. Things would be better next week. They had to be. Nothing could be worse than what she'd already endured.

A sharp pain stabbed into her armpit. She winced silently, glanced at her watch and moaned. No wonder her body felt like it was falling apart. She should have taken her medication three hours ago.

After scrounging through the cluttered interior of her purse, she extracted several prescription bottles and shook the proper dosage of each into her palm. With some effort, she hauled her aching body up, went to the neat galley kitchen and washed the pills down her parched throat.

As she leaned against the counter, her weary gaze fell on the refrigerator, which was barely visible beneath a layer of

papers held with bug-shaped magnets. She should eat, of
course. The doctor had warned her that regular meals were
an important part of the recovery process. Nevertheless, her
stomach rebelled at the thought. Perhaps she could make up
for lost calories by eating twice as much tomorrow, when
she'd had a chance to rest and recover from the grueling
events of the day. Right now, all she wanted was a hot bath
and a soft mattress.

She flipped off the kitchen light and went into the ad-
joining living area, pausing to gaze out at the twinkling city.
The view always took her breath away. That vast, night-
time panorama was why she'd spent her entire trust fund on
a cramped condo instead of purchasing a conservative home
in the suburbs. Her mother and stepfather had been appalled, citing city crime rates and the decay of metropolitan
property values. As always, Jessica had listened politely then
done exactly what she wanted to do. She hadn't regretted it.
At least, not yet.

But then impulsive acts and snap judgments had always
been part—some might say a flaw—of her nature. Jessica
had never considered her decisiveness to be a problem. God
wouldn't have given people brains if He didn't want them to
be used for weighing evidence, assessing options and making informed decisions. Sometimes those conclusions could
be wrong, of course. Her initial reaction to Devon Monroe
came to mind.

Two years ago, she'd considered him to be coarse, crude
and completely lacking in consideration for his father's
feelings. But today she'd noticed something different about
the brash young journalist, a secretive sadness that was
deeply stirring.

After seeing the two men interact at the hospital, Jessica
realized that her original assessment had been tainted by her
own bias. To her, Crandall Monroe had been a dear friend
and trusted confidant; to his son, however, he'd been cool
and withdrawn. That had shocked and saddened her. It had

also thrown a major monkey wrench into her plan to facilitate a truce between the two men.

Rubbing her chilled arms, she turned away from the window. Healing the emotional rift between father and son would take a lot more effort than she'd imagined. The first step would be to learn the root cause of their mutual mistrust and hostility. Then perhaps she could do something to help. Jessica had learned how fragile life was, and how fleeting. When those we cherish are gone, it is too late to regret postponed kindnesses and unspoken affections.

Crandall Monroe had supported Jessica during the bleakest moments of her life. Now she wanted to repay him with a gift more valuable than gold. She wanted to give him back his son.

The first thing Devon saw as he drove into the condominium's guest parking lot was a hunter green Jaguar with its hood up. The second thing he saw was a curvaceous derriere protruding from the engine compartment. He hit the brake, staring in disbelief. There was no doubt in his mind that Jessica Newcomb was the proud owner of that lovely round bottom, but he couldn't fathom why in hell a prissy and proper socialite would be folded into a greasy car engine.

Thoroughly intrigued, Devon pulled his father's beige Mercedes into the nearest parking space. The Jaguar was parked a hundred feet away, beside a hose bib located toward the rear of the building. Jessica didn't look up as he slammed the car door or as he crossed the warm asphalt. There was an open toolbox beside her sneakered feet, along with a plastic bag from a local auto parts chain. A smudged towel that had been spread over the Jag's gleaming fender was cluttered with a variety of box wrenches, bolts and washers.

Just as he came up behind her, she levered herself on tiptoe and dived deeper into a tangled hose mass, her fleece-clad elbow jerking with rhythmic twists.

He peered politely over her shoulder. "What's the problem?"

She instantly reared up, her strangled gasp becoming a howl of pain when her skull smacked the underside of the raised hood. Before Devon could do more than extend a helpless hand, Jessica spun away, clutched her head with both hands and skewed him with an accusatory glare. "Do you enjoy scaring the liver out of people or are you just an inconsiderate boob?"

Feeling stupid, Devon offered a conciliatory shrug. "I'm sorry. I should have known better."

Apparently deflated by the apology, her pale brows knitted into a charming frown. "Yes, you should have." She delicately probed the top of her skull and winced.

Devon stepped forward, extending his hand. "Let me see—"

"No!" Hanging onto her skull as though she expected it to bounce off and roll away, she stumbled backward until her shoulders scraped the building's concrete wall.

Taken aback by her reaction, Devon lowered his hand. "I just want to make sure you're all right."

"I'm fine," she replied crisply, patting her perfectly styled hair as though adjusting a helmet

Devon noted that something about the prissy Miss Jessica seemed different today. Softer. More vulnerable. Perhaps it was her freshly scrubbed face, now devoid of cosmetics, that he found so appealing. Perhaps it was the worn jeans and sloppy sweatshirt making her seem, well, less rigid. He was, however, struck by the incongruity of such casual attire combined with her sophisticated and scrupulously arranged coiffure.

In truth, he didn't much care for her new hairdo. It was too stylish and reflected a touch-me-not formality that he found off-putting. Two years ago her blunt-cut tresses had been sleek and shiny, brushing her shoulders with just the merest hint of curve. They'd been silky and inviting, the kind of hair a man yearns to run his fingers through. Devon felt a strange pang of loss at the memory.

His wandering thoughts were interrupted when Jessica stopped fiddling with her hair, crossed her arms and confronted him. "What are you doing here?"

"Hmm? Oh. Checking on you."

Her chin drooped. "What on earth for?"

"Apparently my father has been trying to call you all morning and kept getting the answering machine. He was concerned enough to telephone the house and insist that I make certain you were all right." Actually, Crandall had seemed a great deal more than concerned. When the jangling telephone had rocked Devon out of bed this morning, the crackling voice on the other end of the line bordered on hysteria. "What did he think I'd find, anyway?"

A furious flush crept along Jessica's jaw. "I have no idea."

Devon wasn't buying that. "Hey, I've just been jarred out of a nice warm bed at the crack of dawn—"

"Ten o'clock is hardly the crack of dawn."

"On Saturday it is. Besides, I'm still on European time, which means that today is really tomorrow so in theory I haven't slept in two days."

"I'm sorry you were inconvenienced."

Devon shifted uncomfortably. "I guess my father's agitation wore off on me. I figured that if he was that worried, he must have a reason."

"Crandall's just a bit overprotective, that's all."

"Overprotective? You're putting me on, right?" The thought was so ludicrous, Devon nearly laughed out loud. "Look, my father is a lot of things but overprotective certainly isn't one of them. When I was growing up, he trav-

eled ten months out of twelve and I considered myself lucky
if he called home twice a year."

"That's terrible." She touched her throat, seeming genuinely dismayed. "You must have been so hurt."

The compassion flooding her soft green eyes took his
breath away. He coughed away a sudden lump in his throat.
"He was a busy man. I, uh, understood that."

"No child understands parental abandonment."

Shifting restlessly, Devon hooked his thumbs in his pants
pockets and avoided her perceptive gaze. "It was a long time
ago. I got over it."

"Did you?"

"Yes." Annoyed by the conversation's direction, Devon
irritably raked his hair and turned the topic back to her. "So
you and my father have some kind of personal relationship?"

Her head snapped around. "Excuse me?"

Puffing his cheeks, Devon blew out a breath and wondered why in hell he couldn't spit out a single word without
putting his foot in his mouth. "I didn't mean to imply that
there was anything unsavory going on."

"How gratifying."

Wiping his moist forehead, he managed a thin smile. "I
was just curious about your position . . . uh . . ." He winced
at the unintentional innuendo. "At ElectroSonics, that is. I
mean, I was just wondering what kind of job requires you
to be available on weekends."

She smiled sweetly. "Don't foreign correspondents ever
work weekends?"

Sighing, he gave up and propped one hip against the car
fender. "I'm just trying to make conversation."

"Why?"

Irked to have lost control of this ridiculous situation, his
response was brusque and to the point. "I haven't the
slightest idea."

She cocked her head prettily. "You don't like me very much, do you?"

Startled by her candor, Devon studied her curious expression and found no trace of either sarcasm or anger. "I haven't made up my mind yet."

To his surprise, Jessica flashed an amused grin that warmed him to his toes. "I haven't made my mind up about you, either."

His own lips curved without permission. "So should we call a truce or what?"

"That would probably be the adult thing to do."

"How dull."

"It's only until Crandall gets back on his feet," she promised, her eyes twinkling as she reached into the bag and extracted a tiny, oblong box. "Then we can declare war again and go back to behaving like a couple of bad-tempered adolescents."

"Sounds like a plan," he murmured, watching in fascination as Jessica extracted a new spark plug from the box, whipped a feeler gage from her hip pocket and expertly adjusted the ground electrode until the plug gap measured exactly 0.75 millimeters. "Where'd you learn to do that?"

"Hmm? Oh, my stepfather. Ralph was his car for almost fifteen years." She blew on the plug's core nose and slid the gage back into her pocket. "When I graduated from college, Dad gave me the Jag on the condition that I learn how to take care of it."

As she moved in front of the vehicle, Devon stepped aside to allow her access. "What have you got against professional mechanics?"

"Not a thing but I've never seen one on the freeway at rush hour. Besides, I'd much rather handle my own problems instead of wringing my hands like a helpless twit until someone comes to my rescue."

Somehow Devon suspected that telling statement summed up Jessica's opinion of life itself. Despite her irritating snippiness and a high-handed attitude that irked him to the bone, he also realized that the woman he'd once written off as a haughty snob was gutty, self-reliant and admirably independent. Most importantly, Jessica Newcomb was different. She was a challenge.

And Devon had never been able to resist a challenge.

When she hoisted up on tiptoe to reach into the engine compartment, he leaned forward and plucked the long-necked rachet from her hand. "I'll finish this up," he said pleasantly. "You go relax, put your feet up, have a cup of coffee."

She stared at him as though he'd suggested piercing her tongue with a lug bolt. "Are you trying to be nice?"

He blinked. "Well, yes."

"Ah. Then I'll refuse your offer politely instead of pointing out how annoying it is to be patronized." She held out her hand. "My plug wrench, please."

"I was just trying to help."

Her foot tapped an impatient rhythm on the asphalt. "I don't need help and I don't want it. I thought I made myself clear on that point."

Embarrassed and unreasonably irritated, Devon slapped the tool into her palm and decided that female independence wasn't quite as admirable as he'd first thought. The woman was impossible. Talk about a lousy attitude.

Devon folded his arms. He didn't need this aggravation and asked himself why he was still standing there. The silent answer suddenly rolled through his mind, surprising him. Jessica Newcomb had all the charm of a starving grizzly but she was still the most intriguing woman he'd ever met. He simply couldn't bring himself to walk away.

Ducking under the hood, Jessica angled a furtive glance at the fuming man. She knew that she'd overreacted, and regretted snapping the poor guy's head off just because he'd offered to help. The thing was that he hadn't exactly offered. When he'd stepped in and taken over, she'd felt inept and foolish. That wasn't his fault, of course. He had no way of knowing why she was so sensitive. And she had no intention of telling him.

Still, she succumbed to an urge to make amends without enduring the humiliation of a full-blown apology. "Actually, a cup of coffee really does sound kind of good, doesn't it? I'll make some as soon as I'm finished here."

He answered with an indecipherable grunt.

As he studied a puffy cloud, she studied him, noticing that the rumpled fatigues had been replaced by crisply tailored beige slacks, a nylon Windbreaker and a cobalt golf shirt that gave his eyes a crystalline spark that was exceptionally appealing. His freshly shaved jawline was firm and strong, the perfect setting for a full-lipped, well-sculpted mouth.

All in all, he'd cleaned up surprisingly well. Well enough, in fact, to be a distraction. After twisting the wrench until the final plug was seated snugly, she chanced a quick glance at the lean hip that was propped against the fender. Her pulse increased instantly. The man was definitely attractive. Too attractive. She roughly withdrew the plug rachet, snuck another admiring glance and accidentally knocked off the socket head, which clattered through the engine and settled on a steel ledge at the bottom of the compartment.

Alerted by her frustrated groan, Devon peered into the engine. "I think I can reach it from under the car," he said, then looked up warily. "Unless, of course, you'd rather do it yourself."

She managed to smile. "Go ahead. My ego can handle the fact that your arms are longer than mine."

Chuckling softly, he knelt behind the driver's wheel, twisted awkwardly under the vehicle and felt blindly along the engine frame. "Am I close yet?"

Jessica pushed the air hose back for a better view. "About six inches forward... that's good. You're almost there. Watch out for that sharp—"

"Ouch!"

"Oh, good grief!" Jessica spun around the fender and helped the struggling man to his feet. "Are you all right?"

"Yeah." He opened his hand to reveal the shiny plug socket and a palm full of blood.

With a gasp of dismay, she tossed the socket aside and tried to look at the wound. "Let me see."

He pulled away. "It's nothing."

She yanked it back. "What are you afraid of?"

He stiffened indignantly. "I'm not afraid of anything."

"That's what I thought." She bit back a smile. "Now, let me see if you need stitches or not."

He reluctantly complied. As she studied the jagged cut at the web of his thumb, he sullenly eyed the toolbox. "I hope you don't have a suture kit in there."

"No. I use staples." Laughing at his horrified expression, she released him long enough to reach into her car and pull a wad of tissues from a box beside the driver's seat. Pressing the tissues against the wound, she folded his thumb into his palm to stem the bleeding and led him toward the underground parking garage.

"Where are we going?"

"Up to my lair," she said cheerfully. "That's a nasty cut but it's not very deep. A bandage and some antiseptic ought to fix you up just fine."

For a moment, she thought he was going to argue the point. Instead he followed passively, watching with interest as Jessica slid a plastic card into a slotted lock in the wrought-iron security gate. The gate slid open. Jessica tucked her card back into her pocket, extracted her apartment keys and led her wounded assistant through a honeycomb of concrete pillars.

Devon glanced around the dreary structure. "Is this where the residents park?"

Jessica poked an arrowed Up button between two elevator doors. "Yes. Homey, isn't it?"

"That's not the word I'd use. How many times have you been mugged down here?"

"Never," she replied with exaggerated indignation. "I'll have you know that this is an excellent neighborhood. Of course, once you leave the building, all bets are off."

When the elevator doors opened, Devon emitted a low whistle. "Classy," he murmured, eyeing the mirrored walls and crystal fixtures. "What happens if I bleed on that fancy carpet?"

"My association fees will go up, so please keep your bodily fluids to yourself."

Devon chuckled and shook his head. "You're a hard lady to figure," he said as the elevator hummed upward. "One minute you're playful as a kitten and the next you're cold enough to freeze meat. Are you deliberately trying to keep me off guard or do you have some kind of aversion to consistency?"

She looked away. "Probably a bit of both."

She could almost feel his gaze on the back of her neck as he waited for clarification of the obtuse statement. He'd have a long wait. Jessica couldn't clarify what she couldn't understand and, quite frankly, was as bewildered by her erratic behavior as was the poor man himself.

After having spent most of her life distancing herself with practiced civility, she suddenly found herself on an emotional roller coaster. Devon Monroe was a thrill seeker, a man who'd abandoned his father for fame and glory. He represented recklessness, irresponsibility and a wanton disregard for the sanctity of life. Yet she was fascinated by him.

In the close confines of the elevator, his musky aftershave enveloped her like a lover's arms. His skin was warm to her touch, the corded muscles of his wrist pulsing against her hand. Her mouth went dry; her heart pounded; her knees lost some of their strength.

When the elevator doors glided open, Jessica rushed into the hallway, vaguely aware that she'd hauled him out so roughly that he'd nearly tripped over his own feet. She managed an apologetic smile and guided him down the short corridor to her apartment.

After opening the door, she released his hand and tossed the keys on the wobbly TV tray that served as a lamp table. She gestured toward the kitchen. "Have a seat. I'll get the first-aid kit."

Devon stepped inside and inspected her eclectic decor with an expression of disbelief that would have been comical had Jessica not been so embarrassed.

She sighed. "Not what you expected?"

"Hardly." He frowned at the vintage dinette, a chrome-stripped hangover from the 1950s.

"It's almost an antique," she explained. "In a few decades, those vinyl chairs will be worth a fortune."

The corner of his mouth tilted in a quirky half smile. "If you say so."

Moistening her lips, she backed awkwardly toward her bedroom, acutely aware that she hadn't so much as fluffed the pillows on her unmade bed. "You can see the ocean from the balcony. I'll, uh, be right back."

With that, she ducked into her bedroom and shut the door before he got a glimpse of the mess inside. Sighing, she glanced around the disheveled room. A pile of clothing had been heaped over the chair that served as a laundry hamper. Her dresser was covered by loose change, costume jewelry and an untidy assortment of cologne bottles. A silky hunk of satin protruded from a nearly closed drawer.

All in all, it looked like the result of a bomb blast. She'd planned to tidy up later. Of course, it always seemed like housecleaning was more plan than action. She'd never been particularly meticulous about such things, although before illness had sapped her strength she'd certainly done a better job of shoveling away the biggest chunks of clutter. Since she rarely had company, there hadn't been much incentive to exert herself. Now Devon was in her tacky living room, probably wondering how anyone could live in such a pig-sty.

Swallowing her humiliation, Jessica reminded herself that all the man wanted was a bandage. It wasn't her job to impress him, or anyone else, for that matter. She lived the way she lived. If he didn't like that, tough.

Thus fortified, she went into the bathroom, wincing at the intimate display of lingerie draped over the shower rod. She cleared a spot on the littered vanity and rifled through her well-stocked medicine cabinet.

A few minutes later she returned to the living room with the supplies. The French doors were open and Devon stood in the doorway with one foot on the balcony.

He looked up as she entered the room. "You're right. The view is great."

"That's why I bought the place." She set the first-aid supplies on the counter, grateful that a pile of dirty dishes were concealed in the dishwasher instead of heaped in the sink.

After closing the balcony doors, Devon joined her in the kitchen. "I like your place. It's ... cozy."

Aware that he was watching her closely, Jessica avoided his gaze as she carefully removed the saturated tissues and held his hand under a thin stream of lukewarm water. If he was waiting for an explanation as to why a pricy penthouse was furnished with Goodwill discards, he'd be sadly disappointed. Her financial situation, like her personal life, was nobody's business but her own.

The pipes rattled as she turned off the faucet with more force than necessary. Without a word, she grabbed a clean towel and dried his injured hand. His fingers were lean and strong, with clean, well-groomed nails and a faint wisp of dark hair accentuating each knuckle. It was a handsome hand, rugged, tanned, exquisitely masculine.

Gracious, it was warm in here. She wiped a forearm across her moist brow then inspected his palm. The jagged cut was about an inch long, extending from the base of his thumb into the fleshy webbing. "This will heal better with a butterfly bandage."

With his head bent forward, his breath warmed the top of her head. "You're the doctor," he said softly.

She issued a jerky nod then snatched up a tube of antibiotic ointment and went to work.

When she'd finished, he held up his bandaged hand and flexed his fingers. "As field triage goes, this would definitely pass muster."

"You're too kind."

Smiling, he glanced around the kitchen. His gaze lingered on the electric coffee machine beside a black glass cooking top. "Say, didn't you mention something about making coffee?"

Jessica fidgeted, increasingly uncomfortable with his nearness and her own peculiar reaction to it. "I may have to give you a rain check on that."

He pursed his lips, regarding her thoughtfully. "Have I upset you?"

*Yes,* she thought miserably, *but not the way you think.*

"Not at all." Sidling a safe distance away, she casually gestured toward the blinking light on her telephone answering machine. "It's just that I should return Crandall's call."

The excuse was as lame as a three-legged mule and they both knew it. Fortunately, Devon proved himself too much of a gentlemen to call her on it. "All right," he said pleasantly. "Another time."

"Yes." She clasped her hands together and followed him to the front door. "I'll look forward to it."

He opened the door and hesitated. Jessica held her breath. Finally, he lifted his bandaged hand and said, "Thanks again."

She exhaled all at once. "You're welcome."

He touched two fingers to his forehead, spun on his heel and was gone.

Trembling, Jessica closed the door and sagged against the jamb, wondering what on earth had come over her. She glanced at her watch. Since her next dose of medicine wasn't due for hours, that obviously wasn't the reason for her sudden weakness. Changing spark plugs hadn't been strenuous enough to account for her physical symptoms and the minor chore certainly had nothing to do with the erotic images flashing through her troubled mind.

Cooling her face with her palms, she issued a lusty sigh and returned to the kitchen, realizing that life would have been a whole lot easier if her boss's son had turned out to be a real dog.

She shook off the distracting thought and pushed the Message button. Crandall's voice boomed out of the machine. "Jessica? Pick up.... Are you there? Dammit." *Click.*

The tape whirred into another message. "Jessica? Call me at the hospital. It's important." *Click. Whir.* "Where are you, Jessica? Why haven't you called back? If I don't hear from you in fifteen minutes—" The worry in Crandall's voice stabbed her like a guilty sword. She couldn't stand to hear another word and pressed the Next Message button. "It's been fifteen minutes, Jessi—"

She hit the button and was startled by her stepfather's soft voice. "Hello, sweetheart. Give me a call when you can. We have to... make arrangements."

Gasping, Jessica quickly shut off the machine. Her blood ran like ice in her veins. Dear God, it was time. She'd have to go home soon. And that scared her to death.

## Chapter Three

Devon drove directly from Jessica's place to the hospital He found Crandall sitting up in bed, calmly studying what appeared to be a financial report and looking much stronger than he had yesterday afternoon. The IV tubes had been removed and much of the color had returned to Crandall's ruddy complexion.

Massively relieved by his father's obvious improvement, Devon stepped inside the room and closed the door. "Since you're not screaming at the 911 operator, I assume you've heard from Jessica."

Crandall peered over his reading glasses. "Yes. She called a few moments ago."

"Did she tell you that I found her in the parking lot with a wrench in her hand and grease on her nose?"

"Really? What on earth was she doing?"

Devon dropped his jacket on the tubular steel footboard and pulled up a chair. "Changing spark plugs."

"Ah." Crandall nodded sagely, readjusted his glasses and returned his attention to the fat sheath of bound papers.

"You don't seem surprised to hear that."

"I'm not, actually. She repaired a forklift once."

For some reason, that news wasn't particularly shocking. Devon was getting the idea that there was very little Jessica Newcomb couldn't do if she put her mind to it. "Don't you have mechanics to handle that sort of thing?"

"As I recall, the incident occurred after-hours." Still staring at the report in his lap, Crandall cleared his throat. "By the way, your efforts this morning were appreciated."

"No problem." Devon leaned back in his chair and propped his ankle on his knee. "Since you expect her to be at your beck and call, I'm surprised you haven't gotten her a beeper."

Crandall's bushy brows dipped in an irritable frown. "She refuses to use one."

"Good for her." The more Devon learned about the elusive Jessica Newcomb, the more he liked her. "So, what was the emergency?"

The older man glanced up apprehensively. "Emergency?"

"Yeah. Your call this morning sounded like a matter of life and death."

"Oh. I, uh..." Crandall bought a moment by searching the cluttered nightstand for a pen. He plucked one from beside a boxed deck of cards, removed the cap and tediously fitted it over the plastic handle. Only when the writing instrument was poised over the paper did he brusquely respond to his son's query. "I needed a file from the office."

"A file," Devon repeated dumbly. "You dragged me out of bed to chase down a woman on her day off so she could bring you a lousy file."

The pen tapped a nervous cadence on the crisp white margin. "All of my executives are brilliant, effective and extremely well paid. They understand, as you apparently do not, the competitive demands of a global economy."

"So that gives you the right to work people into the grave and turn a vibrant, beautiful woman into an exhausted shell?"

Crandall threw the pen into the folds of the report and slammed the cover shut. "It gives me the right to expect excellence and loyalty, two more terms with which you are evidently unfamiliar."

Stung, Devon leapt to his feet and lashed out in anger. "What the hell would you know about loyalty? You've never pledged allegiance to anyone but yourself and your unending pursuit of the almighty dollar."

"Those dollars bought you the fanciest clothes and the finest schools," Crandall snapped. "And you took it all, soaked up luxuries like an ungrateful sponge then refused to give anything back."

"I refused to become your clone, if that's what you mean." The memory of his father's previous manipulation throbbed like a raw nerve. Two years ago, when Devon had turned down his offer of an executive position with the company, Crandall had secretly informed the Associated Press that their prized correspondent was burned out and emotionally unstable.

The underhanded ploy hadn't succeeded, of course, but Devon had been infuriated by the attempt. "That still galls you, doesn't it? You can't stand the fact that after pulling every devious trick in the book, you still couldn't break me, couldn't get want you wanted."

Leaning back into the pillows, Crandall emitted a snort of disgust. "I offered you a future."

"Bull," Devon snapped. "You tried to destroy my career."

"That career nearly killed you! What was I supposed to do when my only son comes home with a bullet in his gut and a leg full of shrapnel?" Frustrated, Crandall raked his fingers through hair that was still as thick and dark as was his son's. "There's no reasoning with you. You're just like your mother."

The comment struck with the force of a fist. Then an image floated through Devon's mind, a vision of the smiling, blue-eyed woman that he'd seen only in photographs. He swallowed a sudden lump and spoke softly. "I wouldn't know."

Crandall looked away. "No, you wouldn't."

Balling his fists into painful knots, Devon stared out the window, stifled by silent recrimination. All he knew about his mother was that she'd been young and beautiful and that she'd died giving him life.

Although Crandall had never directly blamed his son, the resentment had been reflected in every frigid look, every stinging word. As a child, Devon had guilelessly knelt beside his bed asking God to return his mother and take him instead. He'd thought it a fair trade, one that would make his father smile again. Apparently the Almighty hadn't agreed because Devon had always awakened each morning, disappointed and besieged by shame.

That shame had never gone away.

Sighing, Devon gazed out from the tenth-story vantage point absently watching miniature cars moving along a distant freeway, and trying to ignore the palpable tension that always existed when he and his father were in the same room. It seemed that they were bound only by blood, sharing nothing except common ancestry and bitter memories. But Devon was tired of the pain and anger. Life was too short.

So he pushed the hurt aside and changed subjects. "I hear you're going to be released on Monday."

"It's about time," came the peevish reply. "The production schedules are already a week behind."

Devon glanced over his shoulder. "You do realize that it'll be a few weeks before you can go back to the office."

"In a few weeks I'll be bankrupt." Crandall's jaw set into a stubborn line. "I've got a business to run."

The idiotic rationale set Devon's teeth on edge. "And who do you suppose is going to run the damned company after you've worked yourself into a massive coronary—those brilliant executives you keep bragging about?"

"What difference does it make?" Crandall flung the report onto the nightstand and sent an empty plastic water glass and the box of cards clattering to the floor. "You sure don't give a damn."

Devon spun away from the window, his voice rising to a shout. "If that's what you think, then what in hell am I doing here?"

"I didn't ask you to come." Crandall, too, was shouting. He leaned forward in bed, his puffy face growing redder by the minute. "Go back to the career that means so damned much to you. You're not needed here."

"Yeah. I can see that." Snatching his jacket, Devon strode furiously to the door but as he grabbed the knob, an echo from the past whispered in the back of his mind.

*I didn't ask you to come back...! I don't need you...! I don't need anybody...!*

Devon remembered the moment as clearly as if it had happened yesterday. He'd been studying in the dorm room with Larkin and Roberto when one of the vice-chancellors had shown up. Devon had been told to pack his things. Fifteen minutes later, he'd been marched to the administrative office to face the father he hadn't seen in months.

Crandall had pinned him with frigid eyes. "My son the car thief. How proud you make me."

Deep inside, Devon had been shattered by his father's contempt but had long ago learned that displaying weakness was a fatal flaw. Besides, Crandall's fury had hardly been unexpected. After all, a man without anger doesn't abandon his son to a state lockup for three months.

So Devon merely lifted his chin and held his father's cold gaze with one of defiance and said nothing. After a moment, Crandall emitted a scornful snort and strode to the door, holding it open. "Hurry up," he growled. "I've just spent twelve hours on an airplane. I'm hot, I'm tired and I'm definitely not in the mood to indulge a dawdling child."

Devon followed without remarking that he was no longer a child. He'd tasted terror; he'd seen death. He was a man now. A cowardly man.

The drive to Bel-Aire was a silent one. Only when the big Cadillac pulled into the gated drive did Crandall announce that Aunt Emmaline would not be there to greet them. "Your aunt has been relieved of her guardianship responsibilities," Crandall told him. "Please don't delude yourself into the mistaken belief that you can continue to run wild in the streets. The new housekeeper has been instructed to keep me apprised of your every move."

With a stoic shrug, the sullen twelve-year-old conveyed that he couldn't have cared less. Besides, he'd always disliked his Aunt Emmaline, who found caring for her nephew to be a bothersome, albeit lucrative, lifestyle interruption. Devon doubted the new woman would be an improvement. It didn't matter one way or the other. Devon didn't care about anything anymore. He was dead inside.

The moment Devon stepped into the house, he was swept up in a pair of strong, loving arms. *"Gott im Himmel! What a handsome boy you are!"*

Startled, he dropped the small suitcase he'd been carrying, pushed frantically away and stumbled backward, gaping at the brick of a woman whose bright blue eyes reflected sudden bewilderment.

"Forgive me. I forget my place." Tossing the fat ecru braid back over her shoulder, the woman managed an awkward curtsy and respectfully bowed her head as Crandall entered the foyer.

"This is Gunda Meineke," he told Devon brusquely. "Make no mistake, she is quite capable of making you tow the line. Isn't that right, Gunda?"

"*Ja, mein Herr.*"

"Good. Thank you, Gunda. You are dismissed."

"*Jawohl.*" As she turned away from Crandall, her solemn expression broke into a sunshine grin. Her sly wink was for Devon's eyes only and conveyed more deftly than words that the two of them were going to get along just fine.

After Gunda left, a cold silence settled over the room. Devon picked up his suitcase, eyeing the stairs and longing for the solitude of his bedroom. "Can I go now?"

"No." Crandall clasped his hands behind his back and stared sternly over his son's head. "There are some things we, uh, need to discuss."

Devon's heart sank. He ducked his head and studied his sneakers.

"I realize that the past weeks have been difficult for you," Crandall said. "I wish things had turned out differently, of course, but there's nothing to be done about that now. Hopefully, you have learned something from this unfortunate experience." He absently glanced at his watch, a habitual gesture that never failed to make Devon feel as though he were keeping his father from something that was really important. Like making money. "Unfortunately, we'll have to continue this discussion in a couple of weeks. My plane leaves in two hours."

Devon's head snapped up. "Where are you going?"

Annoyed by the sharp question, Crandall spoke with exaggerated civility. "Back to Europe, of course. Since this trip was arranged without proper notice, I wasn't able to clear my calendar. There are some things that must be attended to before I can schedule another visit."

A cold pit of fury opened up in Devon's skinny chest. "Don't bother!" he shouted as hot tears filled his eyes. "I didn't ask you to come back in the first place! I don't need you! I don't need anybody!" Dropping the suitcase, he spun around and stumbled up the stairs.

Crandall hadn't followed. It had been eight months before the Monroe men had seen each other again.

Twenty years later Devon stood in his father's hospital room watching the past collide with the present. It was ironic that although their roles had now been reversed, the same hurtful words concealed the same pain and fear of rejection. Back then, Devon had needed his father and needed him desperately, just as Crandall now needed his son. This time, the cry for help would not go unanswered.

Glancing over his shoulder, Devon saw the older man staring out the window with a feigned stoicism so like his own that it took his breath away. He swallowed hard, then ambled casually across the room, dropped his jacket on the foot of the bed and swung the extension table across his father's lap. Crandall's head remained immobile but his dark gaze followed his son's every move.

Devon picked up the cards from the floor and sat down. "Gin or canasta?"

Crandall's eyes narrowed. "Gin."

Devon shook the cards from the box and shuffled them. "I should warn you that I'll cheat to win."

"Of course you will. You're my son." Crandall smiled. "Now shut up and deal."

Jessica opened the hospital room door and jolted to a stop, unable to believe the sight that greeted her. Devon was hunched in his chair scrawling on some kind of pad while Crandall, with his reading glasses set low on his nose, shuffled like a Las Vegas cardsharper.

Originally Jessica had brought the deck to Crandall's room because he'd been having trouble sleeping and she'd thought solitaire might be a relaxing diversion. At the time he'd seemed irked by the gesture, insisting that games of any kind were a stupid waste of time. Now, however, he was so engrossed that he hadn't even noticed her presence. The entire scene was so alien, so unlike her stodgy, no-nonsense boss that Jessica wouldn't have been more shocked to catch him doing the wild thing with a night nurse.

Crandall squared the deck and smirked at his son. "That last hand put me so far out of reach, you might as well haul up the white flag."

Concentrating on his calculations, Devon's only response was a muttered, "We'll see." After a moment, he uttered a crow of pleasure and wielded the pencil like a triumphant wand. "You're still five points down."

"What?" Crandall dropped the cards and whipped off his glasses. "Let me see those figures."

Grinning happily, Devon handed over the score sheet. "Read it and weep, Dad. Youth conquers all."

As Crandall irritably snatched the scratch pad, Jessica cleared her throat. The men looked up simultaneously with matching expressions of surprise.

Jessica could barely suppress a smile. "Am I interrupting?"

"No, of course not." Devon stood, offering his chair.

"Thank you." She sat gracefully, back straight, ankles primly crossed, in the socially acceptable manner that she'd been taught since childhood. She laid her pocketbook on the nightstand and scrutinized Crandall's pained expression. "The last time I saw that look on your face, a competitor had just undercut us on a million-dollar contract."

Ignoring the comment, Crandall woefully studied Devon's neatly penciled figures. "Do you have a calculator in your purse?"

"No, I'm sorry."

A sly chuckle emanated from above her right shoulder. "For some odd reason, Dad seems to think that I'm not above cheating to win."

Crandall's thin lips twitched in a reluctant smile. "Damn right." He tossed the scratch pad on the table, eyes gleaming with pride as he regarded his son. "I expect a rematch."

"Great. I'll see you this evening."

When Devon reached for his jacket, Jessica blurted, "You don't have to leave." The words rushed out in such panic that she blushed to her roots. "That is, I didn't mean to chase you away."

"You didn't." He smiled pleasantly. "By the way, where's the file?"

"File? What file?"

Devon angled a narrowed smile at his red-faced father. "That's what I thought."

Jessica glanced from Crandall, who was suddenly besieged by a coughing fit, back to Devon. "Is this some kind of private joke or am I just dense?"

"Let's just say the subject came up during a discussion of how hard you've been working." Devon slid his father a wry look. "Does she at least have Sundays off?"

A pink flush crept along Crandall's ears. "Jessica knows that she can take time off any time she wants."

"Good." With a flick of his wrist, he flipped the jacket over his shoulder. "So, Jessica, do you like the desert?"

"The desert?" she repeated dumbly. "You mean cactus and sagebrush, that kind of thing?"

"No cactus. The place I'm thinking of is more chaparral and buttonwillows. Quite nice, actually. Fresh air, sunshine, no telephones. You'll enjoy it. I'll bring lunch."

She blinked in confusion. "Was there an invitation buried inside that glowing testimonial?"

"As a matter of fact, there was." His heels scuffed together and he bent in a mock bow. "Would madam care to join this unworthy knave for an exhilarating day of exploring nature?"

"Yes, actually. Madam would." Had she really said that?

His grin widened. "I'll pick you up at seven a.m.," he said, then touched two fingers to his forehead and disappeared out the door.

Jessica was still trying to figure out why on earth she'd agreed to such a thing when rustling bedclothes captured her attention.

Crandall swiveled the extension table away from his lap. "Do you think that was wise, Jessica?"

She sighed. "Probably not, but I haven't been anywhere in so long I'm going stir-crazy. Besides, it sounds like fun."

His brows wrinkled in that paternal frown that she both despised and adored. "You must be careful not to exert yourself."

"I will."

"It might be prudent to inform Devon of your illness so he'd be better prepared to—"

"No!" Frustrated, Jessica pushed back the chair and stood. "We've discussed this before, Crandall. I'm not a pathetic, fragile creature and I won't have people treating me as though I am."

"I'm sure that won't happen."

"Oh, right." She issued a dry laugh. "And I didn't have five hysterical messages on my machine this morning because I wasn't available to answer the phone."

He had the grace to look embarrassed. "Perhaps I overreacted."

"A tad."

"I was concerned about you."

Jessica heaved a conflicted sigh. "I know. You're a dear, dear friend and I appreciate your concern." That was true enough although Crandall's frequent "overreaction" had convinced her just how vital it was to maintain secrecy throughout the arduous course of recovery. After all, Jessica had a lot of friends. If she'd told everyone and even half of them mimicked her boss's smothering protectiveness, she'd have been a complete basket case.

As it was, she regretted telling Crandall, although ethically she'd had no other choice. Since Jessica held a key position in the company, Crandall had the right to understand her situation in order to make informed decisions about reassigning her duties. Or terminating her entirely.

Despite horror stories of employers who'd fired ill workers, Jessica hadn't seriously believed that Crandall would ever do such a thing. She had, however, feared a job shuffle in which she might be given a less demanding assignment; but that hadn't happened. Crandall had been unfailingly supportive. She loved him for that, even if his constant fretting about her health drove her crazy.

Crandall spoke suddenly. "There are so many people who care about you, Jessica, people who need the opportunity to support you through this difficult period with their good wishes and friendship."

"I have support," she insisted. "I have my family and I have you. Frankly, that's about all the support I can handle."

Sighing, she sat on the edge of the mattress. The past six months had been a grueling ordeal, emotionally as well as physically. There had been so many lies, beginning with a fabricated European vacation story used to conceal her ten-week recuperation period.

The deception was taking its toll but the alternative would be worse. Jessica feared that if her friends and co-workers found out about her illness, they might treat her differently. She couldn't bear the thought of being clucked over or babied or, God forbid, pitied. It was just easier to keep the whole maudlin mess under wraps, at least for a while.

Crandall cleared his throat. "You realize, of course, that being ill is nothing to be ashamed of."

The unexpected statement jolted her to the core. "I'm *not* ashamed, I'm *angry*. In fact, I'm mad as hell that my body had been invaded by something I can't even see. This thing has violated me. It's taken away my peace of mind. I don't feel safe anymore. I feel vulnerable and that *makes me angry*."

"Jessica, please . . . you mustn't upset yourself."

She massaged her forehead and returned to the chair. "I'm sorry. Sometimes I just need to give the old soapbox a workout. But things aren't that bleak anymore. I'm getting stronger every day and in a couple of months I should be completely back to normal." Another lie, of course. She'd never be normal again but at least she was alive and the chances of her staying that way were increasing by the day. "When this is over—really over—I'll have no problem discussing what has happened. I might even give speeches to other people who are facing the same kind of surgery. Until then, I hope you'll continue to respect my wishes and my privacy."

"You know that I will."

She gave his hand a grateful squeeze. "You're such a fine man."

He glanced away, seeming less embarrassed than thoughtful. "I doubt my son would agree with you."

"Now, that's not true. I know you've had problems in the past but you seem to be working them out. When I came in, the two of you were relating like old chums."

"A few moments out of a lifetime." He stared silently across the room for a moment. "We had another argument this morning."

Jessica's heart sank. "People quarrel all the time. The important thing is that you obviously got through it."

Tiredly massaging his eyelids, Crandall shook away her optimism. "We simply put it aside. The wounds are still there, as deep and raw as they ever were."

Touched by the poignant confession, she chanced the question that had always been off-limits. "Does this have anything to do with what happened two years ago?"

"I suppose it does, although our relationship has been strained for so long that I can't even remember a time when we were close." A sad smile curved one corner of his mouth. "I always considered parenting to be a distraction, an interruption in my life. Apparently my son now shares similar feelings about the expected duties of an offspring."

She wanted to dispute that but simply didn't know enough about Devon's relationship with his father to do so. In fact, she didn't know much about Crandall's personal feelings, either. He'd always shielded his emotions with brusque detachment, so his current candor was doubly surprising.

And his next statement was astounding. "I tried to have Devon fired, you know."

All she could do was stare, certain that she'd misheard.

Folding his arms, Crandall gazed blankly across the room and spoke to the air. "When he came home two years ago, I hardly recognized him. Or rather, what was left of him. Of course, I understood that all young men crave adventure. That's why I allowed him to have his foolish fling with this journalism business. But enough was enough, can't you see? It was time for him to come home and do the work that was his destiny."

A tingle of shock slid down her spine. "What work was that?"

The question seemed to stun him. "The company, of course. I spent my entire life building an empire for my son. I couldn't allow him to throw all that away. You understand that, don't you?"

She closed her eyes and took a shaky breath. "What did you do, Crandall?" There was a moment of silence before he told her. She moaned, shaking her head in disbelief. No wonder Devon had been so furious.

"Do you think I was wrong?" Crandall asked.

"Yes."

"Then what should I have done? Surely you understand that I couldn't sit back and watch my son commit suicide."

Jessica felt like she had a stomach full of lead. She'd always believed Devon to be an irresponsible thrill seeker; now she wondered if he considered life on the edge of danger to be an act of defiance or an escape from perceived tyranny.

In either case, she'd misjudged both father and son. The precipice between them was wider than she'd feared and deeper than she ever could have imagined. Now she wasn't certain there was anything that could bridge that gap of mistrust and betrayal. That made her very sad.


Devon's fingers flexed over the telephone in his father's library. He withdrew his hand, wiped his palm on his jeans and stretched out on the tufted burgundy leather couch. This had always been Devon's favorite room, a secluded enclave walled with row upon row of richly bound books. This place, smelling of ripe leather and the wisdom of ages, was where young Devon's imagination had once soared to faraway places, to endless adventure. No matter how broken his spirit had been, this room had always made him whole.

Now he closed his eyes and breathed deeply, absorbing residual vibrations of happier times. A drowsy warmth radiated from his solar plexus, a peaceful courage that finally made its lazy way to his limbs. Before the comforting resolve faded, he picked up the phone and dialed.

Roberto answered on the third ring.

"Well, whatdaya know," Devon drawled. "I didn't think the feds ever let their crack prosecutors spend Saturdays at home. Shouldn't you be out busting terrorists or something?"

An ageless chuckle filtered through the line. "It's been a slow week, *mi hermano*. Besides, the NBA playoff is on cable."

"Ah, that explains it. I wouldn't want you to miss the Bulls just to keep the streets safe."

"A man's got to keep his priorities straight," Roberto agreed. "So how's your dad doing?"

"He'll be coming home on Monday."

"That's great. Must be a load off your mind."

"Yeah. A big one." Devon hooked a hand behind his neck, realizing how much he'd missed hearing his friend's voice. "So, what's Larkin up to these days? Last time I saw him, he'd just hung a shingle with some Beverly Hills psychiatric group."

"That didn't last long," Roberto said. "The money was good but he wasn't happy being a star shrink, so he opened a practice in Baldwin Park where he can serve—and I'm quoting now—'the people who need him most.'"

"Do I detect a hint of wryness?"

Roberto muttered a frustrated oath. "Come on, man. People in the barrio don't give a bleep about repressed childhood memories or sagging self-esteem. All they want is to work a decent job, have enough food on the table and get through the day without stopping a bullet."

"It's tough out there," Devon agreed. "Maybe Larkin wants to help people deal with the violence and take control of their lives."

A silent moment was punctuated with a long-suffering sigh. "Larkin doesn't know what he wants. It's been four years since the divorce, time for him to hoist up his shorts and get on with his own life."

A lump rose in Devon's chest. After all the years, none of them had changed much. Roberto was still charging headlong into life, muscling through obstacles without fear of consequence. And he was still angry. Devon knew that Roberto wasn't unsympathetic to Larkin's plight, but he was obviously frustrated at his inability to help.

Unfortunately, no one could help Larkin, not even his best friends. After years of punishing himself for his parents' divorce, the breakup of his own marriage had nearly pushed Larkin over the edge. That was, Devon thought, yet another solid argument on why intimate relationships should be avoided like the plague.

Roberto's voice broke into his thoughts. "Lark has always listened to you. Maybe you could talk to him. How long are you going to be in town?"

Devon's mouth was suddenly dry enough to spit cotton. "I'm not sure."

"Think you'll be around next Thursday?"

It took a moment to cough out the words. "Yeah. I'll be around."

A heavy silence fell over the line. Finally Roberto said, "Thursday's Tommy's birthday."

"I know." Devon massaged his forehead, needing no reminder of the significant occasion. Twenty years ago, the three surviving roommates had huddled in the dorm, pricked their fingers and sworn a solemn oath to honor their lost friend every year for as long as they lived.

"Lark and I usually meet at the Steer 'N' Stein on La Cienega," Roberto said. "We can go somewhere else if you'd rather—"

"No. That's fine." Devon cleared his throat. "I'll be there."

"See you then," Roberto said.

"Yeah. See you." Devon hung up the phone. So far, so good. He'd committed to the meeting. Now all he had to do was find the guts to actually get through it.

For two decades Tommy's birthday had been commemorated by the Brotherhood to celebrate their fallen comrade's life and honor his friendship. Each man shared the moment, no matter where he was or what he was doing. Last year, in fact, Devon had been dodging mortars in a Sudanese village when the appointed time had arrived. Hunching behind a stone wall, he'd lifted his canteen in silent salute knowing that thousands of miles away, his buddies were doing exactly the same thing.

Now for the first time in years the Blackthorn Brotherhood could raise their glasses together. It would be a bittersweet reunion. Guilt was such a powerful sword.

## Chapter Four

It was still dark when Devon pulled into Jessica's condominium complex so he was surprised to find her bundled in a thick ski jacket and waiting beside the parking garage gate. He pulled up, letting the engine idle as he exited the car and took a brown grocery bag from her arms. "I told you I'd take care of lunch."

"Yes, but you didn't mention breakfast."

"Breakfast?" Devon's stomach growled hungrily as he peered into the bag. "Is that thermos by any chance filled with coffee?"

"Uh-huh." She slid into the passenger seat and reached out for the bag, which she set on the floor between her feet. "And I hope you like apple fritters. There's a little shop around the corner that makes the best in the world."

The thought made his mouth water. "No wonder my father hired you," he murmured, settling into the driver's seat. "You think of everything."

She laughed happily. "I try."

Devon pulled out of the parking lot, merging into thick traffic that clogged Century Boulevard regardless of the hour. He slid a quick glance to his right as Jessica shrugged out of the oversize jacket, which was evidently too warm for the car's toasty interior. "Just toss that in back," he said.

When she twisted around to comply, she spotted the lunch basket on the rear seat. "Gracious, it looks like Gunda out-did herself."

"Gunda had nothing to do with it," he replied indignantly. "I'll have you know that I prepared everything in that basket with my own hands."

"Really?" She dropped the jacket and resettled herself in the Mercedes's plush bucket seat, absently smoothing a plaid scarf that was draped around the scalloped neck of her casual knit top. "So, how many peanut butter-and-jelly sandwiches did you fix?"

He smiled. "Four."

"Great. Peanut butter is my favorite."

"There's also a fine selection of chips and cheese puffs for madam's dining pleasure."

"Umm. I can hardly wait. But meanwhile..." She rooted through the bag for the thermos, then set two mugs in the dashboard's retractable cup holder and filled them with steaming coffee. "Do you take cream or sugar?"

"Don't tell me you have a quart of cream and a sugar bowl in there, too."

"Not real cream, I'm afraid. Just little packets of the dry stuff." She looked up in alarm. "That's all right, isn't it?"

"If it's all right with you, it's all right with me. I don't use it."

"How about sugar?"

"Nope. I drink coffee straight."

A stoplight gave him the opportunity to watch her reach back into the bag and pull out a wad of napkins, one of which she spread across his lap as if she were a fussy waiter. She wrapped another napkin around the fattest fritter

Devon had ever seen and offered it to him, only to yank it back when he eagerly reached out. "Are you sure you can drive with one hand?"

That seemed a ludicrous question in Los Angeles, where freeways were crowded by drivers known to shave, gargle and squirm into panty hose during rush hour commutes. "Of course I can."

Eyes twinkling with mischief, she wiggled the glazed treat just beyond reach. "But doesn't the vehicle code state that all drivers must have both hands on the wheel at all times?"

The bakery-fresh aroma of tart apples and pungent cinnamon was about to drive him wild. "I don't know what the damn code says. I do know, however, that if you don't give me that fritter in five seconds flat, I'm going to pull over and take it by force."

"You wouldn't!"

He sighed. "No, I wouldn't. But I might fall to my knees and beg."

"That's so demeaning. I'd much prefer a manly grovel."

"You're a cruel woman."

"So I've been told." With an impish grin, she handed him the fritter. *"Bon appétit."*

Since maintaining dignity was now a moot point, he flashed a grateful smile and grabbed the sticky confection before she changed her mind.

Over the next twenty minutes, conversation was limited while they enjoyed their breakfast. When the final fritter had been reduced to crumbly rubble, Jessica tossed the gooey napkins into the bag and shook the thermos. "It sounds like there's another cup left."

"You go ahead. I've had enough."

"Me, too." She put the thermos away and leaned back with a contented sigh. "This was a good idea. Thank you for inviting me."

"You act like the day is over. It's just beginning."

"I know." She idly watched the city blur beyond the freeway railing. "It's just been such a long time since I've gone anywhere fun."

"Why's that?"

"Lack of time, I suppose."

He glanced over and noticed that the bluish tinge beneath her eyes had faded but was still visible. "My father works you too hard."

"Crandall doesn't expect anything from others that he doesn't also expect from himself."

"Is that supposed to be a defense?"

She considered that for a moment. "You're very angry with him, aren't you?"

Devon tightened his grip on the leather-bound steering wheel without answering. They drove in silence for a few minutes before Jessica spoke again.

"I guess you have a right to be upset," she said quietly. "Crandall told me how he interfered with your career."

He skimmed her a skeptical glance. "Did he?"

"Yes. He regrets it, of course."

"The only thing he regrets is that it didn't work."

"That's an awful thing to say." Pulling one knee onto the seat, Jessica turned sideways to face him. "I know that Crandall can be difficult at times, but he's the only father you have. The man loves you, for goodness' sake, and despite your who-gives-a-damn attitude, I think you love him, too."

That was true enough, although Devon had no intention of admitting it. Instead, he listened in rapt fascination as Jessica continued to plead his father's case with perplexing vigor.

"I'm not condoning Crandall's actions," she said. "But it's not unusual for parents to hope their children will follow in their own footsteps. My stepfather, for example, is a successful cardiologist. He's a wonderful man and I love him dearly, but he was so disappointed when I pursued an

M.B.A. instead of an M.D. that he sent a condolence card for my graduation.''

''That must have ticked you off.''

''Not really.'' She leaned back, smiling. ''He meant it as a joke and that's how I took it. The point is that your father's feelings are perfectly normal even though his methods may be a bit, well, extreme.''

Extreme. Yes, that was probably an apt description of the man who'd abandoned his biological son to a juvenile prison so that his emotional child, the Company, would not be inconvenienced. That painful memory, and countless others, had wedged a barrier of mistrust between them, a wall that Devon feared could never be breached.

Jessica's soft voice broke into his thoughts. ''You still haven't forgiven him, have you?''

''Why do you say that?''

She sighed. ''Because your jaw is twitching and you're squeezing the wheel so hard your knuckles are white.''

At that moment his fingers started to ache. He loosened the strangling grip. ''What's done is done,'' Devon replied tightly. ''My father and I both want to put the past behind us.'' That was certainly true, although he doubted that either of them knew exactly how to accomplish such a daunting task.

Jessica regarded him intently. ''I'm pleased to hear that.''

The caution in her voice didn't escape his notice. It seemed a depressing affirmation that she, too, doubted that reconciliation was a viable option. ''Why do you care?'' he asked suddenly.

She blinked, taken aback by his brusque tone. ''Excuse me?''

''You seem inordinately interested in repairing relationships. Did you minor in psychology or is dime-store counseling just a hobby?'' The moment he saw her crushed expression he wished that he could yank back the words and swallow them whole. ''Look . . . I didn't mean that.''

"Yes, you did." She managed a thin smile. "It's annoying to have an outsider poking a snoopy nose into one's private affairs, even if said outsider believes that she has a good reason to do so."

"Do you have a good reason?"

She shrugged. "That depends on one's perspective, I imagine. Crandall has been a good friend to me. I admire him and care about his happiness."

"And you think that patching things up between us will make him happy?"

"I know it will."

Devon slid a quick glance toward Jessica, who was staring thoughtfully at her own lap. Suddenly she looked up, her eyes filled with the most extraordinary sadness.

"Life is so short," she whispered. "In the blink of an eye, those we love can be taken away. The worst grief in the world is the memory of apologies that can never be heard and regrets that are never laid to rest."

Something in her quivering voice touched a chord deep inside him. "It almost sounds like you're speaking from experience."

She turned away, gazing out the window as though engrossed in passing scenery. After several moments she spoke again. "My father—my real father—was the kindest, most gentle man in the world. Every day, rain or shine, he'd take my hand and walk me to school. In the afternoon, he was always waiting with this huge smile, ready to escort me home. I adored him and never realized that he was... different. Then when I was about eight, my friends started taunting me, calling my father Elephant Man." She glanced over her shoulder. "His weight hovered between three and four hundred pounds."

When Devon accepted the explanation with a nod, she returned her gaze to the window and was silent for a long moment.

"Shame is such an insidious thing," she said finally. "It creeps in slowly, month after month, until it permeates every cell, every fiber of your being. You're not the same person anymore. You become cruel, ugly, blinded by the bigotry of others."

Devon's heart went out to her. "Is that what happened to you?"

"Yes. The more my friends mocked him, the more humiliated I became. Eventually, I couldn't stand it anymore. I begged my mother to make Daddy stay home, so the other kids wouldn't see him. Of course, he overheard."

Devon exhaled slowly. "That must have been tough on you both."

"He was very hurt, although he never let me know that. He simply flashed that bright smile of his, told me that I was a big girl now and big girls should walk to school with their friends. I was too relieved to give his feelings a second thought." She wiped her eyes with the back of her hand. "The next week he suffered a massive coronary and died."

"Oh, God." The image of a shattered little girl flickered through his mind, along with another horrible thought. "Surely you didn't blame yourself."

"Of course I did. After all, I'd gotten my wish. My friends stopped teasing me and father never walked me to school again."

"But that was a child's perception. When you grew older, you must have realized that you weren't responsible. Heart attacks are a common complication of obesity."

"Perhaps." She pulled a napkin from the bag and dabbed her red eyes. "But the fact remains that a broken heart is a weakened heart. Deep down, I'll always believe that his death was my fault."

Devon wanted to dispute that but couldn't. Beliefs and feelings weren't based on clinical fact. Emotions existed. They couldn't be swept away or rationalized. Her pain was real, as tangible as a touch and just as potent, and guilt was an emotion with which Devon was all too familiar.

He suppressed an urge to pull off the freeway and gather her in his arms. Instead, he reached out and took her hand, offering what solace he could. She looked surprised but didn't resist.

"I wish I could say that someday you'll feel differently but you probably won't," he said. A tingling warmth radiated from her slender hand, which was completely engulfed by his large palm. "Children are not miniature humans, they're works-in-progress. It's not fair to hold them to adult standards."

"Are you saying that an eight-year-old doesn't understand cruelty or the difference between right and wrong?"

"No, I'm saying that eight-year-olds who've made mistakes are entitled to the same forgiveness as adults." He gave her hand a comforting squeeze. "That little girl has suffered enough, Jessica. It's time to forgive her."

She raised her moist eyes. "And would you and your father also be entitled to absolution for past mistakes?"

"You crafty devil." He shook his head, admiring how she'd managed to corner him with his own words. "All right, you've made your point."

She took a deep breath and leaned against the padded headrest, seeming lost in thought. Devon's gaze ricocheted from the road to his lovely passenger, with whom he was becoming more intrigued by the minute. Her silent tears had born mute testimony to the pain of sharing such an achingly intimate experience, yet she'd endured it hoping to spare Devon a similar ordeal.

Jessica Newcomb was a woman of courage and compassion. That made her special. She was also the kind of woman that made a man start thinking about the future. That made her dangerous.

* * *

By midmorning, they were bumping along a rutted road winding through the jagged canyons of the Tejon Pass. They emerged into a sandy valley, scarred by crisscross bike trails and dotted with blue clumps of desert sage. Dust plumes wafted from the knobby tires roaring over the craggy hills, barren as shark's teeth, that encircled a clearing bristling with recreationalists.

Jessica gasped at the bustling sight. "Good grief, where did all these people come from?"

"All over," Devon replied cheerfully. "From Los Angeles, south to Riverside and Bakersfield, north as far as Fresno. This is off-roaders' paradise."

Pressing her nose against the passenger window, Jessica was awestruck by a plethora of unique machines centered in the busy hive of activity. There were a variety of dirt bikes, which were lean motorcycles powered up for steep hills and treacherous terrain. There was also an odd assortment of dune buggies and ATVs fitted with puffy tires specially designed to handle loose sand or jagged rocks with equal ease.

Casual campsites had been haphazardly established, a random city of tents, campers and recreational vehicles that was populated by a human melting pot represented by all ages, creeds and genders.

Jessica had never seen anything like it. "Do you know these people?"

"It's been a few years since I've been here but some of the old-timers are probably still around." Devon parked the Mercedes in the midst of the chaos and flipped off the engine. He eyed her anxiously. "Well, what do you think?"

"I don't know. It's kind of like Disneyland on wheels, isn't it?"

He chuckled, then pointed through the windshield toward a cleft in the hills. "Beyond those rocks is a wild canyon with one of the prettiest creeks in the Tehachapi mountains. We can ride in there later, if you'd like."

"Ride on what?"

Shrugging, he encompassed the scene with a casual sweep of his hand. "Take your pick...two wheels, three wheels or if you're really hinky, I can find something with four wheels."

"You mean these people will loan their vehicles out to total strangers?"

"Not exactly." He flashed a secretive grin. "But I have my ways."

Her eyes narrowed. "Are these 'ways' of yours legal?"

"Of course." In a rather effective Richard Nixon imitation, he held up two fingers on each hand, puffed his cheeks and croaked, "I am not a crook."

Laughing, Jessica clapped her hands in delight. "Such talent! Can you do Bogart?"

Devon curled his upper lip and lisped, "Of all the gin joints in this crazy world, why'd she have to come into mine?"

Moaning, she covered her eyes and shook her head. "I don't think that quote is accurate."

"I paraphrased. Besides, it's the delivery that counts. I do a great Cagney, too."

She held up a restraining palm and regretted having encouraged him in the first place. "Another time."

He shrugged philosophically. "Okay. Meanwhile, I'll keep my day job."

"Good idea." She stepped from the car and was instantly consumed by the aura of excitement permeating the air. "This is so great. Look!" She wiggled a finger toward a half-dozen racers roaring wildly around a makeshift track. Squinting through the rising dust, she was shocked to realize that both the dirt bikes and the helmeted riders seemed inordinately small. "Why, they're just children!"

Devon came up beside her. "Kids are the best racers. They're absolutely fearless."

The words had barely left his tongue when one of the racers leaned too far into a curve and the bike squirted out like a grapefruit seed. Jessica gasped in horror as the roaring pack converged on the limp little body that was sprawled across the track. Before she could exhale, the speeding motorcycles parted, streamed around the helpless child, then reconverged into a harried mass. The fallen rider leapt to his feet, yanked off his helmet and stalked off to retrieve his toppled bike.

Jessica pried her knuckles from her teeth. "Dear God! How can the parents allow those poor children to do something so dangerous?"

"Don't let their size fool you, Jessie. In order to compete in organized track races, those munchkins have proven themselves to be skilled riders." Devon looped a lazy arm around her shoulders. "Ready for a closer look?"

The warmth of his touch both calmed and excited her. She licked her lips and lifted her chin. "That's what we're here for, isn't it?" His affectionate squeeze made her heart leap, then he guided her into the hustling throng.

For Jessica, the next hour was an adventurous whirl of new sights, new sounds and new friends. Devon mingled easily, turning strangers into chums with chatty charm and a relaxed style that politicians would envy. Owners who proudly wheeled their machines out for inspection were treated to Devon's expert appraisal, which was inevitably followed by praise. He had a way of ingratiating himself without seeming pushy.

As much as Jessica admired that, she couldn't help being struck by the paradox between this likable hustler and the surly grump she'd met at the airport two days ago. That ragged, burned-out journalist had stared past her as though she'd been a bland piece of scenery. This new and obviously improved version of the enigmatic Devon Monroe couldn't have been more attentive. He scrupulously included Jessica in his conversations and solicitously asked if she was enjoying herself. Certainly, this was not the behavior of the sullen, self-important jerk she'd first judged him to be.

Even more startling than his unanticipated transformation was her own reaction to it. She found herself watching him in total fascination, transfixed by that silly, crooked grin of his and the way his eyes scrunched when he laughed. He was, she realized, an immensely attractive man. And judging by the admiring glances he was drawing from passing females, Jessica wasn't the only one who thought so.

She studied him silently, watching his casual banter with a burly man named Bill who'd brought his family out for the day. Suddenly Devon turned and caught her staring at him. She flushed and pretended to be inspecting one of the many motorcycles that were parked around the campsite.

Devon said something to Bill, then loped over to Jessica's side. "Can you ride a motorbike?" he asked.

She tensed. "No."

If he was disappointed, he covered it well. "I'd like you to see the canyon," he said amiably. "We can take the car if you want, although it won't make it beyond the creek or..." He let the words slide and cast a longing glance at one of the shiny black motorcycles.

Jessica swallowed hard. "Or what?"

He angled a little-boy look that melted her heart. "Or we could ride double."

The thought scared her to death but she'd have rather eaten glass than disappoint him. "Sure, why not?" she said, and was rewarded by his delighted grin.

"Great! You'll love it."

She rather doubted that but forced an agreeable smile that melted into a wary frown after he returned to where Bill was waiting. Biting her lip, she watched the two men negotiate for a moment, after which Devon peeled a few bills from the cash wad he'd dug out of his jeans. Bill dropped a key into Devon's palm. They sealed the deal with a handshake.

As Bill waddled off to the beer cooler, Devon slid an affectionate hand over the shiny machine and motioned for Jessica. She hesitated, took a bracing breath and complied.

Devon's blue eyes glowed with enthusiasm. "Isn't she a beauty?"

"Uh-huh."

Apparently not noticing that her response was less than enthusiastic, he hoisted a candy-apple red helmet from the handlebars. "Put this on." With a deft flick, he tossed one helmet toward her. It looped lazily and fell into her waiting hands.

She stepped back, eyeing the gaudy headgear. "Do I have to wear it?"

"Yep." Since Devon was already adjusting his own helmet, argument seemed useless.

Sighing, she carefully laid the helmet at her feet, then pulled off her cotton neck scarf and fastened it securely around her head.

Meanwhile Devon had straddled the machine and was inspecting the throttle lever. He glanced up, saw her head scarf and did a double take. "The helmet will protect your hair from wind, if that's what you're concerned about."

It wasn't, of course, but the real reason for the head scarf was nobody else's business. Since she felt compelled to respond, however, she used the first lame excuse that came to mind. "It seemed a polite and tidy thing to do. After all, I wouldn't want someone else using my helmet without taking precautions."

A flicker of amusement lit his pale eyes. "After seeing your apartment, I never would have taken you for the fastidious type."

"I won't dignify that with a response," she said primly, then lifted the helmet and awkwardly lowered it into position.

Devon reached out and fiddled with her chin straps. "How does that feel?"

"Like I have a bowling ball on my head."

"You'll get used to it." He flipped down his plastic visor, then hers. The world took on an eerie gray hue. "There. Are you ready to go?"

She eyed the big machine with growing trepidation. "I suppose so."

"Okay, here's the drill. While we're moving, hang on tight, keep your feet on the pegs—" he pointed to the narrow steel props on each side of the chassis "—and don't let your leg touch the muffler. It gets red-hot. Any questions?"

"Only one." She smiled sweetly. "Is it too late to change my mind?"

"Absolutely." Devon scooted forward on the padded seat, then reached back and patted the ridiculously small portion that was left. "Hop on."

"You're joking, right?" She couldn't see his face through the visor but suspected that he wasn't smiling. "Look, I'll never fit on that tiny thing without, uh, crowding you."

From beneath the tilted helmet came an unmistakable John Wayne drawl. "Haven't you heard, pilgrim? That's the best part."

She rapped her knuckles on the top of his helmet. "Are you leering under there?"

"Yes, ma'am."

"Good. Just checking." With that, she tossed a leg over the seat, held her breath and settled into the intimate position. Her heart was thudding so loudly that it was a wonder he couldn't hear it.

He twisted the key, stomped on the starter and the engine roared to life. While he tested the idle speed, she licked her lips and assessed the muscular back looming in front of her face, wondering whether she was supposed put her arms on the outside or inside of his nylon Windbreaker. Deciding that outside would be more appropriate, she tentatively slid her hands around and lightly touched his firm chest. "No daredevil stuff, okay?"

"I'll pretend you're a crate of eggs."

"How flattering."

He turned slightly. "Hang on."

"I am hanging on," she insisted even though her delicate embrace was too limp to dent a feather pillow.

With a shrug, he revved the engine and kicked the bike into gear. As the motorcycle lurched forward, a startled scream reverberated through her helmet and before they'd traveled fifty feet, Jessica was glued to his back like a postage stamp. The sensation of speed was terrifying. Every time they leaned into a turn, she remembered the tiny body bouncing on the racetrack and thanked God that her will was in order.

After several long minutes of burrowing into Devon's back, Jessica finally gathered the courage to open her eyes and realized that the scenery wasn't moving nearly as fast as she'd expected. When Devon hunched forward, she peered over his shoulder, read the speedometer and flinched. Raw terror notwithstanding, they were only traveling thirty-five miles an hour. Feeling a bit foolish, she began to relax and enjoy the ride.

Despite the chaotic mass of trails cut into the valley floor, Devon seemed to know exactly where he was going. He followed a washboard road to a sloppy T, then took the left fork up into the hills, where the terrain changed drastically. The grade steepened and the narrow road clung to the jagged mountain like a wet ribbon. On one side was a vertical wall of rock; on the other, the ground plummeted down into a deep gorge.

The higher they traveled, the tighter Jessica held on. By the time they emerged into the canyon, she was hugging Devon hard enough to crack his ribs. When he pulled into a scraped-gravel area and turned off the ignition, a massive sigh of relief fogged her visor.

He yanked off his helmet and shook his ruffled hair. "We're here," he announced. "What do you think?"

Lowering one foot to the ground, she reluctantly turned him loose and raised her visor. "Oh my, it's beautiful. There really is a creek . . . and trees! Honest to goodness trees!"

Devon swung a leg over the handlebars, hung his helmet on the rubber handgrip and helped Jessica dismount. His exhilaration was contagious. "See that strip of smooth stone halfway up the cliff? That's an ancient riverbed. There was once a big mining camp here in the canyon. Down the creek about a mile are a couple of broken down cabins. And that cave over there—" he gestured toward a boarded opening in the rock wall "—is the entrance to one of the mines."

Invigorated by the canyon's primitive beauty and Devon's unbridled joy at sharing it with her, Jessica could barely contain her own excitement. "Can we explore? I mean, I've never seen a real mine shaft before."

"The ones around here are off-limits. Too unstable. That's why the Forest Service has them boarded up."

"Oh." Disappointed, she unfastened the chin strap and removed her helmet, being careful not to disturb the head scarf.

Devon regarded her thoughtfully. "If you'd like to see a working mine, I know a place out by Randsberg where a few bucks will buy us a tour."

Her heart leapt at the suggestion. "Do you really think we could?"

"Absolutely."

"I can hardly wait," she said, shocked by a thrill of anticipation. Actually, she'd never given much thought to mines or motorcycles or wild canyons before. Suddenly, she couldn't think of anything else. Never in her life had she felt so liberated, so completely and utterly free. It was as though Devon had opened the door to a new world, a place where exhaustion came from pleasure instead of pain, and the tiniest wonders provided the greatest joys. Gazing around, she heaved a contented sigh. "This is just spectacular."

"I'm glad you like it," Devon said softly. Then he did something completely unexpected by reaching out and caressing her cheek with his thumb. "Has anyone ever told you what a glorious smile you have?"

Instantly tongue-tied, she avoided his warm gaze by staring across the rippling water and stammered, "Look. There's a campground on the other side."

Still stroking her tingling skin, Devon glanced over his shoulder at the scattering of parked vehicles. "It's just a day camp. Overnighters aren't allowed in this area."

As if on cue, a green Forest Service truck rumbled down the road, crossed the creek and pulled up to a group of men who were donning backpacks. The ranger leaned out the window to chat with the hikers, one of whom pointed up into the rugged canyon hills.

"The Forest Service patrols this area several times a day," Devon explained. "The ranger is probably checking their plans and warning them to stay on the trails." He stepped away then, tucking his gentle thumb into a belt loop. "Would you like to go over there?"

A cool breeze swept her face, chilling away the warmth of his touch. She felt oddly bereft. "You mean drive across the creek?"

"I don't think Bill would approve of having his prized dirt bike used as a ferry."

Since the Forest Service truck had just traversed the shallows, Jessica knew that the water was no more than six inches deep. "Then I guess we'll have to walk."

Devon stopped her as she knelt down to untie her shoelaces. "*I'll* walk. Madam will ride."

"But how—? Oh, no!" She pressed her hands to her mouth and giggled. "I haven't had a piggyback ride since I was seven years old."

"Then it's about time, wouldn't you say?" He bent his knees, squatting down to mounting height. "Hop on."

It was, of course, a ridiculous notion. After all, Jessica was a grown woman and grown women do not climb on men's backs. It was unseemly. It was childish. It was foolish. She silently argued with herself for about three seconds, after which she emitted a shriek of delight, leapt up, wound all four limbs around him and clung like a happy tick.

"Alley-oop!" Straightening, Devon tucked his arms under her legs. He turned his head until their noses nearly touched. "Comfy?"

Another girlish giggle spilled out. "I feel silly."

"No, you feel soft and warm." His eyes held hers for a moment, then he gave a jarring bounce and dashed toward the water with Jessica laughing so hard she could barely hang on.

And she laughed for the next two hours.

As they explored the wondrous new world, every insect, every sprouting blade of grass received a share of their attention. Jessica had a million questions—about rocks formed by layers of squished mud and foil-thin flakes of pyrite twinkling just beneath the rippled surface to the gray-leafed thickets that lined the steep side of the creek bed.

With the patience of Job, Devon answered each question the best he could without the slightest trace of irritation. He went so far as to crawl over half-submerged boulders, searching for caddis fly larvae, which he seemed to think were the architectural marvels of the insect world.

After soaking one sleeve to the shoulder, he emitted a triumphant shout and held one up in his palm. Jessica took one look at the tweaked antennae protruding from the creature's sand tube and declared it the most disgusting thing she'd ever seen.

Crestfallen, Devon tried to return the little insect to its home beneath the rock, only to slip and fall face first into the icy water. He emerged, stunned and sputtering, while Jessica dropped to the ground and howled with glee. Devon retaliated by positioning his dripping body above her and shaking like a wet sheepdog. When she squealed for mercy, he flopped beside her.

They were basking drowsily in the sun, enjoying the soothing babble of the creek when the serenity was shattered by a terrified scream.

## Chapter Five

Devon jolted to his feet. "Did you hear that?"

"Yes." Jessica scrambled to her knees and cocked her head, listening. "I'm not sure where it came from."

In less than a heartbeat, a frantic cry for help emanated from a ravine several hundred yards behind them. Jessica stood quickly but Devon was already sprinting toward the sound. She followed with one hand flat atop her head to keep the scarf in place as she ran.

After a hundred yards, her lungs were ready to explode and her legs felt like limp noodles. Gasping, she bent over, hands propped on her knees, cursing her depleted stamina.

After catching her breath, she stumbled into the ravine and headed toward the group of hikers who were now clumped at the base of a craggy ridge. One man was uncoiling a length of thick rope. Everyone else in the somber crowd, seven men including Devon, stood in a circle staring at their shoes. As Jessica hurried closer, however, she saw the yawning pit in the ground and her heart sank.

Praying that no one had fallen in, she came up behind Devon and touched his arm. When he looked over, his grim expression confirmed her worst fears. "Oh, God," she murmured, horrified by the ragged, three-foot opening. "What is it?"

"Could be a hard-rock test hole or the air shaft from an abandoned mine tunnel. At one time, this whole canyon was littered with them. Most have been filled but every so often someone sees a board poking out of the dirt and finds a new one."

Jessica saw the fractured remnants of rotten wood strewn around the area and realized that once the protective planks had been buried by surface debris, they'd be an invisible death trap to anyone unfortunate enough to step on one. Apparently that's exactly what had happened. Her stomach turned at the thought.

At that moment, the man carrying the rope muscled through the human circle. Devon guided Jessica backward, allowing him access to the pit. The Rope Man knelt at the opening and lowered the thick cord down into the pit. "Larry! Can you hear me, man?"

A thin reply wafted up from the darkness.

"Tie the rope around your waist and we'll pull you up." Rope Man stiffened then leaned closer to the hole. "What's that?" He listened for a moment then moaned, sat back on his heels and swore sharply. "He can't use his right arm. Thinks his shoulder's broke."

A lanky, fuzzy-haired fellow stepped forward wringing his bony hands. "What are we gonna do?"

Devon reacted instantly, motioning for Jessica to stay put at the same time he was moving precariously close to the crumbling edge of the shaft. "How far down is he?"

"I don't know for sure. Fifty feet, maybe more."

Devon nodded. "Try to find out if he has any other injuries." He turned to the worried young man. "Is that your four-wheel drive parked by the crossing?"

Fuzzy-Head nodded.

"Do you think you can get it up here?"

Puffing his thin chest, the guy flashed a cocky grin. "I can drive that sucker up a tree if I have to." With that, he leapt over a pile of gear and sprinted down the ravine.

As Rope Man shouted questions down into the hole, Devon turned to the rest of the group. "The CDF ranger has a short-wave radio. He can call for emergency crews and a medevac helicopter."

A paunchy, middle-aged fellow wearing an L.A. Raiders cap lifted a tentative hand. "My car is parked across the creek. I'll go find the ranger." He waited for Devon's nod of approval before loping away to complete his assignment.

"I need flashlights," Devon said to no one in particular. "And leather belts if you have them."

As the group scattered like obedient children, Devon squatted beside the hole. Rope Man looked worried. "It's not good. Larry keeps drifting in and out, like he's having trouble staying conscious. He says his head is bleeding and—" he raked his thinning hair in frustration "—and he says that he's standing in water."

Devon paled. "How much water?"

"Don't know. Every time I ask, he starts mumbling gobbledygook."

Both men stood. There was no need for words. Both realized that if the trapped man lost consciousness, he would probably drown before help could arrive.

Jessica knew it, too.

Sickened and feeling helpless, she stumbled to a nearby rock and sat down, praying that the ranger would arrive quickly and...and do what? Tears stung her eyes as the hopelessness of the situation hit home. Similar rescue attempts she'd seen on television required massive earthmoving equipment and inevitably took hours, sometimes days. The effort was rarely successful.

In this instance, the location was so remote that it would be nightfall before the proper equipment could be moved to the site. That, along with the unstable shaft and the victim's injuries, made the situation seem even more futile.

She glanced glumly toward the rest of the group as individuals scurried about searching for the requested items. For several minutes she watched, both perplexed and fascinated by Devon's authoritative manner, although she couldn't for the life of her figure out what on earth he was doing. The flashlight he'd requested was now dangling from a cord that had been fastened to his own waist. Even stranger, he'd hooked two belts together and looped them around his chest like a bandolier.

She stood slowly, her chest tightened by indefinable fear.

Before she could isolate the source of that fear she was distracted by the distant thrum of an engine. She turned, gazing down the ravine as the roar grew louder. In a moment, a black pickup lurched into view.

Rope Man loped over to meet it. The fuzzy-headed driver rolled down the window and the two men talked, casting agitated glances toward the open pit. After a moment Rope Man stepped away, allowing the compact truck enough room to inch a tedious U-turn between the narrow canyon walls. When the vehicle's tailgate was pointed toward the shaft, the driver shifted into reverse. Hand signals guided the truck backward until the rear wheels were six feet from the opening.

Rope Man climbed into the pickup's open bed. Devon followed, carrying one end of the rope. Using a series of secure knots, they tied the braided nylon line to the steel roll bar arched behind the truck's cab. When they'd finished, Devon jumped to the ground and carefully arranged the rope so it extended over the truck's tailgate.

At first bewildered, Jessica soon realized that they planned to use the truck to pull the man out of the pit and assumed that the rope had been positioned in such a precise manner in order to transfer some of poor Larry's weight from the crumbling lip of the hole to the truck's steel chassis.

The idea would have seemed plausible except for the problem of getting the rope around the victim in the first place. Obviously, the wounded fellow was in no condition to accomplish the task on his own.

As Jessica was mulling over that particular obstacle, the truck moved slowly forward until the rope was stretched flat. At that point, Devon scooped up the free end and looped it around his waist.

Jessica blinked. It took a moment before her stunned brain could react. "What are you *doing?*" Other than a muscle twitch below his ear, there was no indication that Devon had heard her. She crossed the flat quickly and yanked on his arm. "No! You can't go down there. You can't!"

He jerked the final knot, took a shaky breath and patted the fingers that were clawing his biceps. "I have to."

She stepped back, horrified, disbelieving. "No, you don't! Help is coming...experts...people who have the equipment to do this sort of thing."

Devon nodded toward the pit. "He could be dead by then."

"And if that shaft collapses, you'll both be dead!" Frantic, she grabbed his arms and shook as hard as she could. "Look at you! You're white as a sheet and dripping sweat. You know as well as I do that if you go down that hole there's a damned good chance you'll never come up again."

He didn't bother to argue. "Someone has to do it."

"Then why does it have to be you?" she demanded.

"Because I've had similar experiences."

"How similar?"

"Well, I've bellied through guerrilla tunnels in Southeast Asia and I once spent three days in a bat cave." He smiled thinly. "Don't worry. Everything is going to be fine." A shout from the pickup truck caught his attention. He nodded at Rope Man, then lifted Jessica easily and set her to the side. "Stay out of the way. I don't want you to get hurt."

"Please," she croaked, too terrified to say anything more.

After untangling her fingers from the slick fabric of his Windbreaker, he brushed his lips sweetly across her mouth. The brief kiss affected Jessica like a bolt of lightning. She was still reeling when he abruptly released her and went to the edge of the shaft, where Rope Man was waiting to lower him into the abyss.

When the line went taut, Rope Man circled one hand over his head. The truck slowly backed up. As the earth swallowed foot after foot of rope, Jessica watched in horror, her head spinning, her lips still tingling from Devon's kiss. She didn't understand—could never understand—what made Devon Monroe tick. She'd recognized terror in his eyes yet there he was, suspended into the jaws of the earth like so much human bait.

And this wasn't the first time she'd seen him defy death. On the drive home from the airport he'd charged into traffic as though compelled by some deep, intractable force— the same force, perhaps, behind his reputation as a journalist of fearless tenacity and unquestioned courage.

But this wasn't courage. It was madness. All Jessica could do was wait for it to be over.

For what seemed a small eternity, Rope Man continually called down into the shaft, then tipped his ear to catch indistinct replies. Although Jessica was numbed by shock and fear, she heard Devon report that the shaft widened at the base. For some reason, Rope Man considered that to be good news.

Slightly buoyed, she took a shaky step toward the opening. "Wh-what's happening down there?"

Rope Man answered without taking his eyes off the taut rope that was still moving downward. "He's almost to the bottom."

Jessica couldn't look at the hole. Instead, she watched the truck inching toward them. "Then what?"

"That depends on what he finds. If there's enough room to work, he'll try to bring Larry up."

"And if there's not enough room?"

"Then he'll hold Larry's head out of the water until help arrives."

Jessica's knees nearly buckled. "You mean he's going to stay down there?"

"Don't know," he muttered absently. "We'll have to see—" A shout echoed up from below. Rope Man held up a palm and shouted to the truck driver. "Hold it!"

The truck stopped.

Rope Man glanced up apologetically. "Sorry, ma'am, but I'd feel a whole lot better if you'd move back out of the way."

"Oh...of course." Licking her lips, Jessica stumbled over to her rock and sat down, hugging her knees. She closed her eyes and tried to block out the sounds of activity around the pit. A metallic taste of fear flooded her mouth. Feeling ill, she lowered her head and repeatedly told herself that everything would be all right.

Minutes ticked by. She waited. Her jittery muscles ached. Her skin itched. Her head throbbed.

Just when she thought the torture would never end, Rope Man shouted, "Pull 'em up!"

The truck engine revved. Jessica peeled her eyelids open and angled a wary glance toward the shaft. The rope was moving again. This time, it was coming up, inch by painful inch. She held her breath until her lungs ached. The other three men gathered around the opening, blocking her view but she was glued to the rock and couldn't move.

Suddenly there was a flurry of activity. A dirty head emerged from the hole, then another. Jessica was on her feet, sick with relief as both men were hauled onto solid ground.

After unbuckling the belts he'd used to lash himself to the injured man, Devon sat up and brushed sand from his hair. The entire group surrounded the victim and, ignoring his shaken rescuer, dragged the moaning man a safe distance from the shaft. Jessica's attention, however, was riveted on Devon, who was struggling to unknot the rope while uncontrollable tremors rendered his fingers useless for the task.

He was caked with mud and soaked to his thighs. His clothes were filthy, his hair gritty and beneath a cloak of smeared mud, his chalky complexion gave mute testimony to the horror he must have experienced down in that deadly pit.

Forcing her leaden limbs into motion, she went over and knelt beside him, capturing his quivering fingers between her palms. "Let me do it."

Offering no resistance, he dropped his hands limply into his lap. Jessica quickly undid the knot and flung the rope as if it were a snake. Devon covered his face with his hands. He took several shuddering breaths trying to compose himself. When he finally looked up, a startling vulnerability in his eyes took her breath away. The brash daredevil who'd dodged speeding traffic to drag a ladder off the freeway had been replaced by a man at war with himself, a man who needed a tender touch, a reassuring word. A man who needed *her*.

The transformation touched Jessica deeply. Her fingers grazed his smeared forehead. "Are you all right?"

When no sound emerged from his parted lips, he lowered his gaze and issued a jerky nod.

Yielding to a strange compulsion to verify that for herself, she gently probed the muscles of his shoulders then slid her hands down his arms until her fingers slipped into a ragged rip in his sleeve. She stared at the lacerated fabric. "You've torn your jacket."

He didn't spare it a glance. "I never liked it anyway."

Unduly upset by the wounded garment, she started to tremble. "It could have been your arm, you know. Or your leg. Or your throat. You could have died down there!"

Alerted by the rising panic in her voice, Devon offered a conciliatory hand. "It's okay, honey. I'm all right. Larry's all right. Everything turned out fine."

She pulled away, holding her palms up like twin shields. "It's not all right! You've just played Russian roulette with your life and that's not all right at all!"

"Shh." He captured her wrists, pulling her into his arms. "I didn't mean to worry you."

She gave herself to his comforting embrace, pressing her face into the curve of his shoulder and clinging to him with shocking desperation. She'd been more than worried; she'd been terrified to the bone. When she'd watched Devon disappear into that horrible hole, part of her had gone with him. She didn't understand that and didn't want to understand it. All she knew was that something inside her had cracked. Instinctively she realized that she would never be the same.

Slowly the haze of terror lifted and she realized that Devon was murmuring reassuring platitudes and rocking her like she was a frightened child. Embarrassed, she pulled away.

He tucked a thumb under her chin, urging her gaze upward. His eyes crinkled kindly. "Does this sweet concern mean that you'd actually miss me if I were gone?"

A slow heat spread up from her throat. "Of course. And so would your father. If he finds out what you did today, he'll probably have another attack."

The glow faded from his eyes. "Then perhaps we shouldn't mention it."

She studied his clouded expression. Ordinarily, she'd have considered withholding such information as a distasteful breech of ethics. Part of her insisted that Crandall was entitled to know that his son was a hero, albeit a foolish one. Deep down, however, she realized that Devon wouldn't be pleased by the attention such a magnanimous title would garner. So she reluctantly agreed to remain silent. "All right. Crandall won't hear about this from me."

"Thank you." His sad smile plucked at her heartstrings.

Sighing, she removed her head scarf and wiped a dirty smudge from his cheek. "I don't understand this compulsion you have to test fate."

He allowed her to clean his face as though it were the most natural thing in the world. "It wasn't that big a deal."

"Turn your head . . . a little more . . . there." She used the scarf to scour caked mud from the side of his neck. "You'd have thought differently if the shaft had collapsed."

"I figured if that hole had been stable for a hundred years, odds were that it would last a few more hours. Besides, we took every possible precaution."

"If you had so much confidence in those precautions, why were you shaking so violently that you couldn't even untie the rope?"

Avoiding her gaze, he blew out a breath and glanced toward the area where the rest of the group were clustered around their fallen comrade. "I have a thing about being confined in dark places, that's all."

Jessica stared in disbelief. "You're claustrophobic?"

"I wouldn't say that, exactly." His eyes glazed with a faraway look. "It's just that when I was a kid, there was this place, a concrete room so small that you couldn't even lay down. It was dark, cold . . . like a tomb. I hated it. We all did."

Something in his eyes made her blood run cold. "Good Lord, what were you doing in a place like that?"

"Hmm?" He blinked and the wariness returned to his eyes. "It was a long time ago. Old stuff, best forgotten."

"But I don't understand—" She was interrupted by the drone of an engine.

Seeming relieved, Devon gazed past her shoulder. "Here comes the ranger." He stood quickly and helped Jessica to her feet. After indicating that he'd be back in a moment, he strode over to the green truck and spoke to the uniformed man behind the wheel.

Jessica watched quietly, lost in the abyss of her own confusion. Under the best of circumstances, Devon's reaction to the crisis had taken great courage but for a man terrified by enclosed spaces, the act had been one of unbelievable valor. She could only imagine the emotional torment he must have endured yet he'd seemed obsessed by a need to confront his hidden demons, regardless of the cost. That baffled and frightened her, because she feared that someday that dangerous compulsion would demand the ultimate price—his precious life.

Jessica twisted her key in the lock. "I'll put on a pot of coffee."

"That sounds good." Devon followed her inside carrying the plastic bag containing her empty thermos and coffee mugs. "Where should I put this?"

"Hmm?" Jessica draped her jacket on a chair and flipped on the kitchen light. "Oh. Just set it on the table."

She glanced over her shoulder as Devon stepped over a heaping laundry basket and warily eyed the cluttered dinette. Since there wasn't an inch of table that hadn't been piled with magazines, bank statements and junk mail, he looked up in confusion. "What's your second choice?"

A quick peek at the kitchen reminded her that she hadn't gotten around to the dishes for a couple of days. The dishwasher was full and so was the counter. She took the bag from him. "I'll take care of it."

Silently vowing to shovel the place out next week, she propped the bag on a stack of plates in the kitchen sink, retrieved a coffee bag from the cupboard and measured the aromatic granules into her immaculate coffeemaker.

Although embarrassed by the surface mess, she took some comfort in knowing that the kitchen itself was scrupulously clean. Except for a few dishes, of course. Still, she yearned for the day when her body would be back to normal and she'd have enough energy to indulge the nesting instinct that she'd once taken for granted.

After setting the coffee to brew, she found Devon standing in the living room eyeing the floor as though trying to decide the safest place for his next step. She grabbed her briefcase, scooped scattered newspapers from the sofa and tucked a pair of slippers under her arm. "Have a seat."

Before complying, he slid a prudent glance at the sofa to ascertain that the coast was clear.

Jessica tossed the armload of clutter into her bedroom and slammed the door. When she spun around, her cheerful smile froze when she saw Devon extract a purple sweat sock from between the cushions. "So that's where it went." She hurriedly retrieved the item and offered a limp explanation. "Sometimes I watch television while I fold laundry."

He nodded as though finding hosiery in the couch was the most normal thing in the world. She could have kissed him. Instead, she tossed the orphan sock into the laundry basket and sat down with a contented sigh. "Despite all the excitement, this really has been a lovely day."

"I'm glad you enjoyed it." Pulling up one knee, he twisted to face her. "Of course, you're not the one who had to bathe in an icy creek."

"That's because I'm not the one who was covered with muck." She chuckled at the memory. After wading fully clothed into the rushing creek, the poor guy had ducked beneath the frigid water, remained submerged for about thirty seconds then exploded through the surface like a frozen carp. His teeth had chattered for half an hour. Then they'd dined on peanut butter sandwiches while the sun had dried his clothes and warmed his blood. Afterwards they'd spent the rest of the afternoon walking the creek bed in silent communion.

Jessica hadn't wanted to leave. But as the sun dipped toward the horizon, a cold wind had slid in from the north and she'd accepted the sad fact that the day was over. Unfortunately, it had probably been just as well. Although her spirit had been willing to continue the adventure, her body had grown increasingly fatigued. Now, however, after having napped during the two-hour trip home, she felt rested and refreshed. She was also excruciatingly aware that Devon, who was sprawled comfortably beside her, continued to study her disparate decor with disarming interest.

She cleared her throat. "Not the ambience you're used to, is it?"

Startled, he glanced down at her. "What do you mean?"

"After being raised in a mansion, I imagine my place seems a bit, well, common."

"You think I'm a snob?"

"Uh... not exactly."

"Yes, you do." He regarded her with undisguised amusement. "I suppose there's a poetic justice in being hoist with my own petard, so to speak."

She pulled back a bit, eyeing him with perplexed curiosity. "Should I understand what you're talking about?"

Propping an elbow on the back of the sofa, he leaned his chin on his folded hand. "The truth is that I considered *you* to be the snob."

"Me?" She didn't know whether to be shocked or angry. "Why? What on earth have I ever done to make you think that?"

He smiled indulgently. "For one thing, you're just too damned good-looking."

The unexpected compliment knocked the starch out of her sails. Speechless, she could do nothing but stare in astonishment while he cheerfully expanded on the defective rationale.

"Of course, I also considered your expensive sports car and this fancy, uptown condo but the clincher—and this is the good part—was that when we first met, you ignored me. I mean, what was I supposed to think? Obviously any woman able to resist my considerable charms must have a fatal flaw."

"And you judged my flaw to be snobbery?"

He shrugged. "Why not? My ego needed an explanation and that was as good as any."

Shaking her head, Jessica smothered a guilty chuckle. "I should be annoyed as the dickens with you."

"But you're not?"

"No." She slid him a mischievous glance. "Because you're not the only one who jumped to the wrong conclusions. The fact is that I did deliberately ignore you."

"Why?"

"Because I'd prejudged you as irresponsible, self-indulgent and emotionally immature."

"Ouch." Flinching, he pulled an invisible dagger from his heart. "The truth hurts more than I thought it would."

She sobered instantly. "It's not the truth, Devon. I was wrong."

His eyes warmed. "So was I. About you, that is."

A peculiar heat warmed her from the inside out. "Am I to assume that a messy apartment turned the tide in my favor?"

"That was a definite plus. I've always preferred a homey, lived-in look."

"Is that a fair description of your place?"

"My place?" A perplexed crease furrowed his brow. "You mean the flat in Manhattan?"

"That's where you live, isn't it?"

"Sometimes. Mainly it's a convenient mail drop." Leaning back into the soft cushions, he stretched his arm across the back and hooked an ankle over his knee. "Living out of a suitcase and being shuffled between hotel rooms is a hazard of the profession. After a joint commiseration about being homeless, some of my colleagues and I decided to lease a place for use when we're in the States."

"So you have roommates?"

"Only six." He grinned at her astonished expression. "It's not as bad as it sounds. Because we're all subject to long-term overseas assignments, there's rarely more than two of us around at the same time."

She shook her head. "It seems so...transient. I could never live like that."

"No," he murmured, reaching out to stroke her cheek. "I don't suppose you could."

There was a smoldering intensity in his eyes, an intimacy in his gentle caress that made her heart race. She was paralyzed by his touch, barely able to breathe as his thumb grazed an erotic path along her jaw and down to the pounding pulse at the base of her throat. He lowered his head slowly, allowing her time to withdraw. She couldn't.

Without conscious consent, she felt her lips part in silent invitation. He hesitated only a moment before accepting. In the instant before his mouth took hers, her mind screamed a warning that unless she pulled away quickly, life would never be the same.

It was a warning her body refused to acknowledge.

She responded instinctively, winding her arms around his neck with an abandon that would have shocked her rational mind. But she wasn't rational; she was reacting to the warmth of his body, the moist heat of his deepening kiss.

A soft moan flowed from somewhere deep inside her, a secret place that was like sun-warmed butter, slick and aqueous, swelling sweetly until she was filled with its fluid warmth.

The kiss ended as gently as it had begun. Devon's lips hovered inches away, whispering soft words that her addled mind struggled to translate. "You're so lovely you take my breath away." As he spoke, his hands explored the contours of her back, then slid down to span her small waist. She stiffened as his fingers crawled seductively up her ribs. "I've never met anyone like you, so guileless and genuine. There's an openness about you, an honest sincerity that's so rare—" His knuckles brushed her breast.

She gasped and pushed him more roughly than intended. "It's getting late."

He couldn't have seemed more stunned if she'd flung a drink in his face. "What's wrong?"

"Nothing's wrong," she lied. Standing, she smoothed her knit tunic and nervously patted her hair. "I have an early meeting tomorrow."

Devon rose slowly, his bewildered expression raising a lump the size of Wyoming in her throat. "Okay," he murmured. "I understand. I'll, uh, see myself out."

Nodding, she turned away to conceal her misery.

After a moment, footsteps crossed the room and she heard the door open. "Devon?" She glanced over her shoulder as he paused in the doorway. "I really did have a lovely day."

He managed a thin smile. "So did I." Then the door closed and he was gone.

Jessica's shoulders slumped and her breath slid out all at once. She covered her eyes for a moment. When she'd regained her composure, she forced her aching body into the bedroom and undressed for bed.

After pulling a fresh gown from the drawer, Devon's implausible praise circled her benumbed mind. *Guileless. Honest. Genuine.* God, if he only knew.

Jessica removed her partial prosthesis and dragged the perfectly coiffured wig from her stubbled scalp. Then she stood in front of a full-length mirror and wept.

## Chapter Six

"What *are* grunion, anyway?" Jessica took Devon's hand and stepped delicately over a moonlit rock that protruded from the sandy slope.

After guiding her down to the cool flat beach, Devon hoisted the rolled blanket over one shoulder and skimmed an amused glance in her direction. "Everyone in Los Angeles knows about grunion."

"Well, I don't." Looping the canvas tote over her forearm, she paused to roll up the sleeves of her oversize sweatshirt. "Besides, I was raised in Monterey. Monterey doesn't have grunion."

"How do you know?"

"Because I would have heard about them— Ah! Wait!"

A tug on Devon's arm brought him to a stop. When he turned around, Jessica was muttering to herself and hopping on one foot. Instantly concerned, he threw off the blanket and reached out to steady her. "What's wrong? Did you twist your ankle?"

"No." She anxiously eyed the ground. "The sand ate my shoe."

Devon smiled. "I told you not to wear loafers."

"Haven't you heard? I never do what I'm told." Grabbing his arm for balance, she dipped at the waist and scooped up the wayward shoe. She shook out the loose sand, put on the shoe then straightened and gazed around the deserted beach. "This reminds me of the night my cousins took me on a snipe hunt. I ran around with a pillowcase on my head for three hours before I realized that I'd been had."

"Why on earth did you have a pillowcase on your head?"

"Because my cousins convinced me that percale was invisible to snipes and wearing one was the only way to sneak up on the little duffers."

Devon's grin broadened. "You mean it didn't work?"

"Nope. But my stepfather always said that no experience is a loss if one learns something."

"And what did you learn?"

"That a jar of jelly poured in a cousin's sleeping bag is even funnier than a five-year-old with a pillowcase on her head." A sliver of moonlight danced in her eyes. "I also learned that retribution is its own reward. For your sake, Mr. Monroe, I hope I see a grunion tonight."

Devon winced. "If I didn't know better, I'd swear that was a threat."

"Just a friendly warning, that's all." Tossing a mischievous smile over her shoulder, she padded through the soft sand toward the water. Devon blew out a breath and followed until they'd reached a spot several yards beyond the edge of the bubbling tide. Jessica set the tote on the sand and warily sniffed the salty air. "So where are these grunion of yours?"

"They'll be here," he mumbled, adding an "I hope" under his breath.

As she bent to roll up her pant legs, Devon dropped the blanket roll and ran a nervous finger around the crewneck of his sweater. "Funny thing you should mention pillowcases, though."

Her fingers froze on the denim cuffs. Twisting her head sideways, she looked up suspiciously. "What about them?"

He cleared his throat. "I, uh, just happen to have brought a couple with me." With a helpless shrug, he unrolled the blanket and extracted a pair of plain white pillowcases. "Quite a coincidence, huh?"

Straightening, she skewered him with a narrowed stare. "If you try to get that thing on my head, you're a dead man."

"They're used for catching grunion. Honest." He grabbed a case and shook it open. "Look, you roll down the edges like this, so it forms a sack. Then when the grunion run starts, you stand in the shallows and scoop them up." Bending at the waist, he provided a dry demonstration of the proper technique. "See? Nothing to it."

She watched skeptically. "Grunion are fish?"

"Fins and all." He tossed the deflated pillowcase on the sand and proceeded to spread out the blanket. "Every spring during full moons and high tides they come ashore to spawn. There used to be thousands of them from Santa Barbara to Baja but now that civilization has crept to the waterline, they've gotten pretty finicky about which beaches to use."

Frowning, she eyed the desolate coastline. "That's why we came to this godforsaken place?"

"Sure." Devon flopped on the blanket and filled his lungs with tangy air. "Grunion don't like crowds."

After considering that for a moment, Jessica settled down beside him and gazed into the blackness. Watching from the corner of his eye, he was struck by the serenity of her features, the simplicity of her classic profile. She was without doubt a beautiful woman but Devon's attraction went beyond her obvious physical attributes. She exuded an unexpected emotional depth, along with a paradoxical combination of compassion and playfulness that fascinated him. Far from the shallow socialite he'd first judged her to be, Jessica Newcomb embraced a quiet wisdom that was unique in one so young.

Of course, at thirty-one she was well beyond the giddy adolescent stage but despite her playfulness, she seemed to carry an old soul, or what New Age theorists would label a spirit enlightened by many lifetimes. Not that Devon fully accepted such ethereal beliefs but he didn't discount them, either. His years of observing varied cultures had instilled an abiding respect for the diversity of spiritual doctrine.

A cold gust of wind distracted him from further contemplation of karmic theology. Beside him, Jessica suddenly grabbed her head to shield her hair from the stiff ocean breeze. Since the effort was futile, she kept one hand planted atop her scalp and used the other to root through the tote. In a moment, she pulled out the familiar scarf and tied it firmly around her head.

Sighing, she shivered and hugged her knees. "I should have brought a jacket. That wind cuts like a knife."

Although Devon had left his own jacket draped over a kitchen chair, there were other ways to take advantage of the chivalrous opportunity. "Scoot forward toward the edge of the blanket." She looked up curiously but complied without question. When she'd moved down until her toes brushed the sand, Devon pulled the excess blanket over her shoulders and was rewarded by a dazzling smile. "Better?" he asked.

"Much." Holding the edges of the wool tent beneath her chin, she noticed that Devon had moved onto the cold sand to let her have the entire blanket. "Aren't you cold?"

"I'm fine." Except that he couldn't feel his nose and was fairly certain that his lips were blue.

"There's enough room in here for both of us." She swished out an arm, offering him one edge of the blanket.

He hesitated only a moment before moving into the cozy refuge. As their body heat mingled, radiating through the tiny woolen wigwam, Devon slid his arm around her.

With a contented sigh, she nestled against him and laid her head on his shoulder. "Umm. This is lovely, like being inside a toaster."

Squeezing her shoulders, he brushed his lips across the top of her head and kissed cotton. He drew back, frowning. "Do you really need that thing?"

She answered drowsily. "What thing?"

"That babushka."

"Baba-what?" She touched the pleated fabric stretched along her jawline. "Oh. The wind, uh, gives me an earache." She batted her eyelashes. "Actually, I think it's quite chic, don't you?"

He couldn't help but smile. On her, anything would look good. Even an ugly plaid head scarf. "You're probably right. I hear the peasant look is in vogue nowadays."

Her smile was, he thought, a bit strained but before he could examine her expression more closely, she turned away and gazed at the dark ocean. "How's Crandall?" she asked suddenly.

Since she'd seen him that afternoon, the abrupt change in subject suggested that she didn't appreciate being teased about her fashion habits. He made a mental note to keep future comments to himself. "Dad's fine. Coming home seems to have done him a world of good."

That was actually an understatement. Crandall's improvement during the past three days had been nothing short of miraculous. His color had improved, his eyes sparkled and he was barking orders like a three-star general. In short, he was back to normal.

Except, of course, that the doctor had forbidden him to return to work. In the age of electronic miracles, however, that problem had been easily circumvented by a computer modem. Within fifteen minutes of installation, Crandall had been pounding keys like a madman and, according to Jessica, every monitor at ElectroSonics was beeping with E-mail.

Devon was naturally relieved by his father's buoyed spirits, although he couldn't suppress a twinge of concern to see Crandall immerse himself in the same stressful environment that had caused the heart attack in the first place. At least Devon assumed that work had been the cause. Jessica had indicated that there may have been another reason but had clammed up when questioned and refused to elaborate.

In retrospect, Devon realized that his queries had been more confrontational than intended and silently vowed to broach the subject again. When he did, he'd take special pains to be receptive and civil.

Jessica suddenly lifted her head, squinting toward the water. "What's that?"

Devon followed her gaze. "What's what?"

"That." A slender finger emerged from the tent, pointing toward the wet sand at the edge of the ebbing tide. "There's something shiny on the sand."

"Probably just a pull tab or something."

"But it's moving."

Startled, he focused on the appointed spot and saw the tiny flicker an instant before the tide swept it away.

Beside him, Jessica stiffened. "Look! There are more of them."

And indeed there were—a moonlit spark here, a wiggling glimmer there, like blinking fireflies on the sand. Smiling, Devon touched Jessica's arm to keep her from moving forward too soon. "Shh. Those are just the scouts."

Her brows arced to her hairline. "Those things are fish?"

"Uh-huh."

"Grunion-type fish?"

"Yep."

"Ohmygosh." Throwing the blanket back, she yanked off her shoes and would have leapt to her feet except for Devon's restraining grasp. "Let go! I want to see what they look like."

"Trust me. If you'll wait just a few more minutes, you'll have all the grunion you can handle."

She bit her lip and anxiously scanned the waterline. "But what if that's all there is?" At that moment, the tiny glimmers were covered by the foamy tide. Her shoulders slumped. "Oh no. They're gone."

"Nah. They're just reporting in, that's all."

Her eyes narrowed. "If this is a joke—"

"No jelly, please!" He held up a defensive palm. "Look, I've been right so far haven't I? I mean, you've already seen them."

"I've seen something." She folded her arms and scowled into the darkness. "Unfortunately, I don't know what because *someone* wouldn't let me get a closer look."

Smiling smugly, he patted her thigh. "Just watch and wait."

Since she had little choice, she folded her arms and stared unhappily at the rippling tide.

As the minutes ticked by, Devon studied the empty beach with increasing concern. After all, actually being in the right place at the right time for the grunion spawn was a crapshoot to begin with. Truth be told, he was as shocked as Jessica to have lucked out on the first try. Now, as her irked gaze bored into his temple, he wondered if they really *were* gone. Squirming, he slid her a thin smile. "They'll be back any second now."

"Right." She bit off the word and spit it out like a bitter weed.

With a pained flinch, Devon ran a nervous finger around the ribbed neckline of his sweater. "But in case they're not back any second, grape is my favorite kind of jelly."

Her eyes sparkled and the stern expression she'd struggled to maintain finally cracked into a lyrical laugh. "You're funny, Monroe. Maybe I'll let you live."

"I'd really appreciate that."

Their gazes lingered as laughter faded into sensual awareness. He saw in her smoldering eyes a reflection of his own desire and was overwhelmed by a sudden yearning to touch her, to caress every inch of her beautiful body until she cried out with unleashed passion. The powerful image shook him to the core. He wanted her, body and soul, mind and spirit. He wanted her more deeply than he'd ever wanted anyone in his life. He felt something that he'd never felt before, something deep and poignant, something that both intrigued and frightened him.

At that moment, Devon felt that his life had been inalterably changed. And he wasn't at all certain that he wanted that to happen.

Jessica lowered her gaze. Her shoulders heaved once, then stiffened. There was a flash of white as her teeth nipped her lower lip. She took another deep breath. "It's getting late."

Devon felt like he'd swallowed a rock. "Yeah, I guess it is."

She studied a squiggle of moonlight highlighting the crest of each rising swell. "We should probably leave soon."

He nodded miserably.

A strained silence stretched between them before she spoke again. "The moon is so bright that the waves seem iridescent."

After a haphazard glance at the water, Devon did a double take. The waves didn't just seem iridescent. They *were* iridescent, glowing with the refracted light of a million shiny little fish. He raised his arm in triumph and yanked down a fistful of air. "*Yes!*"

Ignoring Jessica's startled expression, Devon quickly untied his shoes. He was tugging off his socks when the first glowing wave crashed, fragmenting into thousands of glittering particles.

"Oh!" Jessica leapt to her feet as the undulating mass coated the sand, turning the entire beach into a twinkling wonderland.

Ignoring the numbing cold, Devon rolled his jeans up to his knees. "Grab your sack. It's show time!"

With her jaw dangling comically, Jessica stood there as if rooted in the sand.

"Come on." He tugged at her arm. "Time's a-wastin'."

Awestruck, she gazed at the sparkling throng. "I've never seen anything like it."

Devon beamed. "Yeah. Great, isn't it?"

Her stunned expression melted into one of absolute delight, then she spun around, and shrieking gleefully, she dashed into the squirming silvery mass. In less than a heartbeat, she was toe dancing in the icy surf with foam licking her ankles and a grin bright enough to light Boston. Giggling madly, she bent to snatch a fish that was flopping at her feet and held it out like a trophy. "Look! I caught one!"

The pronouncement was a bit premature. As she proudly eyed the four-inch creature, it squirted from her grasp and bounced off her nose. Startled, she backpedaled, lost her balance and sat down hard in the wet sand. The ocean rolled in to greet her, covering her thighs with frigid water and passion-crazed fish.

Devon made a game attempt at a rescue but in the end, the sight of Jessica sitting in the surf, squealing and swatting a lapful of slippery grunion was too much. A mirthful snort escalated into uncontrollable chuckles and by the time he reached her, he was convulsed with laughter. He dropped in the dry sand a few feet away, helpless to do anything except hold his side and wipe his eyes.

Jessica wasn't pleased. She did, however, scramble to her knees and was attempting to stand when another foamy surge knocked her face first into the surf. She emerged sputtering and spitting seawater, her soggy scarf dripping like a wet pelt.

Devon howled and flopped back on the sand, holding his throbbing ribs. Something cold and slimy hit his cheek. The effect was sobering enough that he rolled over and reared up on his elbow.

Jessica, who was still kneeling in the surf, was blindly feeling around the murky water. "Aha!" With a smug grin she extracted a wriggling grunion and lobbed it smack into Devon's startled face. "Take that, you cad."

Stunned, Devon numbly watched the finned projectile arc across the sand and disappear with the ebbing tide. He looked up stupidly and saw a silver flash in Jessica's raised hand. "Don't even think ab—" He ducked as the hapless grunion sailed over his head and landed on the damp beach amidst its wriggling mates. He sighed. "So that's how it's going to be, is it?"

Palming the water, she came up with two more thrashing grunion. "Fish fight!"

"You asked for it." Devon easily scooped two of the small creatures in one hand, then he leapt up and sprinted toward her.

Giggling madly, Jessica feebly lofted her catch in his direction, but they flopped harmlessly onto the sand and wriggled away.

Devon had better luck. He splashed into the water and stuffed the wriggling fish down the neck of her floppy sweatshirt.

With a strangled gurgle, she sprang to her feet, stretched out the fleece hem and went into a frenetic tango that was highly amusing, if not technically accurate. After the slippery intruders had been dispatched, she turned on Devon with vengeance in her eyes. Screeching a war cry, she ran straight at him, leapt onto his chest and stuck like a burr.

Unbalanced by her weight, Devon's stiff arms whirled like twin rotors. He bellowed once, stumbled, and fell backward into the water with Jessica still sitting on his chest.

"There!" she chortled gleefully. "Now we're both wet."

A fresh surge of salt water rushed into his ears. "You're a cruel woman."

Grinning happily, she dismounted and wiped her drippy face. "I'll race you for the blanket. Winner takes all." Without waiting for a reply, she took off.

"Hey!" By the time Devon struggled to his feet, she was swathed in a warm woolen cocoon with only her face exposed to the cold night air. He ambled across the sand, shivering. "Comfy?"

She responded to his sarcasm with a contented purr.

Devon rubbed his arms and tried to look pitiful. "Is there room in there for a friend?"

"Maybe." Her eyes gleamed. "It depends on the friend."

Smirking, Devon pulled out his car keys and dangled them in front of her face. "The friend who may not be inclined to share the ride home with a blanket hog."

"Oh. That friend." She heaved an exaggerated sigh and opened the blanket.

Devon pocketed the keys and instantly stepped inside, wrapping the warmth around both of them.

"Umm." Jessica melted into his arms and laid her cheek against his firm chest. She'd never felt so alive, so completely and utterly at peace.

Strange, she thought, that such small events could bring such great joy. She couldn't remember laughing so much as she had during the past week. In fact, she couldn't remember *feeling* so much. Every cell her in body was electrified, intensifying common sensations into exquisite delights. Devon had illuminated her humdrum existence with a new light, showing her the world he saw, a world in which even the most mundane experience became an exciting voyage to adventure.

After all she'd endured over the past months, Jessica had frequently wondered if she'd ever be happy again. But she *was* happy, deliriously so, and it was all because of Devon. She felt deep gratitude toward him...and something deeper. Being with him had filled a void deep inside her, a vague emptiness that she'd never examined too closely, perhaps out of fear that she'd learn something frightening about herself.

But at this moment, the past didn't matter. Here, on a deserted beach, she was ensconced in Devon's warm embrace, feeling safe and cherished. She didn't know why; she didn't care why. All she knew for certain was that after all the agony, all the lonely fears, she was happy. There *was* life after breast cancer; and Jessica was determined to live every delicious moment.

Shifting the telephone against his numb ear, Devon massaged his eyelids and tried to concentrate on the terse voice filtering over the line.

"There were incidents over the weekend," the Associated Press chief was saying. "Scuttlebutt has it that the cease-fire will be broken before the week is out."

Devon's weary gaze fell on the newspaper in his lap. Civilian Slaughter Halts Peace Talks, the headline screamed. The article went on to describe gory details that were already etched in his own memory.

Less than two weeks ago, Devon had stood on the very street where the mortars had landed. He had friends there, some of whom had probably fallen victim to this latest attack, in what had become one of the world's grisliest civil wars. The faces of those people slid through his mind—a wizened matriarch who'd lost her entire family when a round slammed into their apartment; the eight-year-old twins who'd been orphaned by sniper fire; newlyweds who'd died sprinting toward the border in a frantic bid for freedom. These sad images and hundreds of others continued to torment him. For the year Devon had covered the evolving story, he'd watched a thriving populace deteriorate into benumbed zombies and a hauntingly beautiful city reduced to bloody rubble by the darkness of human hate.

When he'd learned of his father's heart attack, he'd left instantly, but not without mixed feelings. Although relieved for the temporary reprieve from the carnage, he also suffered deep-seated guilt at having deserted those about whom he'd come to care deeply. They were his friends and he had abandoned them. Some of them were probably dead now. Had he been there, perhaps he could have done something to stop it.

Intellectually he understood the irrationality of believing his presence could alter the course of a mortar shell. Viscerally, however, he couldn't help but ponder the possibility that if he'd chosen a different course of action, some of those people—like Tommy—might still be alive.

An irksome buzz in his ear brought him back to the present. Momentarily perplexed, he glanced numbly around his father's living room before remembering that his bureau chief was still on the telephone. Devon cleared his throat. "Sorry. I didn't catch that."

A long-suffering sigh filtered through the line. "I said that the city's defense line has cracked and humanitarian shipments are being held up at the border. There's talk that the Allies are threatening air strikes on some of the artillery positions surrounding the city."

"We've heard that before." Devon glanced up as Crandall entered the room. After acknowledging his father with a nod, he returned to his conversation. "But if anything should happen, Callahan can cover it. He's a damned good reporter and he's spent almost as much time in the city as I have."

"Callahan *is* good," the chief acknowledged. "But not as good as you are."

"Hell, no one's as good as I am," Devon said drily. "But Callahan's damned close. He'll keep on top of things until I get back."

Across the room, the color drained from Crandall's face.

"When exactly *will* you be back?"

The chief's question pulled Devon's attention from his father's sudden pallor. "Hmm? Oh. I'm not sure. Maybe the end of the month."

Crandall stood suddenly, went into his library and shut the door.

Devon would have followed if not for the irksome voice scratching at his ear. "I'm going to lay my cards faceup, Monroe. We need you in the field and we need you now."

Devon's worried gaze was riveted on the library door. "I'm on vacation, remember? I have two weeks left."

After a long pause, the chief tried another tactic. "How's your father doing?"

"Better, but still not back to par."

"You must be quite concerned."

"Yes, I am." The silky ploy didn't fool Devon. He knew perfectly well that the only thing on his boss's mind was getting Devon back to work. "Look, I'm not going to catch the next jet out of LAX so let's put that option to rest right now."

"Oh." He heaved a sigh. "So, what are your plans?"

"Just to keep an eye on things and play it by ear."

"Something's going to break in the next week," came the ominous reply. "I can feel it in my bones."

"When you read it on the wires, give me a call. Until then, try aspirin." Devon cradled the receiver, realizing that this was the first time he'd ever balked at a superior's request. Fortunately, the bureau chief hadn't been willing to take the extra step of turning the request into an assignment. Refusing a direct order would have been a termination offense and a death knell to his career as a foreign correspondent. Certainly, that was a risk Devon wasn't willing to take.

Still, there'd been a time when Devon would have been pacing the halls, suitcase in hand, begging for an assignment. Now he found himself dreading the inevitable day when he'd be forced to board that plane and return to the only life he'd ever known. And he didn't know why.

Shaking off the moody contemplation, he went to his father's library and knocked on the door. When there was no response, he called out, "Dad? Are you all right?"

"I'm busy. Go away."

Irritated by the curt reply, Devon glanced at his watch. "Busy doing what? It's after six. Everyone at the office has gone home to relax, which, according to doctors' orders, is exactly what you should be doing."

A grumbled suggestion of where doctors should store such orders filtered through the carved panel door, then Crandall added, "I'm not going to sit on my butt while a bunch of lazy nine-to-fivers flush everything I own down the damned commode."

Frustrated, Devon entered the room. Behind the heaped desk, Crandall was riffling a sheath of papers beside a blinking computer monitor. He spoke without favoring his son with a glance. "I told you I was busy."

Devon crossed the room and slammed both hands on his father's desk. "No wonder you're gray as wood ash. You're not supposed to work more than three hours a day. Does the phrase *no stress* mean anything to you?"

"Yes, as a matter of fact. It means bankruptcy."

Tossing his hands in the air, Devon stunned himself by raising his voice to a shout. "You already have more money than you could spend in a lifetime. What in hell do you want?"

Crandall slowly removed his glasses and fixed Devon with a cold stare. "At the moment I want to be left alone so I can get some work done."

Somehow Devon managed to reel in his anger, along with a burgeoning sense of panic. He took several calming breaths and softened his tone. "I'm sorry. I don't want to add to your pressure."

"Then don't." Crandall turned away and refocused on the report he was editing.

Devon recognized the abrupt dismissal. God knows, he'd seen enough of them over the years. This time, however, he stood his ground by snatching away the report and tossing it onto a nearby credenza.

"What the—" Crandall's complexion went from pale to beet red in thirty seconds flat.

Devon responded by reaching over the desk and shutting down the computer.

Crandall exploded from the chair and pounded the desk with his fist. "What the hell do you think you're doing?"

"Trying to keep you alive. If you don't slow down, your next heart attack may be fatal."

"And if you don't give up traipsing through war zones," Crandall snapped, "your next Pulitzer may be posthumous."

At the chilling pronouncement, the older man's complexion again faded to a pasty hue. Devon swallowed hard, then turned away, raking his hair. Over the years, he'd never once considered that the dangers he faced in his own career might also affect his father. It simply hadn't occurred to him. Now the fear in Crandall's eyes struck Devon like a bullet. For the first time in his life, he viewed himself through his father's eyes and saw an arrogant young man, indifferent to himself and disregarding the concerns of those who were foolish enough to care.

And his father *did* care about him.

That alone was a stunning realization, one that left Devon numb and nearly speechless. Cooling his face with his hands, he gazed over his fingertips and saw the clock ticking on the wall. He spoke without turning. "I'm late for an appointment but tomorrow...maybe we could talk about this."

The silence was deafening. Finally, there was a strained rumbling, the sound Crandall used to clear his throat. "All right, then. Tomorrow."

Devon closed his eyes, took a deep breath and managed a curt nod.

Crandall's voice stopped him at the doorway. "This appointment of yours. Is it by any chance with Jessica?"

"No. Just some friends reminiscing about old times."

"Oh." Crandall considered that for a moment. "You know, son, Jessica is a fine woman."

The pronouncement took Devon by surprise. "Yes, she is."

After tucking his glasses into his shirt pocket, Crandall emitted a series of throaty rumbles, as though wanting to say something else but unable to articulate the words. Finally he gave up and reseated himself behind the desk. "Well then, have a nice time with your friends."

"Thanks." Devon hesitated, suspecting that his father had been on the verge of offering information about Jessica. To say that Devon was fascinated by Jessica Newcomb was an understatement. She was the most alluring woman he'd ever known and Devon was desperate to know everything about her.

But the clock continued its relentless march. The Brotherhood was waiting.

## Chapter Seven

The steak house was busy but not crowded, with plenty of vacant tables scattered between cozy groups of diners. Ambience was muted, softened by warm candle sconces that cast golden light pools on the rustic pine walls. Most of the activity was focused around a massive circular bar which formed the centerpiece of the room. Smiling servers floated between tables, offering customers unhurried attention to enhance the relaxing atmosphere.

As Devon gazed around the dim dining area, a hostess appeared with several menus tucked demurely under her arm. "Good evening, sir. This way, please."

The pleasant woman wound a path toward the secluded table where Roberto was waiting. When he saw Devon, he stood and flashed his trademark smile. "*¡Hola!* It's good to see you, *mi hermano.*"

Grinning, Devon grasped the extended hand. "Hey, Bobby."

After the perfunctory handshake, the friends embraced briefly and ended the greeting with affectionate shoulder slaps. As they seated themselves, Roberto spoke to the hostess. "We'll order after Mr. McKay has arrived." The woman smiled an acknowledgement, discreetly melting into the shadows. The handsome Hispanic turned to Devon. "Larkin will be a few minutes late. One of his group therapy patients had some kind of crisis."

"Not serious, I hope."

"He didn't elaborate but I doubt it. He didn't sound particularly concerned." Roberto leaned back with a smug expression. "Now when he gets here, be respectful. The man has a Ph.D., after all, so be sure to call him *Dr.* McKay."

"I thought Lark hated that title."

"He does." A mischievous gleam danced in Roberto's dark eyes. "It'll drive him crazy."

Devon shook his head. Nothing, it seemed, had changed over the years. Since Larkin had always been the most sensitive member of the group, he'd always been the perfect foil for perpetual teasing and an ingenious assortment of practical jokes. Looking back, it seemed a cruel irony that his closest friends had provided such constant aggravation. The adversity, however, had only served to fortify Larkin's resolve. In many ways, he was now the strongest of them all.

Hooking one arm over the back of his chair, Devon stretched his lean legs beneath the table. "The last time I irritated Lark, he poured two fingers of Scotch down my shirt."

"Ah. Then you definitely deserve a rematch."

"Thanks, but I'll pass. Feel free to go it alone, if you want to risk that slick set of threads." Devon eyed his friend's immaculate business attire. "I didn't know the feds paid their prosecutors so well."

Roberto shrugged off the praise. "They don't. I take kickbacks."

Devon laughed. Outrageous remarks had always been a Brotherhood tradition. "Yeah, right. And I work for Saddam Hussein in my spare time."

"As a matter of fact, I do recall hearing that you won the Pulitzer by threatening the selection committee with a SCUD." He aimed a playful punch at Devon's bicep. "I'd offer congratulations but I know how pained you must be with your success. You've always considered the achievement of wealth as a betrayal of the soul."

Amused by the reminder of his radical youth, Devon rubbed his chin thoughtfully. "I've reconsidered that position. Slightly."

"*¡Dios me libre!*" Roberto feigned horror. "This from a man who once donated his entire fortune to charity rather than risk materialistic contamination."

"If you're referring to the time you conned me out of my allowance—"

"No, no." Roberto protested with an insistent shake of his scrupulously groomed head. "*Conned* is such an indelicate word, my friend. I merely assisted your need to be generous."

Devon regarded him with an indulgent smirk. "You always were full of crap. That's probably why you're such a damned good lawyer."

Roberto's classic features stretched into the brilliant smile that caught most people off guard, drawing attention from the hidden darkness in those intense midnight eyes. Arroya was a fierce friend but he was also a ruthless enemy. Those who underestimated him once would never do so again. For those who crossed him, however, there would be no second chance. His vengeance was swift and merciless.

Given the brutal environment in which he'd been raised, Roberto might well have joined society's dark side. That would have been a tragedy because Roberto Arroya was an intellectual genius, a man destined for greatness—either great good or great evil. Fortunately, the Brotherhood's avenger had chosen the law as his sword.

Roberto suddenly rose, gesturing toward the restaurant's foyer. Devon turned and saw the hostess escorting a clean-cut, bespectacled blonde dressed in casual tweed. The man was ten feet from their table before Devon realized who it was. He blinked in astonishment then pushed himself into a standing position. "My God, Lark, what in hell have you done to yourself? You look like a freaking banker."

Larkin McKay adjusted his silver-rimmed glasses and regarded Devon coolly. "That reaction reflects a deep, psychological fear of intimacy and suppressed envy for those who are quite obviously better looking than you."

Devon chuckled. "Hell, man, everyone's better looking than me."

"Then it's no wonder you're so repressed." Unable to maintain his haughty expression, Larkin's eyes twinkled happily as he wrapped a firm arm around Devon's shoulders. "You old war-horse. Damn. It's good to see you."

"You too, man." Devon settled back in his chair, studying Larkin's strained features. It had been nearly three years since they'd seen each other and Devon was stunned by the change. Larkin, who'd always been chided for his pretty-boy looks, now reflected each of his thirty-one years, and then some. The dignified glasses and silvery streaks in his surfer blond hair did, however, give him a distinguished demeanor befitting his profession.

Considering the number of female heads turning when Larkin had walked through the room, it was evident that his new look was no less attractive to the opposite sex. Larkin hadn't seemed to notice. There was an innate sadness in his eyes that touched Devon to the core, because he knew what had caused that sadness and it damn near broke his heart.

Roberto turned to the new arrival, verbalizing Devon's thoughts. "Are you going to see your kids for spring break?"

"That's the plan. They're flying in next Wednesday."

"Flying in from where?" Devon asked.

"Indiana." Larkin made a production of smoothing a linen napkin across his lap. He cleared his throat. "They live there now, with their mother and ... her husband."

A strained silence fell at the table. Devon stared at the tablecloth for a moment, then looked up. "I'm sorry it didn't work out between you and Bonnie."

Larkin's nonchalant shrug didn't quite come off. "Things happen. I guess we just weren't suited for each other."

Devon and Roberto shared a telling look, but neither man spoke. The breakup of any marriage was tough. For Larkin, who'd idolized his wife and two young children, it had been doubly devastating. His own parents' bitter divorce had been a particularly shattering experience, creating a series of tragedies that had eventually led the traumatized youngster to the hellish environment of Blackthorn Hall. As a child, Larkin had angrily vowed that his own kids, when he had them, would never have to suffer the pain of parental abandonment.

Once again life had spiraled beyond his control. And again, he needed his brothers. Devon reached out and took one of Larkin's hands. Roberto took the other before clasping Devon's free hand. Then, as they'd done uncountable times over the past twenty years, they held up their joined fists in a circle of unity. "One heart, one spirit, one mind," they murmured. "To the Brotherhood."

They were still connected like a six-point star and grinning stupidly when the server's discreet cough caught their attention. "Are you gentlemen ready to order or would you prefer a few more minutes to, uh, practice your routine?"

Roberto leaned back in his chair, absently brushing his immaculate lapel. He smiled without apology. "I'll have the top sirloin—medium—baked potato with extra sour cream, ranch dressing on the salad and coffee."

"Sounds good to me," Larkin said.

Devon agreed. "Make it three."

After scooping up the menus, the waiter slid them a be-mused glance and left. Larkin issued a throaty chuckle. "The last time I saw that look, it was on the face of a red-headed bully from Dorm B who stumbled into one of our boiler room meetings."

Although Devon hadn't thought about that incident in years, he remembered it well. Because each dormitory housed a dozen boys, the Brotherhood was always search-ing for secluded spots where they could gather to share their private thoughts. The boiler room had been perfect, a dark and spooky place declared off-limits by detention facility brass. No one ever went there. No one, that is, except the Brotherhood—and one nosy snitch who'd been spying on them for weeks.

"What was that kid's name?" Roberto asked of no one in particular.

It was Devon who answered. "I'm not sure, but we all called him Howdy Doody because of his red hair and freckles."

Roberto laughed. "Right. And Tommy decided that was too long, so he shortened that to Doo-Doo—"

"Which," Larkin interjected, "was why the kid had it in for us in the first place. That's when Tommy concocted that devious scheme to lure him to the boiler room and con-vince poor old Doo-Doo that we were all sorcerers."

Devon let out a delighted hoot. "I'll never forget the look on that kid's face when he saw us circling a lighted candle wearing towels on our heads and chanting gobbledygook about smiting enemies."

"As I recall, he never came within spitting distance of any of us from that day on." Roberto crossed his arms, leaning on the table with an indulgent smile. "You've got to hand it to Tommy. The guy was a born hustler."

"He always had an angle," Larkin murmured, twirling his water glass.

The table fell silent as the wary waiter reappeared with a coffeepot. When they were alone again, the three men continued their reminiscing with renewed vigor, chuckling about all the havoc they'd caused with childish shenanigans that ran the gamut of silliness, from hiding live frogs in the salad bar to clogging dorm sinks with melted candle wax.

Over the next hour they enjoyed good food and camaraderie with rapid-fire conversation. They reminisced, caught up on each other's current lives and even had time to share a dream or two before Larkin glanced at his watch. "It's almost time," he said quietly.

A subdued mood rippled around the table as Roberto signaled the server and placed their final order.

Devon somberly toyed with his coffee cup, staring into the murky liquid and recalling that the first time they'd celebrated Tommy's birthday had been twenty years ago to the day.

Two weeks after Tommy's death, the Brotherhood survivors had sneaked off to meet in the dank boiler room of Blackthorn Hall. Devon and Larkin had arrived first. They'd laid their flashlights on the stained concrete floor, aiming the beams toward the spot that would be the center of their human circle. Larkin shrugged off his canvas backpack and pulled out a can of cola.

Devon frowned. "Only one can?"

"I only had two quarters." Larkin tossed the deflated pack aside, placed the soft drink in the center of the circle and sat cross-legged beside his flashlight. "One'll be enough. Did you bring the cups?"

"Yeah." To prove that he'd completed his part of the assignment, Devon opened a squashed grocery bag and extracted the four foam cups he'd "liberated" from the administrative lounge. He placed the cups, along with a fat, half-burned candle, next to the soda can and squatted restlessly beside Larkin. "Where's Bobby?"

# PLAY

## SILHOUETTE'S

# LUCKY HEARTS

# GAME

## AND YOU GET

★ **FREE BOOKS**

★ **A FREE GIFT**

★ **AND MUCH MORE**

**TURN THE PAGE AND
DEAL YOURSELF IN** ⟶

# PLAY "LUCKY HEARTS" AND GET...

★ Exciting Silhouette Special Edition® novels — FREE
★ Plus a lovely Pearl Drop Necklace — FREE

## THEN CONTINUE YOUR LUCKY STREAK WITH A SWEETHEART OF A DEAL

1. Play Lucky Hearts as instructed on the opposite page.

2. Send back this card and you'll receive brand-new Silhouette Special Edition® novels. These books have a cover price of $3.50 each, but they are yours to keep absolutely free.

3. There's no catch. You're under no obligation to buy anything. We charge nothing — ZERO — for your first shipment. And you don't have to make any minimum number of purchases — not even one!

4. The fact is thousands of readers enjoy receiving books by mail from the Silhouette Reader Service. They like the convenience of home delivery...they like getting the best new novels months before they're available in stores...and they love our discount prices!

5. We hope that after receiving your free books you'll want to remain a subscriber. But the choice is yours — to continue or cancel, anytime at all! So why not take us up on our invitation, with no risk of any kind. You'll be glad you did!

© 1990 HARLEQUIN ENTERPRISES LIMITED.

"I dunno." Larkin squinted toward the dark hallway that led to the stairs. "Sometimes kitchen duty runs late."

Despite his churning stomach, Devon feigned a confident nod. Roberto's contribution to the ceremony was the most crucial... and the most dangerous. Since Roberto's kitchen chores gave him access to what they needed, the assignment had initially made sense.

Now Devon was having second thoughts. If Roberto got caught, there was little doubt that he'd be relegated to the Box for his crime. He was sickened by the thought of the Brotherhood's youngest member enduring the torture of being locked in a concrete vault so small that standing was impossible and you could only sit with your knees pulled under your chin. No one was ever the same after the Box.

Devon certainly wasn't. He'd never forget the cold, the bone-chilling cold, and the nauseating stench of those who'd been there before him. Now he had nightmares. Sometimes he'd wake up crying, screaming, with Lark and Bobby shaking him. They'd ask what was wrong. Devon wouldn't tell them. He wouldn't tell them about the Box, either. It was too scary to talk about.

Now all Devon could do was pray that Bobby hadn't gotten caught.

Apparently Larkin, too, was worried. He fidgeted with the hem of his tattered T-shirt, staring into the darkness. "Maybe we oughta go look for him."

Devon licked his lips. "Yeah, maybe."

Behind them, the boiler kicked on, hissing and rattling. Neither boy paid attention. They were each concentrating on a different sound, a rhythmic thump echoing down the cinder block hallway. A light emerged from the blackness, feeling its way along the rusted pipes and stained concrete floor.

Larkin's voice was tight with relief. "Geez, man, where've you been?"

Roberto huffed into the room clutching a small paper bag. "I hid in the pantry and waited 'til everyone was gone."

"Weren't you afraid you'd get locked in?"

"Nah." Roberto laid down his flashlight and took his place at the edge of the circle. "I just crawled out through a window."

Devon wiped his wet head and blew out a relieved breath. "So, did you get it or what?"

"'Course I got it." Reaching into the bag, Roberto carefully withdrew an oatmeal cookie the size of a fat pancake. He grinned proudly. "Neat, huh?"

Larkin was unimpressed. "Aw hell, Bobby, you were supposed to get cupcakes."

Roberto's eyes flashed black fire. "All the good stuff went to the staff dining room. There wasn't nothin' left so I stole this from the cook's lunch bag. You got a problem with that?"

Morosely eyeing the immense cookie, Larkin gave a resigned sigh. "It's okay, I guess. Tommy wouldn't care."

Somewhat mollified, Roberto arranged the cookie on the flattened bag and scooted it into the center of the circle along with the cups, candle and can of soda. He glanced at the other boys. "It's almost nine."

"Yeah. I guess we'd better get started," Devon said.

The boys solemnly joined hands and lifted their entwined fists. "One heart, one spirit, one mind. To the Brotherhood." As they murmured the familiar chant, each gaze was fixed on the vacancy, an empty spot in the circle that duplicated the empty place in their hearts.

Swallowing the sudden lump in his throat, Devon lifted the candle, holding it out while Larkin dug a matchbook from his jeans. After two tries, the damp match flared and the candle flickered to life. Meanwhile, Roberto filled four cups with soda. He set one in front of each boy and one at Tommy's place. With that chore completed, all eyes turned to Devon, who was studying the perplexing problem of affixing the candle to Tommy's birthday confection. He finally resolved the situation by seating the candle in a pool of hot wax dribbled on the center of the cookie.

Roberto grinned approvingly. "Cool."

Larkin wiped his eyes and glumly watched the flickering flame. "Who's gonna blow out the candle?"

Roberto's grin faded as he looked anxiously to Devon. They hadn't really thought about this part. Traditionally the birthday boy was supposed to blow out his own candle. Under the circumstances, of course, an alternate would have to be selected. As the leader, Devon made the choice. "You do it, Lark. You and Tommy were best friends."

Larkin shook his head miserably. "I can't."

"We can all do it," Roberto suggested. "You know, count to three and stuff."

That sounded fine to Devon. He turned to Larkin. "Is that okay with you?"

The blond head bobbed twice, then snapped up. Larkin's eyes rounded like saucers. "Look!" He pointed a frantic finger toward the candle just as the flame pulsed to one side and went out.

Three gaping faces were riveted on the smoking wick. After a moment, Devon cleared his throat. "Musta been a draft."

"Yeah." Roberto stared, awestruck. "Musta been."

Larkin was shaking like a windblown leaf. "It was Tommy."

"Don't be a dweeb, Lark." But Devon wasn't as sure as he sounded. He angled a glance toward the empty space, at the circle. It still looked empty. Somehow, it didn't *feel* empty. "Well, the stupid candle is out, so let's get on with it."

"Yeah . . . okay." Roberto's black eyes rolled from right to left, up and down again. "Who's got a knife?"

"Knife?"

Larkin and Devon stared at each other. Roberto moaned. "Great. Now what?"

Muttering under his breath, Devon reached out and broke the cookie into four pieces, setting the biggest piece—the one with the candle—in front of Tommy's place. Then each boy lifted the cookie in one hand and the cup of cola in the other and offered a birthday toast to their absent friend.

Slowly the rust-stained cinder block melted into varnish pine panels and Devon shook off the bittersweet memory. Blinking, he saw the waiter displaying a champagne bottle to Roberto, who nodded his approval. In a moment, the cork was deftly removed but before the waiter could fill the glasses, Roberto took the bottle, dismissing the man with quiet thanks.

When they were alone, Roberto filled the four champagne glasses—an upgrade from soda agreed upon when they'd reached adulthood—then lifted a pink bakery box that had been tucked beneath his chair. After the giant oatmeal cookie was reverently removed and arranged on a plate, Larkin took a small candle from his coat pocket.

Devon reached out. "This is my job, remember?"

Larkin smiled and handed it over. The ritual continued with Devon using the pool of hot wax that formed around the burning wick to seat the candle firmly in the center of the cookie. Then all three men watched the flame, each lost in silent thought. After a moment, the flame flickered and—as always—it leaned to one side and disappeared. They'd stopped questioning the odd occurrence years ago. Instead, they simply used it as a signal that the time had arrived.

The cookie was divided into quarters. Three glasses were raised. The fourth was placed in front of the vacant chair, beside the oatmeal wedge with the smoking candle. Once again, the Brotherhood was complete.

"I'm feeling fine, Mom, better than ever." Holding the cordless phone between her chin and shoulder, Jessica shook out a silky half-slip and awkwardly folded the garment while standing in front of her bedroom dresser.

Aysla Newcomb McKerry's skepticism crackled through her throaty voice. "You're not overdoing, are you? You know what happens when you push yourself too hard."

Jessica arranged the folded slip in her lingerie drawer and sat on the edge of her mattress. "I've had tons of energy this week," she insisted, telling herself that exaggeration wasn't the same as a lie.

There had been moments of exhaustion, of course, but overall she really had felt quite well. Better than well, actually. At times, she'd felt positively radiant. The fact that such surges of emotional buoyancy occurred during her times with Devon were attributable, of course, to pure happenstance. A fluke of nature. Coincidence.

Sighing, she pulled a flannel nightie from the laundry basket. If she had an ounce of courage, she'd admit that coincidence had nothing to do with what she was feeling for her boss's thrill-seeking son. She was obviously infatuated with the man. The realization was not a pleasant one. There was no room in her life for emotional involvement with anyone, least of all a man who was already married to his career.

Her mother's voice interrupted the mental sojourn. "It's been months since we've seen you, dear. Frank and I are both looking forward to your visit."

Jessica's mouth went dry. Stuffing the sloppily wrapped nightgown into the drawer, she knuckled her fleecy scalp as her racing mind frantically sorted excuses. "I want to see you too, Mom, but I, uh, don't know if I can make it this weekend. I've been so busy at work...." The lame words dissipated like so much steam.

A hurt silence filtered over the line. Finally Aysla spoke quietly. "You mustn't put it off again, Jessica. Frank has made all the arrangements."

"I know." Covering her eyes, she flopped back on the mattress, feeling like a coward and a fool. It wasn't the tests that she was afraid of. It was the results; or rather, the potential results.

Periodic reevaluations were absolutely crucial to assure that the cancer hadn't recurred. If microscopic cells were discovered early enough, aggressive therapy was her only chance to stop the silent spread of the disease. Intellectually, she knew that. Emotionally, however, she didn't think she could face another round of the devastating treatment.

A hot rush of tears burned beneath her lids, angering her. She sat up, roughly wiping her moist eyes. "I guess now that my hair is finally growing back, I just wanted to put off the inevitable."

"Recurrence isn't inevitable," Aysla said softly. "Frank studied your surgical records carefully. Since there was no lymph node involvement, there is every reason to believe that the tumor was localized and the prognosis for a good outcome is excellent."

A good outcome was understated medical jargon to describe a live patient rather than a dead one. At one time, Jessica wouldn't have considered simply being alive as a good outcome. Now she understood that to be the only result that mattered.

Eight months ago, she'd thought of breast cancer as a horrible malady that struck other women, other families. Then during her morning shower, she'd felt a small lump. At first, she hadn't been overly concerned, assuming the painless mass to be some kind of benign cyst. But it hadn't been a cyst and it hadn't been benign. The emotional devastation of that diagnosis had been nearly as traumatic as the physical ordeal that would follow.

Jessica's initial reaction had been one of denial, insisting that healthy, thirty-year-old women simply didn't get breast cancer. With her stepfather's medical connections, she'd obtained three concurring opinions and eventually accepted the sad fact that young women did indeed get breast cancer because she had it. Then she'd moved from denial into terror—the terror of dying—and had committed herself mentally and physically to winning the most important fight of her life.

Surgery had been the first step, a lumpectomy that left one breast looking like a half-bitten apple. Still, she'd managed to swallow her vanity, thankful that there was no man in her life so she could focus on recovery without worrying about a lover's reaction to her scars.

Drawing on family support and her own grit, she'd endured weeks of grueling adjunctive treatment that had sapped her strength and caused her lovely blond hair to fall out in ragged clumps. It had been sheer hell but she'd gotten through it once; if she had to, she'd get through it again.

Mentally fortified, she sat up and shifted the phone to her left ear. "When have the tests been scheduled?"

"Friday. I know that's the day after tomorrow—"

"Friday will be fine. Afterward, we'll spend the weekend together."

"Oh, that would be wonderful! The guesthouse has been so empty without you."

Her mother's excitement served to exacerbate Jessica's guilt at having neglected them. It hadn't been deliberate. She loved her parents dearly and was deeply grateful for their staunch support. But since those traumatic postsurgical weeks had been spent at their Monterey home, return visits served as an embarrassing reminder of how helpless she'd been during that painful time. For a woman who valued independence over gold, being reduced to near-invalid status, even temporarily, had been nearly as difficult as dealing with the cancer itself. "But you mustn't fuss over me, all right?"

"Fussing is a mother's prerogative," Aysla replied firmly. "Besides, you'll always be my baby."

Jessica winced. "Prerogative or not, no fussing. Besides, it's your turn to be pampered so I'll take care of the cooking."

"You know that's not necessary, dear. I enjoy doing things for you."

"You also enjoy breakfast in bed and this weekend that's just what you're going to have. And homemade lasagna for supper."

Aysla's melodic chuckle warmed Jessica to her toes. "Have I ever told you what a wonderful daughter you are?"

"Every day of my life," Jessica whispered. "And I love you for it."

A comfortable silence extended between them. Jessica wiped her moist eyes, suspecting that her mother was doing the same.

After a moment, Aysla sniffed audibly and cleared her throat. "So, your hair is growing back?"

"Umm. It's a little over a half inch long now." Jessica absently touched the feathery fuzz. "In a couple of months there should be enough up there to do something...I'm not sure what."

"You'd look lovely with one of those layered pixie cuts."

Jessica chuckled. "Great. I've always wanted to look like Tinkerbell."

"Nonsense," Aysla replied with a smile in her voice. "As soon as you're ready, we'll make an appointment with my stylist. He's absolutely wonderful."

"He'd have to be," Jessica murmured. She caught a glimpse of her reflection in the dresser mirror and decided she was beginning to resemble a blond eagle, which would have been upsetting had it not been such an improvement. At one point, her scalp had looked like a polished cue ball. The effect had been rather humorous, she supposed, although she hadn't been particularly amused at the time. In fact she'd been so horrified that she'd immediately purchased the first wig she'd found that was halfway close to her natural hair color.

By the time she realized that she hated the style, there'd been no way to gracefully reappear in a new one without acknowledging that she'd been wearing a wig. That, of course, would have led friends to question why. Since Jessica couldn't bear to see pity in their eyes, she'd kept the hairpiece and chalked the fiasco up to experience. Even now the ugly thing taunted her from a foam head on the nightstand, where it hung like an unkempt pelt.

Jessica gave it a hateful glance and returned her attention to her mother's cheery voice.

"... and we'll spend the entire day at the salon," Aysla was saying. "Pedicures, facials, the whole works. Won't that be fun?"

"Yes, it'll be great—" Jessica stiffened as the doorbell rang.

"Jessica ... is anything wrong?"

"Hmm? Oh. There's someone at the door, that's all."

"At this hour?"

"It's probably someone from building maintenance. They're famous for showing up at odd times." Standing, Jessica absently tweaked a short tuft at her temple. She glanced at the wig then decided that she didn't give a fig what the maintenance man thought of her cropped hair. "Listen, Mom, I'd better go. I've been complaining about a clogged heating duct for almost a week, I don't want them to put me back on the bottom of the list."

"All right, dear. We'll see you tomorrow."

"Tomorrow," Jessica repeated, heading into the living room. "Love you. Bye."

Clicking the Off switch, she dropped the phone on the coffee table and hurried toward the front door. The bell sounded again. Jessica touched the knob, peered through the peephole and nearly fainted. It was Devon, and he looked like he'd been hit by a truck.

*Chapter Eight*

The door cracked open and a startled eyeball peered through the slit. "My God, Devon! Are you all right?"

"Hmm?" Devon absently glanced down at his torn jacket and smudged jeans. "I had a flat tire on the freeway so I decided to park in a pool of road grease to fix it."

"Oh." The eye blinked in relief before scanning him warily. "What are you doing here?"

He puffed his cheeks, considering that to be one hell of a good question. Unfortunately, he didn't have an acceptable answer. After leaving the restaurant tonight, instinct had driven him to the one person who could offer solace, perhaps even soothe the vague, indefinable ache in his heart. Obviously he couldn't admit that. Jessica would think him a nut case. Devon wasn't sure that she'd be wrong. So he studied his shoes, rubbed the back of his neck and lied. "I was hoping for a cup of coffee."

"Coffee?"

"Well . . . yeah." He cleared his throat, feeling stupid. "I guess it's pretty late, though. For coffee, that is." The eye widened. "I mean, the caffeine would probably keep you awake." Devon moaned and rubbed his face with his hands. "Look, this was a really bad idea. I shouldn't have bothered you."

"No, it's all right."

"It is?"

"Certainly. It's just that, uh—" The eye darted in panic. "I'm not dressed. I'll, uh, be right back."

The door slammed so quickly that Devon reeled backward and grabbed the jamb to steady himself. A rush of footsteps echoed from inside the apartment, fading away, disappearing for a moment, then hurrying closer. In a moment, the security chain rattled. Jessica, looking flushed and harried, opened the door.

"Hi." After the breathless greeting, she patted her perfectly groomed hair and stepped back to allow him access. "Come in."

He regarded her warily, noting that she was impeccably attired in the tailored navy slacks and creamy cuffed blouse that she'd worn earlier in the day. The outfit was accessorized by a muted print scarf, intricately twisted and held in place by a gold broach pinned at the throat. Since it would have been impossible for her to don such a complex ensemble in less than a minute, the excuse of needing to get dressed seemed a bit lame.

Devon peered over her shoulder, half expecting to see a man's shoe poking out from beneath the sofa. The thought was unnerving. "Are you sure I'm not interrupting anything?"

"Of course not." She ducked away to fidget with her hair, then straightened and met his suspicious expression with a guileless smile. "Do you still want that coffee or would you rather have tea?"

"Whatever is easiest." He entered cautiously and was surprised by his own massive relief at finding nothing more than the usual clutter.

After closing the door, Jessica headed to the kitchen, speaking over her shoulder. "Actually, I'm not much of a tea person. I do have decaf, though, if you like it."

"Decaf is fine," he murmured, although he personally despised the stuff.

"In case you'd like to wash up, the bathroom is down the hall."

A quick inspection of his greasy hands proved that to be an excellent suggestion. After depositing his torn, and now oil-stained Windbreaker on the entry coatrack, he followed her directions and was dismayed to discover a sinkful of soaking panty hose. He instantly dismissed the option of removing the intimate apparel—he wouldn't want anyone wringing out his jock straps, after all—and was bent over the tub faucet when Jessica skidded into the doorway with a horrified expression.

"I'll, uh—" a red flush crept up her throat as she sidled toward the sink "—just get these out of your way."

Devon held up his lathered hands and allowed himself an amused grin. "Don't bother. Tub water is the same as sink water. Now, if my only option had been the toilet, I might not be as accommodating."

Obviously mortified, she nonetheless managed to maintain a modicum of dignity. "In that case, I'll just finish up...in the kitchen. With the coffee." Flushing furiously, she spun on her heel and left.

Still chuckling, Devon quickly completed his chore and returned to the living room. As he stepped over a pile of partially sorted magazines, he noticed several family photographs displayed on a curio rack. One informal snapshot, apparently taken at an amusement park, reflected Jessica as a laughing teenager standing beside a happy, middle-aged couple which he assumed to be her mother and stepfather.

Another picture was of a bright-eyed child of about seven with sleek blond hair and a grin he'd have recognized anywhere. In the photo, little Jessica was proudly displaying a puny trout as if it were a prized marlin. Beside her an immense man—obviously the father whom she'd loved so dearly—held up a fishing pole and favored the camera with an infectiously jovial grin. Intrigued, Devon picked up the photograph to examine it more closely.

The kitchen faucet rattled. "I'm surprised to see you," Jessica called over the rush of water. "Crandall mentioned that you had a date this evening."

Devon smiled and returned the photograph to its place beside an untidy stack of credit card receipts. "Just dinner with some old friends."

"Really?"

She sounded so incredulous that he couldn't help but laugh. "Believe it or not, I really do have friends."

She peered anxiously around the wall. "Of course you do. Everyone has friends. I keep forgetting that you grew up in Los Angeles. Were these friends from school?"

"In a sense, I suppose. We met when we were kids."

Jessica again disappeared into the kitchen. A cupboard door closed and in a minute, a can opener whirred softly. "It must be difficult to keep in touch since you travel so much."

"Yes, it is." Devon returned the photograph, still bothered by the vague sensation of displacement and loss that had haunted him all evening. Although aware that his relationship with Bobby and Lark had waned over the years, he'd always assumed growing apart to be the normal result of growing up. Tonight, however, as his friends chatted about moments that the two of them had shared last month and the month before, Devon had felt a distance between them that he hadn't noticed before. Perhaps in the past, he simply hadn't been attuned enough to notice. Or even to care.

But now he did care; he cared deeply.

*Difficult to keep in touch....* Jessica had said. Devon clung to that statement, silently agreeing that his career had been the culprit, the root cause of his emotional isolation. Now, as he scrutinized the secret corners of his heart, he realized that he'd repeatedly used that career as a shield, an excuse to alienate himself from the intimacy of family and friends. What he didn't understand was why.

"Devon?"

Startled, he spun around and stared into Jessica's concerned face.

"Are you all right?" she asked.

His smile was tight enough to crack walnuts. "Sure, why not?"

"You seemed to be a million miles away."

Since there was no accusation in her voice, his smile loosened. "I guess I was. Sorry."

"You're entitled." She cocked her head prettily. "Is something besides the flat tire upsetting you?"

"No." The reply was too fast and sharp to be believed. He sighed and dropped heavily on the sofa. "Nothing gets by you, does it?"

"That nostalgic look in your eye was a dead giveaway." She settled beside him, tucking one foot under her knee and turning sideways. "Do you want to talk about it?"

"No." He did, of course. Inside him, undefinable sensations pulsed with such power that he feared his chest might explode. He closed his eyes, scouring his lids with his fingertips and trying to get control of the emotional perplexing surge.

A soothing warmth touched his thigh. Devon looked at the slender hand resting above his knee. A tingling sensation seemed to be emanating from her delicate fingers, an electric energy that charged his blood and radiated through every cell in his body. The paradoxical effect was one of calm exhilaration.

"Have you and your father had another argument?" she asked gently.

Devon's gaze was riveted on her hand. "We exchanged a few words but no worse than usual."

"I'm sorry to hear that."

Stung by the disappointment in her voice, he suddenly felt compelled to downplay the incident. "It was just a minor disagreement."

"About what?"

"The same thing it's always been about. His work."

Seeming startled by that information, Jessica straightened and retrieved her hand. "I knew Crandall was concerned about the dangers of your career but why would his business cause friction between you?"

"Because it seems to be more important to him than staying alive." He avoided her shocked gaze by studying a greasy smear on his jeans pocket. "A heart attack is a warning to slow down. Evidently, my father hasn't gotten that message."

"So you believe he's working too hard?"

"Let's just say that he thinks the company will collapse if he doesn't exercise personal control over every detail."

Jessica considered that for a moment. "Given his recent health problems, I can understand your concern. What really confuses me is why your father's work habits were such a problem in the past."

Ordinarily, Devon would have clammed up at this point and manipulated the conversation to a less-painful subject. But there was something about Jessica's compassionate quest that made him search his own soul for a truth he'd never revealed. What he discovered was as shocking as it was simple. "I was jealous."

She repeated the word as though she'd never heard it before, then added, "But why?"

"Probably because I was a selfish brat. When I was a kid, my father left me with my aunt and spent most of his time overseas. That ticked me off because I wanted all of his attention." He forced a thin smile. "Sounds pretty shallow, doesn't it?"

"No," she whispered. "It sounds like the normal reaction of a lonely little boy."

"Hey, wipe that pity off your face. I wasn't exactly a stoic little soldier. The truth is that I was a hell-raising trouble-maker with a smart mouth and a rotten disposition."

"I don't doubt that. Children who've been starved for affection are frequently hostile."

The observation was accurate enough to make him squirm. "Look, I've got no one to blame but myself. I crossed over the line."

"How?"

"By turning into a rowdy little street tough." For some reason, Devon realized he was oddly comfortable relating sordid details of his past that he hadn't shared with anyone beyond the Brotherhood. "I started hanging around with a gang of older kids, learning the tricks of the trade."

"What trade?"

"Stealing cars." He grinned at her chagrined frown. "My hero was a tattooed punk who could punch an ignition in less than two seconds. Unfortunately, I wasn't as talented. I'd been struggling with my first yank for nearly five minutes when the police car pulled up. Three of us got snagged that night."

"Oh, good grief. What happened?"

His smile faded. "The usual. We were arrested and hauled into family court. The other kids were given probation and released to their parents but my aunt decided I needed a lesson. She declared that I was incorrigible and had me shipped off to a juvenile detention facility."

Jessica was horrified. "And Crandall allowed that?"

"He'd been out of the country for a couple of months. At first I thought he was in on the deal. Years later I found out that he hadn't known about it."

"But how could he *not* know? Surely the court would have contacted him."

Devon shrugged. "My aunt shared legal guardianship with my father, supposedly so she could handle medical emergencies and the like. As far as the judge was concerned, that was all the authority she needed to sign me up as a temporary ward of the court."

Jessica's response was interrupted by the gurgling hiss of spewing steam, a signal that the coffee was ready. She hesitated then clamped her lips together, excused herself and went into the kitchen.

Unfolding his cramped legs, Devon stretched his feet under the granite-slab table, massaged his forehead and tried to loosen his stiff neck by rolling his head from side to side. The enticing aroma of freshly brewed coffee wafted into the room, along with the homey kitchen sounds of cupboard doors and rattling flatware.

Lulled by the cozy clamor, he stretched lazily on Jessica's sofa and decided that under the right circumstances, domesticity did have its rewards. Not for him, of course, although he could certainly understand the appeal. In fact, the idealistic vision of hearth and home was becoming a dangerous enticement for a man who'd deliberately chosen a vagabond life.

"No sugar, no cream, right?"

He sat up as Jessica set two steaming mugs on the coffee table. "Right. Thanks."

She settled thoughtfully beside him. "How long did you stay in that awful place?"

To postpone a reply, Devon sipped his coffee, barely noticing that it tasted flatter than uncapped soda. Part of him wanted to forget the past and shift the conversational gears toward a more pleasant subject—like the beguiling warmth in her sea-foam green eyes and the saucy spring scent that sweetened the air as she moved. He wanted to tell her how special she was—and how special she made him feel.

But the pressure in his chest was rising and the words rushed out on their own. "I spent almost five months at the Hall."

Her eyelids fluttered shut. She touched her throat and swallowed hard. When she looked at him again, her eyes were bright with empathetic tears. "You must have felt so abandoned."

"I, uh—" He paused for another sip of coffee then deliberately placed the mug on the table. He *had* felt abandoned, of course, and betrayed. But there was no sense sniveling about that now. "Like I said, it was my own damned fault. I needed an attitude adjustment. I got one. Then I got out."

Jessica wasn't buying the abbreviated version. "Your father came for you?"

"Yes."

"But if your aunt never contacted him, how did he finally learn where you were?"

"He got the bills." Devon couldn't keep the bitterness from his voice. "While preparing quarterly reports, the accountant ran across some perplexing invoices from the state."

"You mean people are actually charged for the privilege of being incarcerated?"

"Under the law, parents are financially responsible for the willful misconduct of minor children. Apparently the court believed that attempted car theft fell into that category." Still embarrassed by his youthful stupidity, Devon avoided her gaze and studied a pulled thread on the sofa cushion. "At any rate, a few weeks at a structured rehabilitation facility costs more than your average luxury sedan, so the invoices definitely got my father's attention."

Jessica laid a soft palm on his wrist. "I'm sure Crandall was more upset about what had happened to you than he was about the money."

Devon wasn't so certain but kept that thought to himself. Besides, he'd already paid back every penny his father had laid out on the fiasco. It had taken years, of course, but he'd finally wiped the financial slate clean. The emotional cost was another matter.

After blinking away the image of Tommy Murdock's grinning face, Devon wiped his palms on his thighs and strained to lighten the tone. "The experience may not have been a pleasant one but there were some positive results. After Dad sent my aunt packing and hired Gunda, I learned what real food was supposed to taste like."

Evidently Jessica wasn't fooled by the jocular response. "I suspect you learned a lot more than that. You couldn't have come through something that traumatic without being deeply affected."

Devon dropped all pretense. "It changed my life," he said simply.

Jessica gave his wrist a reassuring squeeze. "Tell me what happened."

"It's not a pretty story."

"Please. I want to know."

"All right." He took a deep breath and started to speak in a voice that hardly shook at all. Over the next half hour, he spoke of the Brotherhood, bonds of friendship that would last a lifetime. But he didn't talk about Tommy Murdock, partly because the memory was too painful and partly because he couldn't face the shame of revealing how his own flawed judgement and cowardice had ultimately contributed to the tragedy.

For her part, Jessica was deeply moved by the poignant depiction of enduring friendship and appalled at the portrayal of how the facility's paramilitary discipline, corrupted by absolute power, had escalated into sadistic acts of cruelty and gestapo tactics inflicted under the guise of authoritarian control.

When Devon calmly described the punitive process of forcing youngsters to stand at attention for hours on end, she couldn't suppress her outrage. "That's criminal! How could they get away with such a terrible thing?"

"Twenty years ago the line between child abuse and discipline wasn't as well-defined as it is now. And if a kid keeled over from heat exhaustion, the complaint was swept under the rug."

"But there must have been dozens of complaints. They couldn't all be ignored."

"No one was going to take the word of a few juvenile delinquents over a respected pillar of the community with a pocketful of credentials." Devon's philosophical attitude suddenly faded. "Besides, these people were masters of mind control. They knew how to instill terror without leaving marks. At least, none that were visible."

The bitterness in his voice sent a frisson of fear down her spine. "How did they do that?"

He gazed across the room, eyes clouded, lips stretched into a hard line. "Isolation."

The succinct reply took her by surprise. "That's all?"

"It was enough." His chest expanded, then shuddered as he exhaled all at once. "The administrative offices were originally designed with a fireproof file vault, kind of a concrete closet, four-foot square, without light, ventilation or heat. I doubt the facility's founding fathers could have foreseen the innovative use to which it was eventually put."

Devon spoke softly, methodically, his glazed gaze focused somewhere in the past as he described the agonizing muscle cramps, the numbing cold, the smothering blackness where a dwindling oxygen supply soon turned each tortuous breath into a desperate gasp for life-giving air.

Jessica covered her mouth, unwilling to believe what she was hearing yet knowing without doubt that it was true. What Devon was describing was his own experience as a terrified child who'd been tortured like a prisoner of war. She swallowed a nauseous surge, overwhelmed by the horror of what he'd endured. All she could do was whisper "Dear God" over and over until her throat clogged with emotion and her vision was blurred by tears.

She wiped her wet eyes with the back of her hand, biting her lip as she studied Devon's ashen face. He was lost somewhere in time, his eyes glazed with past terror, his colorless lips stretched into a rigid grimace. She'd seen that haunted expression once before—when he'd been pulled out of the mine shaft.

He'd mentioned then that he wasn't fond of cramped, dark places. Now she knew why.

Gently framing his face with her hands, she urged him to look at her. "Oh, Lord," she murmured. "After all you've endured, how could you have forced yourself down into that horrible pit?"

His curtained gaze focused slowly. "I couldn't let Tommy die."

"I thought his name was Larry."

A perplexed expression crossed Devon's face. He blinked twice, staring at Jessica as though she'd just materialized. "Yes, of course. His name was Larry."

Jessica's chest swelled with a thousand unfathomable emotions. Still caressing his dear face, she rested her forehead against his chin and fought to control her quivering voice. "When you volunteered for that rescue, I thought you were being a reckless show-off. I was angry with you." She took a shuddering breath and lifted her head to capture his stunned gaze. "I'm ashamed of myself for having judged you unfairly."

Devon seemed genuinely distressed by her words. "I *am* a reckless show-off. It's the only talent I have."

"That's not true." Her hands slid down to give his shoulders an insistent shake. "You're the most courageous man I've ever known."

At the word *courageous* Devon's head snapped up. "Don't say that. You don't know—" He bit off the statement and turned away, refusing to look at her. After a moment he spoke again, more softly this time. "I'm not the man that you think I am."

"You're the finest, bravest—"

He covered his eyes, moaning and shaking his head. "Jessica, please..." The words dissipated like a vaporous cloud as he turned toward her. As he searched her eyes, his own gaze softened, becoming fluid and dusky.

The dark sensuality in his eyes made her tremble. She moistened her lips, realizing that the hand that had been resting on the back of the sofa was now caressing her left shoulder.

He grazed her silken sleeve with his knuckles, then slid his hand down her arm. After lingering at the sensitive curve of her elbow, his fingers moved smoothly up to where her wrist was resting against his collarbone. Still gazing deeply into her eyes, he traced erotic circles on the back of her hand. Each fiery touch sent a tiny spark coursing through her veins, charge after charge until her entire body quivered electric energy.

Then he lifted her hand, reverently turning her palm upward as though exposing a precious gem. Jessica was paralyzed by a surge of intoxicating sensations and barely able to breathe as he slowly, tortuously, raised her hand to his lips. His gaze never wavered, never left her face as he explored her palm with his mouth, delicately tracing each fine line with the tip of his tongue.

Jessica had never experienced anything so erotic, so intensely sexual, in her entire life. His fingertips glided downward, easing the satin cuff back to expose her throbbing pulse. His thumb grazed lazy circles on the tender flesh of her inner wrist. With each exotic revolution, her pulse beat faster and faster still, until her brain was spinning and her skin steaming from his heated touch.

"You are so beautiful," he murmured. "You take my breath away."

She was too entranced to respond, too enraptured by his exquisite seduction. Her pulse pounded until her arm ached yet she was afraid to move for fear he would stop. But he didn't stop. Instead, he replaced his thumb with his lips, kissing her wrist with an urgency that sent shock waves through her entire body.

Devon made love to her wrist, caressing and tasting and nibbling, until Jessica was shaking like a windblown leaf. With a soft cry, she melted against him, wrapping her arms around his neck and kissing him with a fervency beyond anything she'd ever known. The moment their lips met, something exploded, a liquid heat that radiated like lava from a place deep inside her. She moaned in surprise and ecstasy, parting her lips in a silent plea for even more intimacy. It was a request instantly fulfilled.

Devon's control snapped. A groan of passion rumbled from deep in his throat. His hands were everywhere, exploring her face, her throat, memorizing the curve of her spine and testing the span of her small waist.

A rush of air filled Jessica's starving lungs and she realized that Devon's mouth was now blazing a moist path down her throat. She arched backward, her fingers clutching his shoulders like desperate talons. Each breath came as a ragged gasp. Odd whimpering sounds echoed around them. The noises were coming from Jessica but she was too frantic to care. All that mattered was this man, this moment. She couldn't get enough of him. Visions flashed through her mind, arousing images of tangled bodies, naked and slick with passion... *Naked?*

The erotic fantasy faded. Still struggling for breath, she realized that she was pinned beneath Devon's chest as he continued to kiss her throat with unyielding ardor. But something felt odd around her forehead. When her mind cleared, she was horrified. Not only had her wig slipped

down to her eyebrows, Devon's hand was creeping toward
her padded breast.

"Stop!" Jessica slapped his hand away, grabbed her head
and bolted upright so quickly that Devon had to grab the
granite table to keep from being tossed onto the floor.

He sat up, dazed. "What's wrong?"

"Uh...nothing." She ducked away to straighten the
skewed wig. "It's getting late, that's all."

His bewildered expression cut her to the quick. "Have
upset you?"

Unable to look at him, she stood and made a production
out of smoothing her clothes. "I didn't expect this to happen. Everything is moving too fast."

From the corner of her eye she saw Devon stand and take
a shaky step in her direction. "Jessica—" When he reached
out, she skittered away and crossed her arms like a shield.
His hand dropped limply to his side. "I didn't expect this to
happen either. This isn't why I came here tonight. I need for
you to believe that."

"I do." A hot mist seeped into her eyes. She would rather
cut off an arm than to have caused the hurt she saw in his
eyes. But she was confused, frightened by the depth of her
feelings. If their relationship continued to spiral toward the
ultimate intimacy, she'd have to reveal the truth about her
illness and risk being rejected by the man who has come to
mean so very much to her. "Please. I just need some space
right now."

He regarded her warily. "All right."

She forced herself to look at him. It was a mistake. Her
heart swelled with emotions that she dared not reveal, no
even to herself. "This isn't your fault, Devon. You haven'
done anything wrong."

A brusque nod was his only response. He set his jaw and
went to retrieve his jacket from the coatrack. After draping
the torn Windbreaker over his shoulder, he grasped the
doorknob and paused. "Maybe we could talk about this
tomorrow night...over dinner."

She clasped her hands together. "I'm sorry. I'll be out of town this weekend."

A muscle twitched below his ear. "Another time, then."

"Yes, another time."

Before she could beg him to stay, he opened the door and was gone. Jessica stared at the vacant foyer, fighting tears and feeling empty. After several minutes, she sat at the kitchen table and anxiously considered her options.

There were only two—be truthful or continue to lie.

She winced at the harsh word. The fact was that she'd never considered keeping personal business to herself as a lie. An evasion, perhaps, but never a lie. Nor was Devon's reaction to her scars the real crux of her dilemma. Of course she was nervous—who wouldn't be?—but she was more apprehensive about her own emotional involvement, of actually *needing* Devon in her life. That was a line she'd already crossed. There was an emptiness inside her when he wasn't around, a sense of being incomplete that quite frankly scared her spitless.

This wasn't the right time for emotional commitment—not for her and not for Devon. Jessica's future was obscured by a prognosis that although optimistic, was far from assured, and Devon's entire life was one of constant movement 'from one perilous locale to another. She knew he wasn't a man who could ever settle happily into benign domesticity; she also knew that she could never live with the constant fear and uncertainty of his dangerous profession.

They were two diametrically opposed individuals, neither of whom could offer what the other needed. Intellectually Jessica understood that and realized that they had no real future together. Unfortunately, it was a bit too late for such pragmatic revelations. She'd already fallen in love with Devon. And that was the saddest irony of them all.

## Chapter Nine

Devon sat in the dark kitchen nursing his second glass of milk. It had been a long, lousy day and so far, an even longer, lousier night. He'd called Jessica twice, hoping to catch her before she left town—or perhaps hoping that she wasn't really leaving at all. The story could have been an excuse to keep him away. If it had been, he couldn't have blamed her, not after he'd dived on top of her with all the finesse of a bull in heat.

Disgusted with himself, Devon swung his feet onto the table and leaned back until his chair was balanced on two legs. He raked his hair, trying to figure out what in hell had gotten into him last night. Even if he fancied himself a stud—which he didn't—Jessica Newcomb was definitely not a woman to be conquered and abandoned. She was special, so damned special that he couldn't even believe he'd gotten up the nerve to kiss her.

Of course there'd been other kisses—on a moonlit beach and a chaste peck of relief when he'd been yanked out of the mine shaft. Each time the inside of his chest had quivered and a prickly rush had raised goose bumps along his spine.

But last night had been different. Last night, he'd gazed into Jessica's fluid eyes and seen the reflection of his own lonely soul. Last night, he'd seen forever.

That was pretty scary stuff to a man who'd never bothered to contemplate a future beyond his next assignment.

"Hey!" A blinding light nearly knocked Devon off his chair.

Crandall stood in the doorway with his hand on the switch. "Sorry. I didn't know you were in here."

"I couldn't sleep." Shading his eyes against the glare, Devon lowered his feet to the floor and watched his father shuffle toward the refrigerator. "I guess you couldn't, either."

"How can I be tired? I'm not allowed to do anything." Exasperated, Crandall peered into the refrigerator. "There's nothing in here but rabbit food," he grumbled. "Hell, I'm not even allowed to eat."

"You're on a low-fat diet, remember? Have a carrot stick."

Crandall slammed the fridge door. "I don't want a damn carrot stick. I want a steak dripping with fat and mashed potatoes smothered in thick brown gravy."

Devon nodded sympathetically. "Have a carrot stick."

Crandall tightened his robe tie and sat glumly at the table. "I thought you were going out for the evening."

"I changed my mind." Devon shifted in his chair, hoping his father would drop the subject.

He didn't. "Why?"

"I guess lurking around a smoky bar waiting to be picked up has lost its appeal."

"Unless, of course, Jessica Newcomb happens to be there."

"What in hell is that supposed to mean?"

"Nothing." Crandall offered an innocent smile, then his gaze dropped to the glass Devon was twirling. "Is that real milk?"

"Hmm?" Devon glanced down. "Yeah, I guess so."

Crandall sighed wistfully. "All I get is chalk water."

"Skim milk isn't all that bad."

"Would you drink it?"

"Not on a bet." Devon finished his milk and set the empty glass aside. "Now you can explain that remark about Jessica."

Crandall casually removed his spectacles, holding them up to the light for inspection. "There's nothing to explain."

"You implied that she spends her time hanging around bars."

"I did no such thing." Crandall blew on each lens before polishing it with the edge of his velour robe. "The comment was merely based on my observation that you seem to enjoy her company. Of course, I could be mistaken." After a final inspection, he set the glasses low on his nose and peered over the sparkling lenses. "Jessica being away for the weekend is probably coincidental to you sulking in the dark like a lost puppy."

Devon stiffened. "I am not sulking."

"If you say so." Crandall pushed back his chair, eyeing the pantry door. "I wonder if Gunda hid any cookies in there?"

"She threw them away while you were in the hospital."

"Remind me to fire her." After readjusting his chair, Crandall emitted a dejected sigh and propped his elbows on the table.

Devon skewered his father with a hard stare. "You know where she is, don't you?"

Crandall blinked in bewilderment. "Gunda?"

"No, Jessica." Frustrated, Devon crossed his arms and leaned anxiously forward. "If you know that she's left, you must know where she's gone."

A loose string on his robe cuff caught Crandall's eye. He was instantly engrossed, fiddling with the stupid thing as though it was the first thread he'd ever seen. "Perhaps she had some personal business to take care of."

Irritated by his father's evasiveness, Devon gritted his teeth and spoke through them. "You've spoken with her, haven't you?"

Crandall pursed his lips and wound the wayward string around his fingertip. "As a matter of fact, I believe she did call this morning."

Devon tensed, ready to spring as he peppered his father with a barrage of frantic questions. "Was she all right? What did she say? Did she tell you—?"

"Good Lord!" Crandall held up his hands as if warding off blows. "Slow down and let me catch my breath."

Devon unballed his curled fists, forcing himself to lean back in his chair despite the fact that feigning apathy at this point was ridiculous. "I was simply curious, that's all."

"Evidently so," Crandall replied, his dark eyes sparkling. "Now, let's see if I can deal with your, uh, curiosity at a reasonable pace. As far as I know Jessica is perfectly fine. She simply requested a vacation day."

"For what?"

Crandall again seemed fascinated by the stupid string. "It wasn't my business to ask. She did, however, mention that you'd dropped by last night. Apparently she was concerned about something the two of you discussed."

Devon's heart sank. "Did she mention what that something was?"

"She was rather vague, actually." Crandall coughed, cleared his throat and took a deep breath. "But she did state with considerable emphasis that you had something important to discuss with me and she was quite insistent that I should give you the opportunity to do so."

Baffled, Devon thought back to last evening, wondering what on earth Jessica could have been referring to. He didn't have a clue and said so.

Crandall sighed. "She said it was in regards to something that happened when you were a child."

A numbing tingle slid down Devon's spine. There wasn't a doubt in his mind that Jessica had been referring to his time at Blackthorn Hall. He absently fingered a scratch in the table's laminate top, angry that she'd revealed something he'd told her in confidence. Well, she hadn't exactly revealed it, but she'd certainly offered a stingingly blatant hint. He felt betrayed.

When Devon didn't respond, Crandall continued to speak quietly. "Of course, I didn't have any idea what she was talking about but she was so passionately insistent that I spent the entire day thinking about those years and the good times we'd shared together. What I discovered was frightening."

Devon looked up, frowning and wary. "And what exactly did you discover?"

"That I couldn't remember any good times because we hadn't shared any." Avoiding his son's gaze, Crandall stared across the kitchen with an expression of profound sadness. "Then it occurred to me that I couldn't recall any details of your childhood. I didn't know whether your grades were good or bad, or even if you liked school. I couldn't remember what sports you participated in—if any—nor could I recall when you went on your first date or learned to drive a car. One minute you were an infant, the next you were graduating from college. All the years in between are a blur, as if you'd grown up in a vacuum. I don't understand how that happened."

Devon set his chin, hunched over the table and massaged his stiff neck. "You were a busy man. I understood that." That was true enough. Devon had always known that his father's business came first. He hadn't liked it; but he'd understood it. "What I didn't understand is why you wouldn't take me to Europe so we could be together."

Crandall's chest heaved, then he exhaled slowly. "It never occurred to me that you'd want to go. Besides, I was always traveling. Over the years, I rarely spent more than six months in one place. Your home was here, your friends were here. I thought you needed that stability."

"I needed a father," Devon said simply.

"Of course you did. Unfortunately I didn't know how to be one."

"I was under the impression that you didn't *want* to be one."

Crandall took off his glasses, closed his eyes and pinched the bridge of his nose. "You're wrong, son. There was a time that I wanted to be a father more than anything in this world. My desire for a family was so intense that your mother gave up everything to sate it." He shuddered, replaced his glasses and looked Devon straight in the eye. "You're just like her, you know."

Devon straightened. "So you've said, but I don't know how. You rarely talked about her."

Crandall didn't dispute that. Instead, he gazed into space, his eyes warm, his face flushed with the memory of youth. "Marlena and I met in Aspen. She was a world-class skier, training for international competition. I was at the slalom course watching one of her practice runs when she hooked a gate, tumbled halfway down the mountain and slid right into me. I helped her up, brushed the snow off her nose and fell hopelessly in love. We married two months later."

The fact that his mother had been a competitive skier was a jolt. Devon was hungry to know more yet said nothing, fearing even the sound of his voice might break his father's fragile link with the past. He held his breath and waited.

Crandall gazed across the room and smiled. "We were so different. I was always the cautious one, so pragmatic and wary, while Marlena plummeted through life as though it were just another snowy mountain. She was always eager for excitement, always anxious to conquer a new challenge, be it hang gliding, scuba diving or aerobic skydiving. She adored danger and I adored her." The smile in his eyes faded. "We both wanted children, although we'd agreed to wait a couple of years so Marlena could complete her competitive career. But her adventures frightened me. I began to nag her about giving up her career so we could start our family right away. Because she loved me, she agreed."

A heavy silence fell over the room. Devon felt sick. One of the few things he had known about his mother was that she'd died in childbirth; he'd always suspected that his father had blamed him for that. Now he was sure of it. He propped his elbows on the table, using his hands to conceal his anguish. When his throat spasm stopped, he peered over his fingertips. "How you must have despised me."

Crandall jolted upright with a dumbfounded expression that under other circumstances would have been amusing. "Is that what you think?"

"If not for me, she might still be alive."

The older man's eyes were bright with unshed tears. "No, son. I never blamed you. Initially I blamed myself, believing that if I hadn't insisted on starting a family so soon..." The words dissipated like so much steam. Crandall shook his head slowly. "But Marlena desperately wanted children. We both did. The complications that occurred during your birth could just as easily have happened a year later or two or six. Eventually I was able to accept that your mother's death was a fluke of nature, a horrible tragedy for which no one could be blamed."

"But you were never able to accept *me.*"

Crandall considered that without denying it. "At first I was too consumed by grief to do more than acknowledge your existence. I'd convinced myself that you were only an infant, too young to care who held the bottle as long as your belly was full. So I immersed myself in work, not only to alleviate the pain, but because I realized that for the first time in my life, I was establishing a future for someone other than myself.''

Devon placed his hands flat on the table, trying to sort out the surge of conflicting emotions. Empathy for his father's grief still mingled with the anger of abandonment. ''There came a time when I outgrew bottles,'' he said quietly. ''You still weren't around.''

''I know.'' Crandall toyed with his robe cuff. ''The older you became, the more you resembled your mother—that crooked smile, the stubborn way you set your jaw, your fearless nature. You were so like Marlena, inside and out, that I couldn't look at you without reliving her loss.''

Devon was deeply moved by his father's painful disclosure yet it was almost too much information to digest. His head was spinning. ''I wish we could have talked about this a long time ago.''

''Would it have made any difference?''

''I don't know,'' he replied honestly. ''I'm not sure our relationship would have been any different but I might have felt better about myself.''

''At the time, I thought it would make you feel worse. Another miscalculation on my part, I suppose.'' Crandall sighed. ''If I'd done things differently, you wouldn't have felt the need to punish me by repeatedly risking your life.''

''What?'' Devon straightened so quickly his chair rattled. ''My job has nothing to do with you.''

''Doesn't it?'' Crandall smiled sadly. ''You are your mother's son, but you also have my blood in your veins. From me you've learned that work is an escape, a way to shield your heart and bury your anger. It's the only lesson I taught you. I wish I could take it back.''

Devon sat there, stunned, while his father gazed across the room with a bemused expression.

''You know,'' Crandall said suddenly. ''Watching you and Jessica together reminds me of how things were between Marlena and I. Of course the roles are reversed, but the interaction between free spirit and pragmatist is very much the same.'' He swung around in his chair and looked straight at his son. ''You care about Jessica, don't you?''

Taken aback by his father's directness, Devon found his words stumbling over his tongue. ''I . . . well, of course . . . she's, uh, a very nice person.''

''Actually, she can be a bit prickly at times.''

''She speaks her mind, if that's what you mean.'' Devon didn't bother to hide his annoyance at the criticism. ''I appreciate her candor.''

Crandall's smile widened. ''Do you, now?''

''Yes, I do.'' Devon folded his arms and glared across the table. ''What's more, I think she probably has more business sense than any of those pompous vice presidents of yours who earn twice her salary.''

''Ah. So you believe her talents are being unfairly exploited?''

Devon swallowed a cross retort and realized that his father was enjoying this verbal repartee entirely too much. The shrewd sparkle in the older man's eyes reflected a hidden agenda that gave Devon pause. ''What's going on here?''

Crandall smugly steepled his fingers. ''We're simply discussing a mutual acquaintance. As I recall, you were the one who initially broached the subject.''

Devon watched his father with a narrowed gaze. ''I asked if you knew where she was this weekend. Your answer was evasive, to the say the least.''

''Yes, it was.'' Crandall's satisfied expression suddenly faded. ''Jessica is a courageous and fiercely independent woman. I admire her. I respect her. I wanted to see that same admiration and respect in your eyes before—'' He glanced away but not before Devon saw the sadness in his eyes.

A frisson of fear tickled his nape. ''Before what?''

''Before I betray her confidence.'' He faced Devon squarely. ''Jessica planned to tell you next week but these next few days will be difficult for her. If you have the strength and the love to help her through them, I'll tell you what you want to know."

Devon's gaze wavered. He was being asked to label his feelings with a word he'd never uttered or implied, a word that conjured images of permanence, commitment, emotional vulnerability and struck fear in his bachelor heart. He didn't know how to respond because he didn't know what love felt like. So he silently searched his soul; and Crandall awaited the answer.

After heaping a final mound of mozzarella atop thick layers of pasta and sauce, Jessica glanced at the wall clock in her mother's tidy kitchen. Since the lasagna wouldn't go into the oven for a while, she covered the baking pan with foil and set it aside.

Normally she enjoyed cooking, particularly for an audience as appreciative as her parents. Today, however, she was physically tired, emotionally drained and simply grateful that the bulk of her kitchen duties were done. She glanced through the doorway and saw that Frank, her stepfather, was still in his study, immersed in work. She felt suddenly alone, with the walls of the comfortable home closing in on her. Outside the birds were singing, the sun was shining and the ocean glimmered like a sea of sapphires.

Desperate for fresh air and sunshine, Jessica wiped her hands on a kitchen towel, protected her sensitive scalp with a baseball cap and went into the garden. A cobblestone path meandered between beds of lush foliage and colorful blooms, providing a restful stroll from the main house to the guest cottage. At the hub of the garden was a small fountain surrounded by a circle of terra-cotta pavers, each of which had been lovingly laid by her stepfather.

Beyond the fountain, a ribboned sun hat protruded above a hedge of emerald cotoneaster. The hat appeared to levitate a moment before a pair of exquisite gray eyes appeared

beneath the straw brim. "I thought I heard footsteps."
Aysla stood, still clutching a garden spade in her gloved
hand. "I was hoping you'd join me."

As Jessica wound her way through the hedge to the patch
of freshly turned soil where her mother was working, an
impressive array of bedding flats caught her eye. "Did you
grow these in the greenhouse?"

Aysla smiled proudly. "Yes. Aren't they lovely?"

"Your green thumb never ceases to amaze me." Jessica
stepped over the cultivated bed and found a cushy spot on
the immaculately clipped lawn. "You should send a video
of this place to that garden show on TV."

"I doubt they'd be interested," Aysla murmured, although her eyes lit up at the thought. "My little place isn't
all that exotic."

Jessica hugged her knees, gazing across the expansive
lawn to a spot where the land ended at a rocky bluff overlooking the Pacific Ocean. "I think it's the most beautiful
place in the world."

"Thank you, dear, but I suspect you're a bit biased."
Nonetheless, Aysla was obviously pleased by the praise.
With a satisfied smile, she absently dusted leaf litter from
the glossy cotoneaster before settling beside her daughter.

They sat quietly, as comfortable with the silence as they
were with each other. Jessica and her mother had always
enjoyed an extraordinarily close relationship. When they
went out together, people frequently mistook them for sisters, which was no surprise considering Aysla's youthful
appearance.

Even now, with her freshly scrubbed complexion
smudged by garden soil, it was difficult to believe such a
lovely woman could have a thirty-one-year old daughter.
Her lean legs, exposed by shorts that would have seemed
inappropriate on most women her age, were still as lithe and
tan as those of a supple adolescent. In fact, Aysla's only
concession to age were a few deepening lines at the corner

of her eyes and mouth, along with a smattering of gray in her delicate blond hair.

But Aysla's beauty was far from skin-deep. She was the sweetest, the wisest and the most sensitive person Jessica had ever known.

And using that sensitivity, she suddenly pulled off her work gloves, then reached out and took her daughter's hand. "Something is bothering you," she said simply.

Jessica hesitated, then squeezed her mother's hand and forced a thin smile. "I'm just a little tired."

Her mother's eyes filled with sympathy. "Of course you are. Between the trip up here and all those awful tests, you must be completely exhausted."

In truth, the short flight from Los Angeles had been quite relaxing. The tests, however, had been another matter. Not that they'd been painful—although technicians had drawn enough blood to supply a city of vampires and taken so many nuclear scans that she'd probably set off Geiger counters in the next county. After spending all of yesterday and the better part of this morning being shuffled between labs, Jessica was sick of needles, sick of having body parts squeezed, squashed and X-rayed, and generally sick of being sick.

Besides, she hated seeing her mother worry. "I'm fine, really. In fact, I've felt nearly as strong the past couple of weeks as I did before the surgery."

But Aysla would not be consoled. "After all you've been through, I can't believe I actually left you to slave away in the kitchen like an indentured servant."

Jessica chuckled softly. "Honestly, Mother, you're so melodramatic. You really should have taken your drama coach's advice and gone into theater."

Lifting one perfectly tweezed brow, Aysla made a noble attempt at indignation but an amused twitch at the corner of her mouth gave her away. "In that case, I shall save future performances for someone who can appreciate them."

"Like Frank?"

At the mention of her second husband, the woman's smile broadened into a melting grin. "Yes. He hasn't seen through me yet."

"Of course he has. He just loves you anyway." Jessica fiddled with a blade of grass. "You know, it occurred to me that you and Frank will be celebrating your twentieth anniversary this year."

"Gracious," Aysla murmured, seeming stunned by the realization. "Time does fly."

"We should do something special."

"Every day Frank and I are together is special." She cocked her head, regarding her daughter thoughtfully. "What is it, Jessica? You look so sad."

"Do I?" She forced a brighter expression but it crumbled beneath her mother's reproachful gaze. "All right. I suppose I am feeling a bit, well, sentimental. I've been thinking a lot lately about—" she slid her mother an apprehensive glance "—about Daddy."

Aysla's eyes clouded. "I think about him, too."

For some reason, that was surprising. "You do?"

"Of course. I loved your father deeply." She idly fingered a clod of rich dirt. "I still miss him, you know."

"But you have Frank."

"Yes." Her eyes were suddenly moist. "Some people live their entire lives without experiencing the kind of love that has blessed me twice. I'm a very lucky woman."

Jessica swallowed a guilty twinge and was unable to meet her mother's eyes. "I'm glad you're happy."

"Hmm. Is there an unspoken *but* at the end of that sentence?"

"No. I really mean it. Frank is a wonderful man. He's always been a good father to me and I love him."

"I know you do." Aysla brushed her palms. "I also know that there was a time that you didn't like him very much."

Jessica winced. "Was I that transparent?"

"All ten-year-olds are transparent, although you tried very hard to keep your feelings to yourself." Lazily stretching out on the cool grass, Aysla propped herself up on one elbow. "Don't be so hard on yourself, Jessica. It's perfectly normal that you'd have resented seeing another man in my life. After all, your father had only been gone a couple of years."

Still staring at the green blade in her hand, Jessica replied with a somber nod. "I think it would have been easier to accept Frank if he hadn't been so good-looking."

The comment so startled the older woman that her hand slipped away from her head and her entire body jerked in response. "Why on earth would that make any difference?"

Feeling shallow and petty, Jessica shrugged in much the same way she'd done as a child. "It's just that you two made such a stunning couple—everyone said so—and it got me thinking about why you'd chosen Daddy when you could have had your pick of men...because you were so beautiful, that is...and Daddy, well, he wasn't very, uh...oh, shoot." Frustrated, she tossed the shredded grass aside and flopped on her back. The sudden movement jarred off her cap. She didn't bother to retrieve it. "I sound like an idiot. Forget everything I've just said."

Aysla chewed her lip, staring into space though contemplating something quite profound. After a moment, she spoke quietly. "The first time I saw your father was at a college track meet. There were a lot of people in the bleachers that day but your dad stuck out like a sore thumb." She chuckled at the memory. "Here was this mountain of a man wearing a psychedelic shirt and absolutely surrounded by beautiful young women. At first I thought they were posing for some kind of joke photograph."

Jessica rolled to her side and levered up on her elbow. "But they weren't?"

"No. The women were his friends, as were the half-dozen men in the group." Aysla gave her daughter's cheek a maternal caress. "The very first time I looked into your father's beautiful eyes and saw the glory of that gentle soul, I understood why everyone loved him. Because I loved him, too."

A lump rose in Jessica's throat. She blinked away the gathering tears. She wanted to speak, to blurt out the hidden fears behind her superficial query but found it impossible to articulate feelings that she didn't even understand. For some reason, it was desperately important to know how love felt, to be assured that the sweetest of all emotions really was blind to the flaws of human flesh.

But as always, her mother's wisdom exceeded her own. "We don't choose love," Aysla said quietly. "Love chooses us. It's not always easy to recognize, particularly when fear erects a barrier around the heart. The important thing is that love looks beyond the surface." She reached out and took her daughter's hand. "When love chooses you, my darling, your scars won't matter. You know that, don't you?"

"Yes," Jessica whispered. "I know it here—" she touched her forehead "—but sometimes when I look into the mirror, something inside of me weeps. I know it's trite and self-centered because my scars are minor compared to those of so many others. And I tell myself that a man looking for physical perfection is a man I don't want."

"You've been giving yourself very good advice. But do you believe it?"

"Yes, I do believe it."

"Then what is it that is frightening you?"

The words slipped out before Jessica had time to consider them. "Loss frightens me." Looking stunned, Aysla released her daughter's hand while Jessica struggled to explain. "I'm more afraid of losing love than of never finding it at all."

"Why do you think you would lose it?"

"Because nothing is forever. When we lost Daddy, the grief nearly destroyed us both. That's one reason I was so upset when you married Frank. I just couldn't believe you'd take the chance of going through that again." Avoiding her mother's shocked gaze, Jessica gathered her courage and finally expressed the secret fears that had haunted her since childhood. "I know that death is a part of life but I always shoved thoughts of it to the back of my mind . . . until I got sick."

Aysla went white. "You're not going to die, Jessica. The cancer is gone. You're cured and you're going to live for a long, long time."

While conceding that was probably true, Jessica was nonetheless aware that recurrence was always a frightening possibility. Her own life, however, wasn't at the crux of her fear. It was Devon's. How could she have fallen in love with a man who challenged death at every turn? Life was so fragile. That lesson, which Jessica had repeatedly learned, was one Devon seemed destined to ignore. How could she allow herself to love him, to risk another agonizing loss?

And yet, how could she not?

Frank's tense voice echoed from the back porch, breaking Jessica's silent meditation. "Aysla, dear, could you please come into the house? Quickly, please."

"I'll be right there." She frowned, apparently as perplexed by her husband's strained request as was Jessica. She stood and dusted herself.

Jessica rose to her knees, glancing over her shoulder. She saw nothing but cotoneaster leaves. "He sounds upset."

"He's probably misplaced his reading glasses. You know how annoyed Frank becomes if the least little thing is out of place." She laid a hand on her daughter's shoulder to keep her from rising. "Stay here and relax. I'll be back in a few minutes and we'll talk some more." With that, Aysla followed a worn path through the hedge and disappeared.

After a moment Jessica heard her parents' hushed voices. Then the back door closed and the yard fell silent. Jessica sat there, alone, lost in thought as she gazed out at the sliver of ocean visible beyond the cliff. It was, she thought, like the edge of forever.

Forever. It was an enticing word, yet a frightening one. Nothing was forever . . . was it?

And then, as though responding to her silent question, the cotoneasters rustled at her back. When Jessica turned, she realized that forever had a face.

## Chapter Ten

For an instant Jessica thought she was seeing a mirage. Then a light breeze cooled her scalp—her *bare* scalp—where Devon's astonished gaze had settled. Embarrassed, she quickly replaced the cap and yanked it halfway down her forehead. A prickly flush warmed her face. She avoided his gaze and forced a nervous laugh. "When I have a bad hair day, it's a doozy."

Instead of smiling, his eyes filled with what Jessica interpreted as pity.

She went rigid. "What are you doing here anyway?"

"I needed to see you."

"You've seen me. Now go home. Please." That final tremulous word would have seemed like an afterthought except for the desperation of its delivery.

Devon stood his ground like a traumatized statue. "Why didn't you tell me?"

"Tell you what? That I have a lousy hairdresser?"

"Why didn't you tell me that you're ill?"

The fact that he'd carefully avoided saying the word *cancer* didn't escape her notice. "I *was* ill. Now I'm recovering." Sighing, she rubbed her eyelids. "How did you find out?"

"My father told me."

For some reason, that wasn't a surprise. "I wish he hadn't."

"And I wish you'd trusted me enough to take me into your confidence." There was no accusation in his voice; only sadness.

Jessica folded her arms and gazed across the yard. "It isn't the kind of thing you blurt out to a casual acquaintance. After we became, um, friends, I was afraid you'd treat me differently."

"Differently? How?"

She shrugged, unable to put into words the devastating effect of an anxious glance, an apprehensive frown, a pitying stare mingled with relief that it had happened to you instead of them. "I was planning to tell you next week," she said finally.

He considered that for a moment. "After you got the test results?"

Her head snapped up in shock. "Crandall's briefing was really quite thorough, wasn't it?"

"It's not entirely his fault. I was pretty relentless."

"No one browbeats Crandall Monroe. Your father never says anything that he doesn't want to say." She set her jaw, angry that Crandall had betrayed her trust.

"My father knew this weekend would be difficult for you," Devon said. "He thought you could use a friend."

"I have friends," she replied tightly.

"How many of them know what you've been dealing with for the past eight months?"

"A few."

"How few?"

"Damned few, all right?" She planted her feet and jammed her fists against her hips. "This is a boring subject and I don't want to talk about it anymore."

"Why couldn't you tell them? Having cancer is nothing to be ashamed of—"

Jessica exploded. "I'm getting sick and tired of explaining that I'm *not* ashamed," she shouted. "I'm *angry*. A bunch of renegade cells that can't follow genetic instruction have turned my entire life upside down and that ticks me off, okay?"

"Jessie—"

"No!" She held up her palms, sidestepping his outstretched hand. "I don't need anyone to hold me up, thank you. I can walk on my own like a big girl. As for why I didn't tell my friends, I didn't want them to put their own lives on hold because they felt obligated to hover over me like irksome insects. And last but certainly not least, I didn't want my friends looking at me the way *you* are looking at me right now."

Devon jerked as if he'd been slapped. "How am I looking at you?"

Jessica was stung by his crushed expression. Her anger drained away as suddenly as it had appeared, leaving her hollow inside. She sighed. "You're looking at me like I'm a pitiful puppy, abandoned on the road and left for dead."

Devon hooked his thumbs in his jeans pockets, rocked back on his heels and stared thoughtfully at the ground. When he looked up again, his eyes flashed with indignation. "I'll plead guilty to being sympathetic. If that's a crime, shoot me. But if you think I'm here for a pity party, you're very much mistaken."

"Which brings up the same point," she replied tartly. "Why *are* you here?"

"At the moment, I'm asking myself the same question. I didn't spend six hours on the road so you could insult my motives."

He was so clearly exasperated, so endearingly irked that Jessica could barely bite back a smile. "I would *love* to insult your motives. Unfortunately I don't know what they are."

Devon continued to stare grumpily at his shoes. "You are without a doubt the most aggravating woman I've ever known."

"I'll take that as a compliment."

"You would." He peeked up, squinting into the late-afternoon sun. "So, can we call a truce here or what?"

"We're not at war, Devon."

"You could've fooled me."

She looked away, pricked by guilt. "I'm sorry. When I'm upset, I tend to get a bit surly. But you've come all the way up here trying to be nice and I've treated you badly. I apologize for that."

"I am not trying to be nice." Devon took hold of her shoulders and gave her a gentle shake. "Listen to me, Jessica. I'm here because I want to be with you. Don't ask me why. All I know is that I spent yesterday wandering around like a lost soul, wondering where you were and what you were doing and why you wanted to do it without me." Her eyes widened. When she started to speak, he touched a finger to her lips. "Look, maybe I have been insensitive, bursting in like this and violating your privacy. I should have picked up a clue from the third degree your parents just gave me but it wouldn't have mattered. They got the message that I wasn't going to leave without seeing you."

Jessica angled an involuntary glance toward the house. "So that's why Frank sounded so tense."

"Yeah. For a while there I thought he was going to fold me in half and dump my bleeding body in the street."

"I don't believe it," she murmured, astounded by the image of her prim and proper stepfather locked in confrontation with anyone, let alone a man of Devon's considerable stature. "Frank can't even close the door in a salesman's face."

"Evidently he didn't consider the salesman to be a threat to his daughter." Devon released Jessica and rubbed the kinks out of his neck. "Not that I blame the guy for being protective. That's what fathers do. The truth is that I found Frank to be pretty likable, in a stoic sort of way."

Devon slid a covert glance toward Jessica and saw she was looking at him as though he'd sprouted antlers. For all he knew, he might have. He was too numb to tell. Ever since learning about Jessica's secret, Devon had been thrashing through a mental fog. This morning, he'd finally stepped into the sunshine. Everything that had happened over the past weeks suddenly made sense—her frequent fatigue, the stupid head scarf she'd used to tie on her wig and the way she'd shied away when his touch when it became too intimate.

He also remembered how pale she'd been during their grueling motorcycle tour of the desert and could have kicked himself for having put her through it. If that hadn't been bad enough, he'd dragged her out in the middle of the night and practically thrown her into the icy surf. In her weakened state, she could have come down with pneumonia. The thought scared him half to death.

The bottom line was that his friendship had damn near killed her. That he'd never again subject her to such physical jeopardy was little consolation. If anything had happened to Jessica, he wouldn't have been able to bear the guilt. Or the pain of having lost her.

Now, as she absently chewed her lip in adorable, childlike fashion, his heart was so full he feared it might burst. He wanted to sweep her into his arms and fight the world to keep her safe. He'd glimpsed vulnerability beneath her veneer of staunch independence and found a woman who yearned for love; a woman who needed him.

But not necessarily a woman who wanted him.

He jammed his hands into his pockets to keep from touching her. "If you tell me to leave, I will."

He held his breath while she considered the option. After several incredibly long seconds, she lifted her cap, wiped her forearm across her brow and gave him a penetrating stare. "Do you like lasagna?"

"Uh . . . sure."

She settled the cap back on her head and squinted toward the sea. "Then you might as well stay."

After dinner, Jessica guided Devon to a rocky bluff overlooking the ocean. They stood silently for a while, watching the reflection of a fuchsia sunset riding distant swells.

Devon reached down and took her hand. "The view is spectacular," he said. "I can't imagine growing up surrounded by so much natural splendor."

"I didn't exactly grow up here. My parents bought this place while I was in college. Before that we lived in a subdivision over there." She pointed toward a cluster of rolling hills a few miles to the east. "We couldn't see the ocean but it was only a short bike ride away."

"Did you spend a lot of time at the beach?"

"I practically lived there during the summer. The rest of the year I went every weekend that it didn't rain. And Mom would always show up around noon, carrying a little sack lunch for me."

"You're kidding. Every day?"

"Hmm. That way she could make sure I was okay without seeming overprotective. I'd have been mortified if my friends thought she was checking up on me."

"Sounds like you've always been an independent little cuss."

"To a fault, I'm afraid. Fortunately—or unfortunately, depending on one's point of view—my mother has always indulged that side of my nature with subtle guidance, after which she'd charitably allow me to believe that I'd made my own decisions."

"Aysla seems like a very special woman."

"She is." Jessica gazed at the brilliant horizon, remembering other sunsets she and her mother had watched from this very spot.

During those times, however, Jessica hadn't been particularly enthralled by a sky smeared with crimson and wispy clouds splashed with magenta reflections of the setting sun. The beauty had been dimmed by the pain of recent surgery and fear of the future. But Aysla had never allowed Jessica to give in to those fears or to the depression that had seemed so overwhelming. Instead, she'd reacquainted her daughter with the small joys that made life a treasure to cherish rather than an ordeal to be endured.

As Jessica recalled details of her mother's staunch support, she didn't realize that her thoughts had become words. "I could never have gotten through it without her."

"Through what?"

Blinking, Jessica looked up and was instantly lost in Devon's gentle eyes. "Through everything," she murmured. "The surgery, the emotional aftermath—you name it, she got me through it."

Devon lifted her hand to his lips. He delicately kissed each knuckle, then pressed her palm to his cheek in a gesture so gentle and loving that it brought tears to her eyes. "I don't know Aysla very well, but I doubt she'd take that much credit. You were the one who suffered. God, I can't even fathom what you must have gone through."

"Please . . . you make me sound like Joan of Arc."

He kissed her palm once more before releasing her. "In my eyes, you are."

"Heavens, no." She emphasized the denial with a vehement shake of her head. "Nothing could be further from the truth. When I was first diagnosed, I was scared out of my mind. I screamed and cried and railed like a thwarted child.

I kept asking 'why me?' After a while I realized that I was never going to get an answer because there wasn't one. Cancer doesn't ask for volunteers. I had to deal with it because I didn't have any other choice.''

"And you *have* dealt with it."

"Correction—I *am* dealing with it."

The sudden fear in his eyes cut her to the quick. "But it's gone, right? You're cured."

"I hope so. The signs are all good. I was very fortunate that the tumor was still quite small and there was no evidence that the malignancy had spread. But cancer cells are insidious little devils. Even with aggressive radiation and chemotherapy treatments, a few cells occasionally escape."

Devon looked sick. "What exactly does that mean?"

"From what I understand—and from a technical aspect, I don't understand all that much—sometimes they tuck themselves away and go dormant for a while."

"How long is awhile?"

She shrugged. "It varies but after five years without a recurrence, the patient is usually considered to be cured."

*"Five years?"* His incredulous expression melted into one of absolute horror. "You have to live with this for five years?"

"It's not as bad as it sounds. Naturally, I'll have to be meticulous about scheduling routine tests and physical examinations. The truth is that by taking such good care of myself, I'll probably end up healthier than those people who are more likely to have regular checkups of their cars than of their bodies."

Devon seemed unconvinced by the assurance. He studied her face, gazing into her eyes with a power that shook her to the soles of her feet. Then he suddenly embraced her, cradling her against his chest as if she were more precious than gold.

She melted against him, enveloped by his heat, his strength, the safety of his loving embrace. All she could think about was how extraordinary this moment was. It hadn't been so long ago, during the height of indignity and despair, that Jessica had feared she'd never again feel the warmth of caring arms or the rhythmic throb of a masculine heartbeat pulsing against her cheek.

She pushed away a tiny doubt about Devon's motives; whether he felt sympathy or compassion or even pity didn't matter anymore. All that counted was the gentleness of his touch, the yearning she'd recognized in his eyes. He not only cared about her, he wanted her the way a man wants a woman.

The wondrous realization made her want to weep with joy.

Even now, as Devon reverently cupped her head, he stroked her silky new hair as though it were a velvet crown. She shivered, not from cold but from the tingling tenderness of his touch. It had been so long, so achingly long since she'd felt such inner peace. And yet there was a vague elation stirring inside her, a euphoric premonition that something wonderful was happening, something that would change her life forever.

She went limp inside, giving in to a convergence of arousing sensations. Devon's unique scent surrounded her, an intoxicating blend of subtle spice and musky man. She breathed deeply, taking that ethereal part of him deep into her lungs and holding him there, beside her heart, until reluctantly forced to let him go. She exhaled slowly, dizzied by the unexpected intimacy, and greedily repeated the process to absorb more of him into herself. The experience was incredibly erotic.

Devon moved against her, dipping his head until the moist heat of his breath warmed her brow. His mouth rested against her forehead, a feathery kiss that seemed too fragile to be real. "Thank you," he whispered.

Startled, she twisted to look up at him. "For what?"

"For being a fighter, for not giving up no matter how difficult things were." He tilted her chin up with his thumb. "Thank you for hanging on until I could find you."

Then his mouth touched hers in a kiss so sweet, so filled with love that she feared her heart might explode from sheer happiness. Her chest throbbed; her knees buckled; her mind swirled with kaleidoscope colors. The effect was both thrilling and terrifying, yet she clung helplessly, praying the sweet moment would never end.

But it did end. Devon suddenly stepped back, looking stunned and shaken. Had he not been holding her up, Jessica herself would have sagged to the ground in a quivering puddle. She took a ragged breath, then another. The numbness dissipated slowly. When her limbs had gained enough strength for support, she released her death grip on the front of his shirt and made a game attempt to stand on her own.

Beyond the expansive lawn, perhaps a hundred yards away, a graceful curve of twinkling lights outlined the footpath of her parents' garden.

Jessica managed a limp smile. "We should probably go back to the house."

Devon didn't return her smile. He simply stood silently, his gaze penetrating so deeply that she could almost feel its touch. "Have I been out of line?"

"No, not at all." She absently fanned her face with her hand. "It's just that the bluff can be dangerous after dark, when you don't have a clear view of the edge. There have been accidents."

"Here, on your parents' property?"

"No, thank heavens. But farther down the ridge where the public has access to the beach, there were a couple of incidents before the county finally put up a fence."

As she spoke, Devon automatically tightened his grip on her arm and guided her away from the cliff. When they were a safe distance away, he stopped and pivoted to face her.

"Jessica, I..." The anguished words evaporated like so much sea spray.

Alarmed by his sorrowful tone, Jessica laid her palm intimately against his chest. His heart was racing. "What is it, Devon? What do you want to say?"

Tilting his head back, Devon appeared to be staring at the moonless sky but night shadows concealed his expression, along with any emotion that might otherwise have been revealed. He issued a poignant sigh. "I don't know what I want to say. Everything's all jumbled up in my head."

That kind of bewilderment was something Jessica could relate to. "I know the feeling. Sometimes everything seems so disjointed that I wouldn't recognize a cognizant thought if I had one." She chose not to mention that this was definitely one of those times.

Devon studied her face for a moment, then slid a possessive arm around her shoulders.

They walked the gilded path in silence, stepped through the cotoneaster hedge and followed the paved walk to the circular fountain in the center of the garden. Light bulbs concealed beneath the brick rim illuminated the arching water, which swirled up from the crystal pool like an aqueous ballerina. Echoing through the settling mist, the fountain's soothing gurgle joined other sounds of night—a chorus of chirpy crickets, the rumbling croak of a hopeful toad and the muted moan of the eternal sea.

Devon seemed transfixed by the fountain's dancing water. "It's getting late," he said, still staring at the twinkling display. "I should be leaving."

"So soon?"

"It's a long drive."

"You're going back to Los Angeles tonight?" She couldn't hide her dismay.

Alerted by the distressed quiver of her voice, Devon questioned her with a look.

She swallowed hard. "I, uh, was hoping to give you a tour of the house."

"I've already seen the house," he replied, obviously perplexed.

"I was talking about the—" a nervous cough nearly smothered the final words "—guesthouse."

He stared at her, mystified. "I thought you were staying in the guesthou—" His eyes widened with sudden enlightenment. He blinked twice, swallowed once and roughly cleared his throat. "What would your parents think about this, uh, tour?"

The truth was that they'd been so concerned about her dearth of relationships that they'd probably uncork a bottle of bubbly and celebrate. Naturally, she had no intention of revealing that to the man that she had, for all intents and purposes, just invited into her bed.

She glanced away, feeling suddenly shy and wondering what had possessed her to be so incredibly bold. But she didn't regret it—not yet, anyway—and so she answered Devon's question with as much casual candor as she could muster. "Trust me, they won't mind."

He studied her for a long moment, then lifted her hand to his lips. "I'll let you lead the way."

Somehow Jessica doubted he was referring entirely to their short walk to the cottage. Instinctively she recognized his subtle promise to allow the evening to progress at whatever pace she selected. Since she was already nervous enough to jump out of her skin, his sensitivity was deeply appreciated.

The guesthouse was nestled at the far side of the garden amid a lush forest of foliage. Barely visible from the main house, the cottage provided complete privacy and a comforting sense of isolation. It was, Jessica thought, rather like a secluded vacation bungalow snuggled in the tropics of an island resort. She loved it here. Over the years, the tiny cot-

age had been her haven, her retreat from a world that had
not always treated her kindly.

Now she opened the plain wooden door, wondering if
Devon would find it as inviting. He stepped inside, glancing curiously around the compact interior. Jessica anx-
ously followed his gaze from the tiny kitchenette, with it's
miniature refrigerator and RV-size range, to the sitting area
consisting of a mauve-and-burgundy-print sofa and matching recliner, along with two tables and a brass floor lamp.

She clasped her hands together. "What do you think?"

He didn't answer right away. Instead, he strolled across
the small room, eyed the half-read newspaper sprawled on
the coffee table, then plucked a wadded sweater and a pair
of socks off the back of the chair. He held up the garments
and grinned. "I like it. It's you."

The goofy look on his face made her laugh. "Make
yourself comfortable. I think there's some wine in the
fridge."

"That sounds great." He draped the socks and sweater
over the chair before settling onto the sofa. "This place reminds me of a flat I once had in Belfast."

Jessica took two wineglasses from the cupboard and
glanced over her shoulder. "Is there anywhere in the world
that you haven't been?"

"There are a few islands off the coast of Greenland that
I've missed. I flew over them once, though, if that counts."

"It doesn't." After uncorking a half-full wine bottle retrieved from the refrigerator, she filled the glasses and took
them into the sitting area. "Don't you ever get tired of
traveling?"

A peculiar sadness clouded his eyes. "Sometimes." He
took the glass she offered, smiling his thanks. "But moving
around goes with the territory."

Jessica sat beside him, sobered by the reminder that
Devon Monroe was a man for whom permanence was not
an option. Last week, she'd been philosophical about that

simple truth; tonight, she was deeply disturbed by the real
ization that sooner or later he would leave. Her heart twiste
at the thought. She took a sip of wine, trying to compos
herself. It tasted bitter. She set the glass aside.

Feeling even more apprehensive, she squirmed restlessly
acutely aware that for the first time that evening they ha
nothing to say to each other. The strained silence stretche
on as Devon savored his wine and Jessica fretted, wonder
ing if intimacy between them would be a mistake.

She'd had a few such relationships in her life, friendship
that had evolved slowly into love affairs. The result had a
ways been the eventual loss of both the friend and the love
Inevitably, the men in her life had wanted more than she'
been willing to give. They'd wanted permanence; she'
wanted freedom. They'd been in *love;* she'd been in *like*.

Now the situation had apparently been reversed. It wa
she who had stars in her eyes and Devon who was the res
less one, with his yearning gaze glued to the horizon. H
couldn't promise her forever; all he could offer was now
And because she loved him, it was all she would ask.

But if they couldn't share a life, they could share memo
ries, memories created tonight—if she had the courage.

A gentle *thunk* broke into her thoughts as Devon ha
placed his half-empty wineglass on the table. He propped a
ankle on his knee and turned to face her. "I'm not going t
bite you, Jessica."

She felt her face heat. "I know that."

"Do you?" He studied her for a moment. "I'd rather cu
off an arm than to hurt you."

"I know that, too." She slumped against the soft cush
ion. "I guess I'm a little nervous."

He absently tugged his earlobe. "So am I."

The surprising confession caught her off guard. "Why?"

"This is kind of a big step for me," he said, with
sheepish grin that tugged at her heartstrings. "To tell yo

the truth, it's been a long time since I've been seriously involved with anyone."

The fact that he considered lovemaking to be a serious involvement was a great relief. This was also a big step for Jessica, an emotional commitment that was as frightening as it was exciting.

Devon slid an arm around Jessica's shoulders, drawing her onto his lap. He sighed contently as she laid her head on his shoulder. "I guess we're just a couple of sexual wimps."

She smiled and nuzzled the exposed flesh at the base of his throat. "I think it's too soon to make that evaluation."

A fine mesh of goose bumps emerged as the tip of her tongue traced a corded muscle from his collarbone to just below his ear. He shivered. "I think you could be right."

"Hmm." As she continued her tactile exploration, his scent enveloped her with dizzying results. Her heart beat faster. A slow heat throbbed deep in her belly. She felt as though the room were revolving around them.

Devon's flesh quivered beneath each delicate nip, each sensual taste, until a slick film of perspiration misted his face and a gratified groan rumbled from his chest. His reaction empowered her, filling her with the exquisite joy of having given him pleasure. Soon she was completely immersed in exploring his body, testing the firmness of his muscular chest, savoring his tangy taste, absorbing his masculine heat until she wasn't certain where he left off and she began.

When her fingers tangled in the annoying fabric of his shirt, impeding her progress, she tugged irritably at the buttons. In less than a minute, the cloth parted to expose a sculpted chest defined by an enticing spatter of silky hair. She touched him gently, reverently, following the firm contours with her fingertips. She laid her palm over his heart, feeling the power of each rhythmic beat beneath a tickle of fine hairs.

Then she saw it, a jagged red scar extending from the base of his shoulder to where his arm folded against his ribs. She bit her lip, gingerly touching the thickened tissue with her fingertip. She lifted her face, searching his eyes, and would have asked about the wound except that he silenced her with a kiss so sweet, so deep that everything else was wiped from her mind.

She whimpered deep in her throat and wound her arms around him, pulling him closer, and closer still. His hands framed her face with erotic desperation. His desire burned through his touch, his kiss, the ragged throb of his pulse where his wrist pressed against her ear.

Jessica felt as if she were falling, plummeting through time and space in a dreamlike swirl. She sank into a soft cloud, pressed there by the weight of Devon's body. There was a tugging at her waist, then a fluttering sensation skimmed her ribs.

Her mind cleared slowly. The cloud became the sofa cushion on which she was reclining. She vaguely realized that her blouse had been loosened; and although Devon's lips were busily investigating the tasty flesh of her throat, his fingertips were grazing her bare midriff. A shaft of panic stiffened her spine. She struggled to sit up.

Devon levered up on one arm. "What's wrong?"

"Nothing." She quickly rearranged her blouse to cover her bare skin. The light emitted by the room's two lamps seemed suddenly blinding. "I just think we'd be more comfortable in the bedroom." And in the dark.

He sat up. "Are you sure?"

The question referred to more than changing rooms. "Yes, I'm sure."

Seeming relieved, he stood and helped her up. She gave his hand a reassuring squeeze and led to the only door other than the entry. She hurried across the darkened room, scooped a small pile of freshly folded linen off the bed and set it on the dresser.

Backlit by the living room lamps, Devon's silhouette loomed in the doorway. Jessica saw his hand touch the wall, searching for a switch. "No lights," she said quickly.

He hesitated briefly, then lowered his hand. "All right." He stepped inside and closed the door. Except for a thin shaft of moonlight from the window, the room was engulfed by darkness.

Jessica took a deep breath, felt around for the edge of the quilted bedspread and turned down the covers. As her eyes adjusted to the dimness, she spoke to the shadowed figure still positioned by the door. "The bed is ready."

"Okay. Great." Feeling the air with stiffly extended arms, he moved cautiously forward. After two steps, he rammed into the corner of the dresser, spun around, tripped over Jessica's open suitcase and with a surprised bellow, flopped face first onto the mattress.

Horrified, Jessica frantically patted the mattress until she found a warm, quivering hunk of flesh. "Are you all right?"

"Sure. I just like to make a memorable entrance." Devon chuckled, rolled onto his back, and burst into laughter.

Jessica straightened, not sure if she should be insulted. Then she realized that two adults groping around a pitch-black room like a couple of shy adolescents was pretty funny stuff. She smiled, as amused by Devon's howls as she was by the ludicrous situation. A snicker slid from her own throat, then another and another. She threw herself on the bed, laughing, and patted the pillow beside her. "Come here."

Devon gasped for breath. "I don't know where you are."

"Here's a clue." She grabbed the pillow and aimed a swat at a dim shadow hunched at the foot of the mattress.

"Aha!" The shadow lunged.

Jessica squealed and they rolled into a giggling tangle of limbs. Their laughter died slowly, comfortably, as they settled into each other's arms.

As Devon lazily stroked her arm, Jessica sighed. "You must think I'm really strange, making you go through all this."

He brushed his lips across her brow. "Being bashful isn't a crime. In fact, I think it's kind of adorable."

Jessica cringed inside. Her feelings went beyond being adorably bashful. She wanted to be perfect for Devon and her body would never be perfect again. It was as simple and as complicated as that. She'd thought she'd come to terms with her scars; now she wondered. Certainly Devon knew those scars existed—she'd been honest about that—but for some odd reason, she couldn't shake off the irrational feeling that if he didn't actually see them, he might forget about them.

Or perhaps, she might forget.

The melancholy contemplation was interrupted by a delicious shiver when Devon kissed the sensitive pulse point at the curve of her throat. "You taste so good," he murmured. "Like honey on sweet cream."

She arched her throat, thrilled by his moist kisses and the soft tickle of his fingertips teasing the delicate flesh of her inner arm. Moaning, she pushed at his open shirt, shoving the fabric over his shoulders. He shrugged the garment off and tossed it aside.

The mattress dipped as he swung his legs over the side to remove first his shoes, then his jeans and finally his socks. He returned to her side wearing only his briefs.

Following his lead, Jessica pulled off her canvas skimmers and dropped them beside the bed. She was nervously fiddling with the front button of her slacks when Devon's warm palm slid over her hand. He whispered in her ear, "Let me."

She gratefully relinquished the task, allowing him to undress her with royal care. He slid the linen slacks over her hips, pausing to kiss each thigh, then each knee and finally each trembling ankle before draping the deflated garment over the foot of the bed. Jessica lifted her arms, allowing him to ease the knit top over her head. She stopped him as he reached for her bra clasp. She simply held his wrist, saying nothing, too embarrassed even to look up. His response was to sweep her into his arms in an embrace so loving that it took her breath away.

The sweet sensations intensified slowly, methodically, like the sensual strains of *Bolero* building to a crescendo of passion. Every kiss lit another flame in her burning belly; every scorching stroke of his fingers sent sparks down her spine until she was on fire, burning with a hunger that only this man could sate.

She craved the feel of his masculinity, the warmth of his furred skin against her palm. She longed to memorize the landscape of his body with her fingertips. And so she touched him, gingerly at first, barely skimming his firm abdomen with her knuckles, then more boldly, tracing the thickening path of hair from his naval, over the elastic border and finally laying her palm over the thin cotton which covered the part of him that she sought. The strength of what she felt was awesome, pulsing with power and with a hunger equal to her own.

His body shook beneath her touch. His breath came in tortured gasps. Finally, when he could endure no more, he hooked his thumbs beneath the elastic and removed the obstructing garment. All of him was now hers.

She measured him with her hand, massaging, stroking, pleasuring him until he cried out in desperation. He turned the tables quickly, sweeping away her lace panties and initiating a sensual caress that made her crazy. She thrashed, she moaned, she clutched at his shoulders. Then, when she was certain she was actually dying, he moved over her and positioned himself at the threshold. She arched up to meet him.

He framed her face with his hands, whispered her name, and gave her his love.

\* \* \*

Holding Devon's sleeping head to her bosom, Jessica stared into the darkness and fought a rush of tears. She'd tried to convince herself that sweet memories would keep her warm after Devon had gone. Now she wanted so much more. She wanted his heart. She wanted his love. She wanted forever.

But all she could keep was the memory. It simply wasn't enough.

## Chapter Eleven

It was a lovely dream.

Jessica felt as if she were a complacent kitten curled in a warm lap. Loving fingers stroked her furry head. The soothing sensation made her all floaty inside. She was safe. She was loved. She purred with contentment.

After a delicious stretch, her groggy mind wakened slowly, with a gentle slide into ambiguous awareness. She felt sunlight on her face. It was morning. Instinctively she realized that it was a beautiful morning—perhaps the most beautiful morning of her life—but she hadn't awakened completely enough to remember why.

But she still felt like that purring kitten nestled against a warm body. And someone was definitely petting her head.

She blinked and was immediately blinded by a shaft of sunlight from the undraped window. Moaning, she covered her eyes, pulled up her knees and scrunched her face into the pillow. Something tickled her nose. Odd, she thought. Not only did the pillow seem unusually firm and warm, it was also hairy.

When her eyelids sprang open, the first thing she saw was a man's wristwatch. Then she saw the wrist to which it was attached and beyond that, a masculine hand dangling partially over the mattress in comfortable repose. Even with all those clues, it took a moment for her to realize that she was using the crook of an arm as a pillow. And a moment longer to realize that the arm belonged to Devon Monroe.

The fingers that were stroking her head slid down to caress her cheek. "Good morning, sleepyhead."

Murmuring a slurred greeting, Jessica levered up on one elbow and wiped a sluggish hand across her face. A shake of her head helped clear the fog from her mind.

"Did you sleep well?" Devon asked.

"Hmm." She covered a yawn, then absently reached back to massage her neck. "And you?"

"Never better." He grazed the inside of her raised arm with his thumb. "Has anyone told you how lovely you are in the morning?"

She was considering a flippant reply when she suddenly moved her leg against his bare thigh and remembered that he was naked beneath the covers. Even worse, so was she. Except, of course, for the bra she'd refused to remove. That modest garment, along with the concealing darkness, had cloaked her disfigurement. But now the room was awash with sunlight brilliant enough to magnify even the tiniest flaw.

She was even more horrified to realize that her arm was tossed carelessly over her head to reveal the ugly scars extending beyond the concealing fabric of her bra. She yanked down her arm, pinning it to her side, and snapped a stunned glance over her shoulder. The look on Devon's face indicated that the gesture was too late.

Before he could do more than call her name, she whipped off the covers, hopped out of bed and dashed into the bathroom. She sagged against the vanity and tried to compose herself. Devon's expression hadn't been one of revulsion. He had, in fact, seemed rather thoughtful. Still, the harsh light of day had been known to cool more than one man's ardor and Jessica wondered with increasing trepidation what might be running through his mind.

As to what was going on in her own mind, well, that was utter chaos. Her heart ached in the afterglow of their glorious lovemaking yet she was sobered by the stern warnings of her anxious mind. For a few intoxicating moments, reality had been suspended; they'd savored a veritable feast of tactile delights and inflamed passions. For those sublime and all-too-brief hours, Jessica had pushed everything else out of her mind—the past, the future, the reality of their divergent lives. But now tomorrow had arrived and with it, the paralyzing fear that last night might be all that they would ever have.

A soft knock at the door made her gasp. "Jessica? Are you all right?"

She spun around, touched her throat, and fought for an even tone. "I'm fine. I'm just, uh—" she fumbled with the faucet "—brushing my teeth." A thin stream of water bubbled into the basin. "I'll be out in a few minutes."

Except for the dribbling faucet, the room was silent. Then Devon said, "No hurry. I'll put on the coffee."

"Thank you."

Jessica held her breath. When his footsteps moved away from the door, she exhaled slowly, leaned over the sink and splashed her face with icy water. She turned off the faucet, glimpsed her reflection in the vanity mirror and as was her habit, automatically turned away. A small voice in the back of her mind chided her for the foolish avoidance. It was a voice she hadn't noticed before. So she listened.

*Take a good look,* it said. *If you can't accept what you see, neither can anyone else.*

That was true, of course, although grudging acknowledgement didn't make the task any easier. She forced her reluctant gaze forward and saw a terrified woman staring back at her. Except for the buzzed hair and a smear of slept-on mascara, the woman wasn't completely unattractive. Jessica scrutinized her image closely. Her cheeks were a bit hollow, but she didn't really look as gaunt as she once had. The five pounds she'd put on in the past month had helped more than she'd realized.

But it wasn't her face she was concerned with. With stoic determination, she stepped back until her upper torso appeared in the mirror, then raised her arm to inspect the scars Devon had seen. They were still there and they were still ugly.

The worst was a thickened red welt just below and to the front of her shoulder joint. This, and similar scars in her armpit, had resulted from a precautionary lymph nodes extraction. The incisions had healed well, although the area was subject to bouts of edema and was painful when she overexerted the weakened arm muscles.

For the first time, she studied the disfigurements with a modicum of objectivity and decided that the periphery blemishes, although not particularly appealing, weren't as repugnant as she'd once thought.

The breast itself was quite another matter. Along with the tumor, a marginal amount of tissue had been removed from the outside portion of her right breast. The result was a puckered cavern the size of a golf ball and a tweaked nipple that pointed to the right rather than straight ahead.

Despite her fretting, Jessica was well aware that she was more fortunate than many women for whom mastectomy had been required. Just having a nipple, tweaked or otherwise, would be a benefit for reconstructive surgery, a future option she hadn't considered until now. Meanwhile the contours of her custom brassiere provided the outward appearance of normalcy.

Jessica studied her reflection, sobered by the realization that although no cancer victim could ever be considered "lucky," her own optimistic outcome had made her more fortunate than many others. Wallowing in angst over what couldn't be changed was pointless, puerile and a waste of precious time.

*Right on,* echoed the voice in her mind.

She sighed. Mental pep talks were easy; being rejected by a man you're crazy in love with, now that was a bitch.

But nobody ever said life would be easy.

Puffing her cheeks, Jessica blew out a breath and decided that she couldn't lurk in the bathroom all day. Tempting as the option was, she had to face Devon. If he regretted what had happened last night, well, she'd find the strength to deal with that, too.

But she couldn't deal with anything while wearing nothing but a bra and a terrified expression. Fortunately, a fresh supply of laundered lingerie was slung over the shower rod, so she slipped into a pair of fresh panties, pulled a cotton duster from the door hook and hurriedly completed her morning routine. Then, with clean teeth and a freshly scrubbed face, she took a deep breath and opened the bathroom door.

Devon was at the window, shirtless, his jeans slung low over his hips. He turned as she entered the room, regarding her warily. "Hi."

"Hi." Jessica tightened the duster's cloth belt, deliberately averting her gaze from the tousled bed. She stared instead out the open door toward the kitchen. "Did you find the coffee?"

"Sure. It's almost ready."

"Good. That's good." She closed her eyes with a silent moan. This was without a doubt the most awkward moment of her life. She wanted to leap into Devon's arms and cover him with kisses. She wanted to press his dear face to her heart and confess that she'd fallen in love with him. She wanted to feel his hands all over her body, thrilling her with the warmth of his tender touch.

She wanted all of those things; so why were they talking about coffee?

Because she was a coward, that's why. Despite her mental fortification, her determination to "deal with" reality, Jessica was deathly afraid of rejection. She couldn't look at Devon for fear of what she'd see in his eyes. She couldn't look at the bed because the memory of what had happened there sent delicious chills down her spine. So she stood there like a stupid rock, doing nothing, saying nothing, resolving nothing.

And the miserable silence stretched on.

From the corner of her eye, Jessica saw Devon fold his arms and lean back against the wall. He cleared his throat. She stiffened.

"I guess this morning-after stuff isn't what it's cracked up to be," he said lightly.

She chanced a glance and saw a forced smile contradicting his guarded gaze. "No, I guess it isn't."

His smile faded. He shifted restlessly and stared across the room. "You look like a woman with a pocketful of regrets."

"Me? Oh, no. I thought you were the one..." Confused, she fiddled with the limp cotton belt and allowed the words to die naturally.

Devon measured her with a penetrating gaze. "What was it that you thought, Jessica?"

She managed a listless shrug. "I thought you might be a bit put off."

"Put off? By what?" When she didn't respond, he crossed the room and took hold of her shoulders, forcing her to look at him. "By your scars?" Her darting gaze supplied the answer. He moaned. "Look, I know sometimes I come across as a shallow jerk but—"

"I've never thought that."

He smiled at her indignant denial. "Never? Not even once?"

"Well...maybe before I got to know you, but I was wrong."

"Were you?"

"Of course I was. You're one of the finest men I've ever met. You're understanding and sensitive and...and...why on earth are you grinning like that?"

"I was just wondering why you'd believe such a sensitive, understanding man would give a fat flying fig about a couple of little pink scars."

Her face was suddenly hot enough to glow. "You haven't seen them all."

He sobered instantly. "You don't get it, do you?"

"Get what?"

"The fact that I don't care about the scars. I don't care whether or not you even *have* a breast. Can't you understand? It just doesn't matter."

Bewildered by his vehemence, Jessica searched his eyes and said nothing.

Devon set his chin. "You don't believe me, do you? You think for some perverse reason I'm just spouting whatever you want to hear."

"I think you mean what you're saying but..." She chewed her lip and looked away.

"But what?" He tightened his grip on her shoulders. "But once I see the horror of disfigured flesh, you think I'm going to run screaming into the night?"

She winced at the harsh words. "Not exactly."

After releasing Jessica so abruptly that she swayed, Devon took several steps backward until he was standing flat-footed in the center of the room. "So, you want to talk about physical imperfections?"

Actually, that was the last thing she wanted to talk about but before she could say so, Devon was pointing to the jagged scar on his upper chest, the one she'd noticed earlier.

"This," he said dramatically, "is what happens when one attempts to break up a knife fight in Milan."

"Oh, Lord! That's awful!"

"And this little jewel—" he swung around to display an ugly puckered circle below his left shoulder blade "—was compliments of a Somalian sniper. Attractive, huh?"

Jessica felt sick. "Please . . . you don't have to do this."

"Ah, but it gets better." Facing her again, he unbuttoned his jeans and pushed them into a denim puddle at his feet. "These shrapnel scars are from Beirut." He pointed out a horrible road map of lumpy tissue on his left thigh then directed her attention to a similar mass spidering out from a deep cavern in his right calf. "And this is Ethiopian shrapnel. Of the two, I prefer the Lebanese version— quicker, cleaner, blows out less muscle."

"Ohmygod." Jessica pressed a hand to her mouth. "How can you joke about this?"

He straightened, smiling cheerfully. "Why shouldn't I joke about it? It happened. It's over. I lived through it. Since these little mementos aren't going away, I might as well have some fun with them."

"Fun," she repeated lamely.

"Sure. I named the one on my shoulder Duck 'n' Run as a reminder of what I should have done when the altercation started. The Somalian souvenir is called American Dog, because that's what the sniper yelled before he pulled the trigger."

"You're making this up."

"Nope." His fingertip traced a quick cross over his heart. "Remember the old saying, 'There are a million stories in the naked city'? Same thing, only in my case it's a naked body."

He looked so smug, and so silly standing there in his shorts with his jeans rumpled around his ankles that she couldn't help but smile and go along with the gag. "So what do you call Beirut?"

"Ah." He affectionately patted his scarred thigh. "This one is my favorite. I call it Cross Fire—the reason is obvious—and the one on my calf is named Drumstick because—"

She held up her hand and groaned. "Let me guess. You christened it Drumstick because it looks like a chewed chicken leg."

He brightened. "Right. Say, you're really getting the hang of this."

She shook her head, trying not to chuckle and losing the battle. "You've made your point."

"Not quite. There's one more grossly maimed part of my anatomy that you're entitled to see." With that, he yanked down his briefs and turned around to expose another puckered bullet scar. This one was in his right buttock. "I call it the Ego Buster."

A tickled snort slipped out. Jessica covered her mouth, trying desperately to hold back the laughter. She couldn't. Her shoulders vibrated. A series of muffled giggles escaped her smothering palms to waft audibly across the room.

Devon pulled up his briefs and feigned a stricken expression. "I hope it's just the scar you find amusing and not something more personal."

At that point, Jessica lost it completely. She let out a howl, spun around and clung to the bathroom doorjamb, laughing so hard she couldn't have stood on her own if she'd wanted to. She laughed until tears rolled down her cheeks, her knees buckled and her ribs went into a spasm. Then she sank onto the floor in a quivering, giggling heap. "Ohh." She sniffed and wiped her wet eyes. "I'm s-sorry. I don't know wh-what's gotten into me."

"You were obviously overcome by the sight of my adorable bottom."

Jessica was seized by a coughing fit, after which she took a wheezing breath and held up her hand in surrender.

"Enough," she whispered, gasping. "If you don't stop making me laugh, I'm going to have an attack."

Devon hiked up his jeans before joining her on the floor. He sat cross-legged, elbows on his knees and he leaned forward. "So, are you okay or should I start doing the mouth-to-mouth thing?"

Still shaky, she propped her head against the wall. "Now that you mention it, a little resuscitation might be just what the doctor ordered."

The soft glow in his eyes sent shivers down her spine. "That's a prescription I'd be happy to fill."

Sliding two fingers beneath her chin, Devon gently tilted her face upward, then leaned slowly forward and fitted his mouth over her waiting lips. The kiss was so sweet, so incredibly sweet, that wave after wave of liquid warmth flowed through her veins. She whimpered deep in her throat and rested her limp fingers on his collarbone. The room was spinning again. Her bones felt like rubber.

When the kiss ended, Devon looked as shaken as Jessica felt. He took a deep breath, blew it out and took another. He slid a yearning glance toward the bed. "I suppose your parents are expecting you for breakfast."

She used her fingertip to trace a tiny line at the corner of his mouth. "Yes, but it's early. Besides, they have no choice but to wait for me."

"Why's that?"

"Because I'm cooking."

He shuddered as her fingertip slid around to tease his earlobe. "You certainly are."

Smiling to herself, Jessica nuzzled the curve of his throat. "Would you like waffles or bacon and eggs?"

"Hmm?"

"For breakfast."

"Am I invited?"

She sat back, startled that he would even ask. "Of course. Did you think I was going to hide you in the closet and let you starve?"

"I thought you might slip me a piece of toast or something."

"That's not funny." Jessica used both hands to steady his face and looked him right in the eye. "I'm not embarrassed by our relationship. Are you?"

He turned his head to gently kiss her palm, then cradled her hand against his cheek. "I think you deserve better than me and I suspect your parents will feel the same way. Having said that, I'll confess that being with you has made me happier and more at peace with myself than I've ever been in my life."

A rush of relief nearly choked her. "I'm glad," she whispered. "I want you to be happy."

His eyes filled with wonder. "I know you do. I'm just not sure I understand why."

She wanted to grab his head, shake it and shout, *Because I love you, you dolt.* Instead she managed a serene smile. "Because you're a good and decent man."

Devon's gaze slipped away. "Ah, yes. That's me, a real champion of humanity." His sudden sadness tore at her heart but before she could question him, the poignant mood dissipated as quickly as it had arrived. When he looked at her again, his gaze smoldered with familiar intensity. "How much time did you say we had before breakfast?"

"That depends on what you have in mind." The coquettish murmur was nearly drowned out by the sudden acceleration of her heart. Of course, she knew exactly what he had in mind and shivered with anticipation when his hand slid sensually along her thigh.

He slipped his thumb beneath the thin cotton robe, drawing back the fabric to expose her bare leg folded demurely and tucked beside the curve of her hip. "I thought I

might be able to interest you in a few more minutes of qual-
ity time together."

"I think that can be arranged." She barely recognized the
husky whisper as her own. But with his fingers grazing a
sizzling path across her bare flesh, she was grateful to have
any voice at all.

Besides, her gaze was suddenly riveted on his chest. She
marveled at how truly exquisite it was, tanned and well
muscled, with sculpted contours defined by just the right
amount of dark, masculine hair. His abdomen was solid,
with rigid muscles rippling beneath the surface. It was odd,
she thought, that she'd always considered Devon to be a lean
man, well proportioned but not particularly powerful. How
wrong she'd been. Beneath his loose fatigues and the baggy
casuals he favored was a body to die for, a body silently
beckoning her touch.

The exploration began slowly, more a tentative pet than
a sensual caress. Her shy fingers skittered softly around the
edges, teasing his ribs, moving along the outside of his arms
to his shoulders, then tracing the ridge along his collarbone
before starting the circle again. Last night in the darkness,
she'd memorized the topography of his body by touch.
Now, gleaming by sunlight, his golden skin took on an
ethereal glow that made him seem almost omnipotent.

She was particularly fascinated by his nipples, swarthy
orbs dusted ever so gently with a smattering of silky hairs.
They stood like erect little soldiers, rock-hard and stoic, each
guarding its own muscled hill. She itched to touch them, to
feel the roughened tips scrape against her palms.

As she worked up courage for the intimate caress, her
fingers feathered down to brush each sensitive peak. The
reaction was instantaneous. Devon sucked in a harsh breath
and went rigid.

She yanked her hands away. "I—I'm sorry—"

"Shh. It's okay." He caught her wrists, kissed the throbbing pulse of each, then pressed her hands to his chest. "Don't stop."

She hesitated, amazed by his rapturous expression. She'd never considered a man's breasts as an erogenous zone but as she gently rolled each nipple with her thumb, his shudder of sheer delight proved the fallacy of that errant assumption. His entire body vibrated beneath her touch, empowering her to bolder and bolder exploration. When at last she leaned forward to kiss him there, he groaned low in his throat while a final, violent tremor shook him to the bone.

Suddenly Devon scooped his hands under Jessica's arms and rose to his feet, lifting her with him. With trembling fingers he parted the bodice of her robe, exposing her throat to his seeking mouth. As he kissed the curve of her neck, he pushed the duster over her shoulders, then reached down to tug at the knotted belt. In a moment, the robe slithered to the floor.

With sun-warmed air caressing her back, she grappled with the button on his jeans, sighing in relief when it finally sprang open. Devon's bulging anatomy completed the chore. The zipper parted; the jeans slid lazily down his lean hips and were kicked aside.

The next moments were a frenzy of searching hands and desperate kisses, of passions aroused to the breaking point and beyond. Each ragged breath floated in the thick air; soft whimpers harmonized with ragged moans until the room was filled with the seductive symphony of their love.

He cherished her body with his lips, touching and tasting every curve with delicate flicks of his tongue. Then he knelt before her, pressing his face against her soft belly. As he slid her silken panties slowly down her thighs, he whispered her name like a prayer and kissed her inner thighs. The sensation was so exquisite, so incredibly erotic that she tangled her fingers in his thick hair and bit her lip to keep from crying out.

Devon rose up on his knees, wrapped one arm around her waist and the other around her hips, then placed a gentle kiss on each lace-clad breast before nesting his face in the valley between her ribs. "I've never met anyone like you," he whispered against her skin. "You do things to me, things I don't understand. Sometimes it scares me to feel this way."

Cradling his head in her arms, Jessica leaned down to rub her cheek against his soft hair. "How do you feel, Devon?"

"That's the thing...I'm not sure." He twisted his head to look up at her, his eyes filled with wonder. "Maybe I just want you so bad it hurts."

She smoothed a mussed strand of hair from his face. "I'm right here."

"Yeah," he murmured, as though shocked by the realization. "You are, aren't you?" Still holding her, Devon stood in the circle of Jessica's arms. His kiss was deep and sweet, with a trembling intensity that betrayed the fierce passion pulsing just below the surface.

Their bare torsos moved sensually, stroking, caressing, pressing closer, tighter, teasing themselves into an excited frenzy. Gasping and half-crazed, they broke apart long enough for Devon to discard his briefs. When he reached for her again, she held him back with a gentle hand on his chest. As her gaze slid down his battered body, her heart filled with compassion and with love. He'd trusted her enough to bare himself, body and soul. She could do no less.

Raising her gaze, she looked deeply into his eyes and slid each bra strap over her shoulder in a slow, sensual striptease. He questioned her silently, found the answer he sought, then reached back between her shoulder blades and pinched the clasp. The bra, weighted by its padded contours, lurched drunkenly forward, slid down her arms and plopped to the floor. Jessica swept it aside with her foot, then continued to stare at the rumpled garment and was overwhelmed by a sudden urge to cover herself. Her arms instantly folded across her chest with fisted hands tucked under her chin.

Without speaking, Devon caressed her arms with long, gentle strokes. After a moment, her knotted muscles relaxed like melted butter and her arms dropped to her sides. She held her breath, unable to meet Devon's eyes.

Tender fingers feathered below each breast. "Is it still sore to the touch?"

She clamped her lips together and shook her head.

"Good," he murmured, moving his hands up to cup both breasts. "Now it's my turn."

Ignoring her tiny gasp of surprise, he instantly stroked both nipples with his flat palm, adjusting to their directional differences as if it were perfectly normal for one breast to point north and the other northeast. Before she could mentally assimilate what had just happened, an electric excitement skittered down her spine. Her lips parted; her eyelids fluttered shut. She automatically arched, moaning as he had done when she'd teased and tantalized him in the same way.

In less than a heartbeat, her body was alive with sensation, a million tiny sparks traveling every nerve, igniting every cell, arousing every fiber of her being. And when she thought she could endure no more, he used his lips to drive her into an aroused frenzy. A moist heat exploded deep inside. Her body convulsed. At the moment she cried out, Devon lifted her hips. Embracing him with loving thighs, she took him into her body, into her heart and into her soul.

She felt whole. She felt loved. And for that sweet, delicious moment, she forgot that nothing is forever.

## Chapter Twelve

Devon entered the guesthouse and tossed an empty soda can in the kitchen trash. He leaned against the counter as Jessica hurried out of the bedroom with an armful of lingerie. She glanced anxiously around the tidy sitting room. "Did you put my suitcase in your car?"

"No. It's over here." He went to retrieve the suitcase, flopped it on the sofa and opened it for her.

Her relieved smile turned into a sheepish grin as she tucked the garments into a silky pocket inside the luggage. "I forgot about the things on the shower rod."

"Why doesn't that surprise me?"

"Now be nice," Jessica admonished cheerfully. She clicked the fasteners into place and straightened. "There. That's everything."

"Have you checked the sofa cushions for socks?"

"Very funny." She flopped down on the sofa, propped an elbow on her suitcase and absently fiddled with the bangs of her wig. "Did you enjoy touring the aquarium?"

"As a matter of fact, I did."

She looked relieved. "You and Frank both seemed rather taken with the shark exhibit."

"Frank wants to put one in the fountain." Devon sat in the chair, amused by her stunned expression. "He thinks it would add a bit of biological interest to your mother's garden."

"Surely he was joking."

"I doubt it. Beneath your father's dignified exterior beats the heart of a true bohemian."

Jessica gaped for a moment before waving the ludicrous statement away. "You ought to drop journalism and take up creative writing."

Feeling pleased with himself, Devon laced his fingers behind his head and grinned. "I had you going there, didn't I?"

She tried for an apathetic shrug but her lips twitched into a grudging smile. "You're impossible."

"I know. It's part of my charm."

Her smile widened slightly, then a peculiar wistfulness clouded her lovely eyes. She looked away, chewing her lip, and gazed across the room with a faraway expression that was strangely unsettling.

"Is something wrong?" he asked.

"Hmm?" She glanced toward him. "No, nothing's wrong. I was just thinking."

"About what?"

A thoughtful frown creased her brow. "There was a big article in the paper this morning about a South American journalist who was killed covering an attempted coup."

Instantly alarmed, Devon leaned forward. "I have a lot of friends working for the South America press corps. Did the article give a name?"

"Not that I recall." She hesitated as if choosing her words carefully. "It made me think, though, and I was, well, wondering if you'd ever considered any other line of work."

"Not really."

She didn't try to disguise her disappointment. "Oh."

"No job is completely without danger."

"Perhaps not, but some are certainly less hazardous than others. Besides, when you first arrived in L.A., you were so—I don't know—burned out and exhausted. You've seemed so much happier since then, I thought perhaps..." She sighed and rubbed both hands across her face. "Never mind. Obviously you enjoy your work."

"I enjoy being a reporter," Devon said slowly. "It's what I do and I'm damned good at it."

She nodded miserably. "I know you are."

A strained silence stretched between them. Devon pinched the bridge of his nose, trying to compose himself. The discussion of his mental state had touched a raw nerve, forcing him to acknowledge secret doubts that had been plaguing him for months. Jessica's perceptive observation had been right on the money. When Devon had left Europe, he'd been a walking shell of a man, incapable of feeling any emotions beyond bitterness and helpless anger.

But Jessica had changed all that. She'd given him a new vision, shown him that life was more than a daily dose of tragedy. Because of her, Devon had met a man he'd never known before—his own father. And he'd liked what he'd seen. The man Devon had now discovered was one who'd earned the respect of his peers and the trust of his friends. He was a man worth knowing; a man Devon was finally beginning to understand. That meant the world and without Jessica's encouragement it never would have happened.

"I'm sorry," Jessica said suddenly. "I've stuck my nose into something that's none of my business, haven't I?"

He looked up and the mere sight of her warmed his heart. "I'd like to think that everything about me is your business...and vice versa."

Her smile was a little nervous. "Actually, I've always loved to travel. It must be wonderful to have a career that allows you to see the world and earn a paycheck at the same time."

At this point, all Devon had to do was agree with her and the subject would be dropped like a hot rock. Since that was exactly what he wanted, he had no idea why he found himself saying, "The world I know isn't worth seeing, unless watching entire cities bombed into ruins is considered a spectator sport. After a while, even death and destruction tends to lose its appeal."

Jessica winced at the graphic image. "Then why on earth do you do it?"

"Because it's my job." He sighed wearily. "No, it's more than that. Ever since I was a kid, I've wanted to be a journalist. I naively figured that once injustice and cruelty were exposed, people would be outraged enough to stop it."

"I don't think that's naive," Jessica said quietly. "I think it's a noble plan."

He emitted a sound of disgust. "Unfortunately, it doesn't work. People can only absorb so much misery before they harden themselves to it. When that happens, the evening news becomes an abstract work of fiction, entertaining enough but no one takes it seriously."

"Then why don't you just give it up?"

He looked at her as if she'd asked him to sever an arm. "Because it's my life."

Jessica lowered her gaze without comment. After fidgeting with her watch strap for a moment, she suddenly stood and glanced around the room.

Devon rose slowly. "What are you looking for?"

"My purse. I thought I left it— Ah. It's on the counter." She went to dig through the trendy leather-and-canvas bag, and pulled out a brown plastic prescription bottle. After shaking something into her palm, she dropped the bottle back into her purse and spoke over her shoulder. "I'm glad we're going back to Los Angeles together. How long will the drive take?"

Devon joined her in the kitchenette. "We should hit town before the ten p.m. news. Why, do you have a hot date?"

"I might." She filled a glass with water and slid him a coy glance. "Depending, of course, on how tired you are."

Devon's gaze was riveted on the tiny pills nested in her palm. "What's that?"

"Tamoxifen."

"What's it for?"

"According to Frank's fancy medical jargon, it helps prevent breast cancer recurrence by 'providing effective adjuvant antiestrogen therapy.'" She popped the tablets into her mouth, washed them down and set the half-empty glass aside. After extracting a second bottle, she offered an apologetic shrug. "I have so many different medications that the mind boggles. The truth is that I've forgotten what half of them are supposed to do, but if I don't take them, I usually end up feeling like a wrung-out dishrag."

The stiff reminder of her illness hit Devon like a fist. He stood there, transfixed, as she casually dispatched two yellow capsules, then tightened the drawstring on her bag and glanced at her watch. "Mom asked us to stop in before we left. Do we have enough time?"

"You look tired," Devon blurted.

Her eyes rounded in astonishment. "Thanks. You look good, too."

"All that walking must have worn you out," he mumbled, stunned by a sudden surge of panic. "I never should have put you through it."

Jessica took a wary step backward. A strange expression crossed her face... apprehension, perhaps. Or annoyance. Then she turned and walked silently into the living room.

Unfortunately Devon was too preoccupied with his own fears to catch the warning look in her eyes because a single, terrifying word kept rolling around his mind. *Recurrence.* That meant the cancer could come back. Even now there could be malignant cells lurking in her body, waiting for a weak moment to mount a new attack.

But that wasn't going to happen. Devon wouldn't allow it.

A rustling noise caught his attention. He glanced up just as Jessica hoisted the suitcase off the couch. When she winced, Devon uttered a gasp of dismay, sprang across the room and practically ripped the luggage out of her hand. "Careful! You'll hurt yourself."

At first she stared up in stunned disbelief. Then her lips tightened and her eyes darkened into ominous shadows. An exquisite sadness crossed her face as she turned and walked out of the house.

Devon shifted his grip on the suitcase and followed, oblivious to all but his own torment. There was so much he had to do now, so much he had to learn. This tamoxifen stuff, for instance. He'd have to check that out and make certain that Jessica was getting the best treatment available. And he'd check out her doctors, too. Nothing could be overlooked or left to chance. There was too much at stake.

Tommy Murdock had died because Devon had done nothing to stop it. That wasn't going to happen again.

Hunched over his father's kitchen table, Devon was pouring over a stack of pamphlets and medical texts as Gunda hurried through the kitchen door with groceries for the evening meal.

She clucked, frowned, and placed her parcels on the counter. "*Bel meiner Trau!* You have not left that place for three days."

Devon barely looked up. "Did you know that bone marrow transplants have been successful in treating certain types of breast cancer?"

"I have heard so."

"Actually, the process is pretty amazing. A person can actually have her own marrow frozen, then after radiation or chemotherapy, it's thawed out and—"

"*Das tut's!* Enough!" Gunda yanked a clump of Swiss chard from the bag and flopped it forcefully on the counter. "I cannot hear such talk while preparing the food."

"Sorry." Devon closed the book, pushed back his chair and went to plant a conciliatory kiss on the housekeeper's fluffy graying head. "Am I forgiven, *Mütterchen?*"

Gunda playfully pushed him away. "I am not your 'dear little mother.'"

"Oh, but you are." Still standing behind her, Devon embraced her thick waist, hoisted her off the ground and spun around the kitchen, ignoring her sputtered protest.

When he finally turned her loose, she shook a pudgy finger in his face and scolded him in her native tongue. Devon spoke some German, although not fluently enough to keep up with her rapid-fire rebuke. He did, however, follow enough to translate a few words and understand that the gist of her remarks had little to do with his frisky frolic around the kitchen.

"Whoa, slow down," he said, then waited until she fell silent. "I caught the word *obsessed* but I can't for the life of me figure out what you're talking about."

"This!" She encompassed the cluttered table with a sturdy sweep of her arm. "Miss Newcomb's car is outside but do you spend time with her? No. You sit with books."

Perplexed by the woman's vehemence, Devon absently scratched his temple. "Jessica's in the study with Dad. They're going over budgets or something."

"And so you think she does not see what you are doing?"

Although Devon was still bewildered, the accusation in Gunda's voice was troubling. "What in hell am I doing?"

The woman sighed. As quickly as her frustration had appeared, it drained away and was replaced by maternal concern. "You care deeply for Miss Newcomb, do you not?"

There was no need to deny it. "Yes, I do."

"Then do not let her feel like ... how do I say this ... a doctor's mouse?"

Devon blinked. "Do you mean a laboratory rat?"

"*Jawohl.*" The housekeeper issued an affirmative nod. "She has been through much, but she is well now, is she not?"

"I don't know. Nobody knows and that's the problem." He raked his fingers through his hair. "According to what I've read, it will take years before anyone can be certain that the disease won't reoccur."

"Does that happen to most people, this reoccurring thing?"

"No. Actually, the odds are that it won't."

"Then why do you worry?"

Because he was terrified of losing her, that's why. And because any chance of that happening, no matter how remote, made him crazy.

When he didn't respond, Gunda laid a warm hand on his cheek. "It is good that you care, that you want to understand this thing that has hurt her, but perhaps you go too far. Show her your love, not your fear. That is what she needs." With a final affectionate pat, the woman returned to unloading her groceries. Suddenly she snapped her fingers. "*Warte mal!* I nearly forgot." Mumbling to herself, Gunda dug through her purse, then chortled happily and pulled out a neatly folded sheet of paper. "This is from Katrina."

Devon admired the crayoned picture, which was an unrecognizable series of multicolored scrawls. "Did she draw this by herself?"

"*Ja.*" Gunda gazed at the colorful smears with undisguised pride. "It is good?"

Considering the fact that less than a year ago, the autistic child had been unable to focus on anything outside the confines of her own fragmented mind, Devon agreed that the drawing exhibited great progress. "It's wonderful," he assured the beaming grandmother. "Put it up on the fridge so everyone can admire it."

Nodding happily, Gunda took the precious picture and Devon returned his attention to the table. As he absently fingered the glossy cover of a chemotherapy pamphlet, the housekeeper's warning rang in his mind. Although Devon didn't really believe he was obsessed with anything, he was nonetheless unsettled by Gunda's observations and had the discomfiting sensation that she might actually be right about Jessica's feelings on the matter.

Since returning from Monterey, Devon and Jessica had been nearly inseparable, spending every spare minute together. They'd shared candlelit dinners, haunted video-rental stores searching for old Cagney classics and had scoured the local mall in a futile quest of a stuffed shark as a gag gift for Frank.

And afterward, they'd made love—sometimes sweet and passionate, sometimes wild and zany, always incredibly, exquisitely wonderful. Then they'd snuggled in each other's arms, basking in the afterglow. Everything had been perfect until the *C* word was mentioned.

At the time, Devon had been too engrossed in relating details of a new treatment or the latest recovery statistics to note the thickening atmosphere, the subtle tensing of her muscles. In retrospect, however, he now recognized how uncomfortable she must have been and was chagrined by his insensitivity.

*Show her your love, not your fear.*

It seemed simple enough; but concealing such an all-consuming terror would be the most difficult feat of Devon's life.

\* \* \*

Crandall adjusted his spectacles and peered over the rimless lenses. "Are you certain these figures have been corroborated by marketing?"

"Both the marketing and finance directors have signed off on them," Jessica replied, thumbing through a thick stack of bound budget pages. "Long-term projections are always somewhat speculative, but the calculation parameters are sound and unless there's an unanticipated dip in consumer demand, I think their figures are reasonable."

"Good." Closing the softcover document, Crandall took off his glasses and wiped his forearm across his brow. "I want the final version in the stockholders' hands by the end of the month."

"That shouldn't be a problem. Everything seems to be on schedule."

"I'm sure it is. You never let me down, Jessica."

Pleased by the praise, she smiled and tucked the draft back into her briefcase. "The budget package is a joint effort. We've all been working on it for weeks."

"But you are the one who has pulled it all together, shipshape and on time." Crandall dropped the fat document on his desk and leaned back in his chair, regarding her with a bemused expression. "Considering the recent upswing in your social life, I'm frankly surprised you've found time for something as mundane as work."

Jessica's fingers froze on the valise clasp. "That was a low blow, Crandall."

"Just a cursory observation, my dear." He smiled and stretched like a sated cat. "After all, I'd have to be blind not to have noticed a certain sparkle in your eyes, a sparkle that my son also displays at the breakfast table. Assuming, of course, that he arrives home in time for breakfast, which wasn't the case this morning. But then, you already know that, don't you?"

Jessica snapped the fastener and set the briefcase aside
"What can you expect? You've been pushing us together fo
weeks. Now that you've gotten your wish, you're com
plaining?"

"Not at all." Crandall steepled his hands and looked ex
tremely pleased with himself. "May I assume that you'v
forgiven me for having breached your confidentiality in th
first place?"

"No, you may not assume that," she replied crisply. "
was my place to tell Devon about my illness, not yours. I'n
still very annoyed with you."

Crandall's elbows slipped off the table. He seeme
stunned by her brusque tone. "I'm sorry. I didn't rea
ize—"

Instantly regretting her abruptness, she waved away th
apology and tried to make amends. "You did what yo
thought was right at the time. It's not your fault."

He leaned forward to scrutinize her unhappy face. "Wha
is it, Jessica? Has Devon been unkind to you?"

"Unkind? Devon? Heavens, no." She laughed at th
irony. "That's the problem. He's too darn nice."

"Oh. Well, that must be very difficult for you." The dr
humor fell on deaf ears. Jessica's smile faded and th
amused twinkle left Crandall's eyes. "You weren't joking
were you?"

"No," she whispered, annoyed by a sudden prick of tears
She roughly wiped them away. "This is ridiculous. Wha
kind of woman complains about a man who can't d
enough for her?"

Crandall considered that. "Perhaps a woman who pre
fers to do things for herself."

Jessica couldn't sit for another moment. Standin
quickly, she crossed the room and feigned interest in th
huge library of first-edition books lining one wall of th
study. She absently fingered the worn spine of one leathe
volume, vaguely noting that the worn gold leaf title ha

been rendered unreadable by years of handling. "That's probably it," she murmured thoughtfully. "I've been on my own for so long, I'm just not used to having someone carry my laundry basket and bring me coffee."

Crandall's chair squeaked. "So you feel smothered?"

"Not exactly. I feel . . ." She paused and looked over her shoulder. "I feel like an invalid."

"Gracious," he muttered, obviously bewildered and at a loss for words.

Jessica returned her attention to the books, wishing she'd kept her mouth shut. How could she explain what she didn't even understand? All she knew was that since Devon found out about her illness, he'd been solicitous to a fault, constantly chiding her to rest and generally treating her as though she might keel over at any moment. It was driving her nuts.

She'd tried to talk to him, to reassure him that she was perfectly fine. He'd listened, too, nodding attentively and stroking the back of her hand with sensual little strokes that inevitably turned her limbs to butter. Within two minutes, Jessica would forget what she'd been saying and fall into his arms. Then they'd make love and she'd be completely overwhelmed by the fire of their passion.

Afterward, she'd convince herself that everything was all right . . . no, better than all right. Everything was wonderful. In bed, Devon didn't treat her as if she were made of porcelain. Their lovemaking was tender, yes, but it was also wild, tempestuous, erotic. He made her feel whole, infinitely desirable, exquisitely loved.

But then the cycle would begin again—the worried looks, the fretting frowns—and Jessica would start to feel fragile, breakable.

Things had changed between them. Devon didn't tease her anymore. He didn't joke about her cluttered apartment. He didn't suggest motorcycle adventures or moonlight swims.

Devon treated her differently now. That was exactly what Jessica had been most afraid of; and it had happened.

Jessica peeked into the kitchen expecting to find Devon still hunched over the kitchen table. He was gone and so was the hateful pile of medical books that he'd buried his nose in for the past several days.

At the stove, Gunda looked up from stirring a pot long enough for a cheery greeting. "*Guten Tag.* You and *mein Hausherr* have completed your work?"

"*Hausherr?* You mean Crandall?"

"*Ja.* It pleases him to be called 'master of the house.'" She chuckled and wiped her fat hands on her apron. "You will stay for supper?"

"I wish I could." Jessica sniffed appreciatively. The enticing aroma of braised meat made her mouth water. "Unfortunately, I still have a couple hours' work left at the office."

Gunda clucked reproachfully. "You work too hard."

"Now you sound like Devon."

The housekeeper's thick shoulders rotated in an unrepentant shrug. "Sometimes he is right."

Jessica smiled. "But not often?"

Gunda neither confirmed nor denied the observation. Instead, she offered a mischievous grin and returned her attention to the stove. "Devon took the books upstairs. He will be back soon."

After brief consideration, Jessica decided not to wait. "I'll see him later." She hefted her briefcase and headed toward the door, pausing to inspect a colorful abstract drawing that had been taped to the refrigerator. "Did your granddaughter do this?"

Gunda brightened. "It is good?"

"Very good," Jessica murmured. "From what I understand, many autistic children aren't able to focus their attention long enough to do this kind of work."

"It is the school. The teachers are so good with Katrina. Every day she learns more."

"Is this a new school?"

"*Ja.* Devon learned about it because he knows many people. I was afraid my Katrina would not be accepted. It was so expensive and I am not rich, but Devon said they had grants . . . from the government." Gunda slid a wary glance toward the doorway, then lowered her voice. "Devon does not know that I found out."

"Found out what?"

"The grants, they pay only so much. Someone must pay the difference."

Jessica was getting the idea. "Devon sends the rest of the money, doesn't he?"

Gunda nodded, then laid a finger against her lips. "He is embarrassed by his own generosity, so this must be our secret."

Bemused, Jessica shook her head. "If it's supposed to be a secret, why did you tell me?"

Gunda's blue eyes sparkled. "Because a woman should know such things about the man she loves."

## Chapter Thirteen

It was nearly 8:00 p.m. when Jessica hurried down the carpeted hallway with a bagful of steaming white cartons. As was her habit, she clutched her keys at the ready but wasn't surprised to find her condominium door unlocked. She'd given Devon a spare key a couple of days ago when she'd been late for their date and found him sitting outside her door like a lost puppy.

Now she was late again. Hopefully a peace offering of sweet-and-sour pork and *moo goo gai pan* would soothe his ruffled feathers.

She rushed through the condominium door, flushed and damp, flashing a smile of genuine delight at the lanky figure slumped across her sofa. "Hi! Have you been waiting long?"

Devon tossed a magazine on the coffee table. "Only two hours."

The tension in his voice caught her attention. She paused at the kitchen entrance, glancing warily over her shoulder. "I called Gunda. Didn't you get my message?"

"I got it. Another crisis, right?"

"During budget time, everything is a crisis." She slid the bag onto the counter then turned around as he followed her into the kitchen. "I'm sorry. I can see that you're annoyed and I don't blame you, but it's my job to get the work done."

"No matter what the cost?"

She propped a hip against the edge of the tile, scrutinizing his thoughtful expression. He didn't really look upset. He looked...well, unreadable. Whatever was going on inside his head was not being revealed by his hooded gaze. That made her nervous. "Crandall will be back at the office next week. He'll only be working half days, but that should still be a big help."

Devon nodded, an expressionless gesture that did little to ease her growing apprehension. He studied her face as though committing her features to memory, then reached out and caressed her cheek. As always, his touch sent a shiver of excitement down her spine. "You must be tired."

She was exhausted. "I feel fine."

"Hmm. Then those dark circles under your eyes must be a fashion statement."

"Absolutely. The panda look is all the rage nowadays. I think it has something to do with environmentalism." She figured that making light of her fatigue was worth a shot but wasn't surprised when Devon didn't so much as crack a smile.

Instead, he simply lifted her hand to his lips and spoke so seriously that he could have been announcing the end of life on earth. "Radiation and chemotherapy treatments can temporarily suppress the immune system. If you don't eat well and get plenty of rest, you could be at risk for secondary infection."

Jessica moaned, retrieved her hand and used it to massage her aching forehead. "I wish you'd throw those damn medical books in the trash. You're driving me crazy."

His crushed expression cut her to the quick. "I'm sorry."

She sighed, slid her arms around his waist and nestled her head against his warm chest. "I didn't mean to be so testy. I know you're concerned, but my immune system is just ducky and so is the rest of me. In fact, I was planning to tell you over celebratory chow mein but now it seems cruel to wait." She twisted her head to look up and couldn't suppress a radiant grin. "Frank called me at work."

Devon went stiff. "The test results . . . ?"

"They came in this morning. Everything is A-OK."

His entire body vibrated and his eyelids sagged shut as though weighted with lead. "Thank God," he murmured. When he opened his eyes, they were too bright, too moist. He laid his palm over her cheek, pressing her against his heart, and brushed a sweet kiss across her brow. "I knew everything would be fine."

She smiled. "Of course you did."

The room fell silent as they embraced. Jessica closed her eyes, listening to the comforting rhythm of his heartbeat and feeling so happy at that moment that she feared her own heart might burst from sheer joy.

When her stepfather had called with the wonderful news, Jessica's first thought had been of Devon. She'd wanted to dash out of the office and throw herself into his arms. Of course, she couldn't. She'd had responsibilities. But she'd wanted to see him so bad her teeth ached.

Now she wanted to share everything with him, every facet of her life—the tragedies and the triumphs, the exciting and the mundane. There was an almost spiritual bonding between them, a closeness she'd never experienced before and suspected she'd never have again. Before Devon, her life had been flat, perhaps even a little empty.

She hadn't known that at the time; in fact, she'd actually considered herself to be happy. The truth was that she'd been content. Real happiness, she'd discovered, was entirely different. It was an explosion in the blood, a lump in the throat, a trembling anticipation. It was a mental image etched in the mind. It was an exhilaration of the senses. It was love.

For the first time in her life, she knew the joy of love and understood why poets wrote odes to its poignancy. There was no emotion more powerful, more profound, more life-altering than this sweet metamorphosis of the soul.

The sensation was almost too glorious to endure. Jessica took a shuddering breath and reluctantly stepped back. "Our celebration dinner is getting cold."

Devon looked away, covering his face to stifle a strained cough, then he discreetly dabbed his eyes. "I'll, uh, just get things ready." He swept up the bag and commenced unloading various sized cartons onto the kitchen table. "This smells great," he said. "Should I break out the paper plates?"

"Heavens, no! This is a special occasion, remember?" She reached into the cupboard and pulled out two plain, stoneware dinner plates. "Use these. And there's some crystal stemware above the refrigerator."

"Wow. They aren't even chipped. We're really getting fancy tonight."

"Nothing but the best," she murmured, distracted by her search for the bottle of aspirin she usually kept in the pantry.

Behind her, Devon rustled through the silverware drawer. "Do we need a serving spoon for every carton?"

"Hmm? Oh, yes." She found the aspirin lurking behind a box of pancake mix. "You wouldn't want spicy Szechuan sauce spoiling the delicate flavor of steamed vegetables, would you?"

Devon shrugged, but dutifully counted out a half-dozen large spoons. "It doesn't matter to me. Everything ends up in the same place anyway."

"What an appetizing thought," she mumbled, shaking two pills into her palm. "You certainly know how to set the mood for fine dining."

"Well, if you're looking for mood, lead me to the candles— Wait a minute. What are those?"

Her hand froze on the water glass. Confused, she followed Devon's suspicious gaze to the twin tablets nestled in her hand. "They're just aspirin."

His brows knit into a furry bridge. "Are you sure you should be taking those?"

"Excuse me?"

"Aspirin might have a negative reaction to some of the other medications you're using."

She stared at him with undisguised astonishment. "It doesn't."

"Are you sure? Maybe you should wait until you can check it out with your doctor."

"This is a joke, right?" One look at his somber eyes convinced her that he was deadly serious. She swallowed an indignant response by reminding herself that he meant well. "I appreciate your concern," she said carefully. "But I can assure you that my doctor and I have already discussed this. Over-the-counter headache remedies are perfectly safe, okay?"

At the word *headache* his eyebrows arched halfway to his hairline. "Your head hurts? That could be symptomatic of—"

"For crying out loud, it's just a *headache*. People get them all the time, especially when they're being constantly aggravated by overprotective worrywarts!"

He blinked pitifully. "You think I'm a worrywart?"

"One of the world's biggest." Her pained sigh evolved into a low chuckle. "It must be an inherited thing. I thought

Crandall was bad but you make him look positively apathetic."

Devon managed a smile, although he was still staring at her as if collapse were imminent. "What does my father have to do with anything?"

"During the weeks after my surgery, he called about six times a day. If, God forbid, he got the answering machine, he went apoplectic. Once I dragged myself out of the most delicious bath to find him pounding on my door and screaming at one of my neighbors to call 911." In retrospect, Jessica secretly admitted that the incident had not been without a certain amount of comic value even though she'd been mortified at the time.

Devon, however, seemed more astounded than amused. "I can't picture my father reacting like that."

"Why not? He worries about you constantly. Two years ago when you showed up on crutches—" The words broke abruptly as she recalled the horrible wound in his right calf. "That was the Ethiopian shrapnel wound, wasn't it?"

After acknowledging that it was, he guided her back to the original subject. "You were saying something about two years ago."

"Oh, yes. Anyway, he was so distraught over your injuries that he considered hiring a platoon of mercenaries to pluck you off the battlefield and whisk you off for deprogramming."

*"Deprogramming?"*

"Sure. As far as Crandall was concerned, anyone who suffered that much grief catering to the public's prurient need to read about death and destruction must have been brainwashed." When his eyes clouded, Jessica laid a reassuring hand on his arm. "When your father said those things, he wasn't diminishing the importance of your work. It was a cry of frustration and of fear. Can't you understand? He was afraid because he loves you."

As Devon stared blankly, Jessica feared he hadn't heard a single word. Then all of a sudden a soft glow illuminated his eyes and an expression of wonder crossed his face. He touched her throat, then swept the tip of his index finger upward until it settled beneath her chin. "Yes," he murmured, tilting her face up. "I understand. Do you?"

For a moment, the meaning of that cryptic question escaped her. Comprehension dawned slowly, although she barely dared to recognize the joyous leap of her heart. Devon seemed to be comparing the motive for his own overzealous concern to that of his father, implying that both were motivated by love. Could it be true? Was Devon trying to say that he loved her? Or had she completely misunderstood his meaning?

Before her buzzing brain cleared enough to respond, Devon plucked the aspirin from her palm and dropped the tablets on the counter. "You won't be needing these," he told her. "I have a much better remedy for headaches."

"What's that?"

He kissed the corner of her mouth, his fingers kneading delicious circles around her tight shoulder muscles. "It starts with a full body massage."

"Hmm-m-m." She closed her eyes, rolling her head to take advantage of the relaxing sensation. "And how does it end?"

"That's the best part," he whispered. Then he swept her into his arms and carried her to bed.


Devon peered into a small carton, poking the contents with a spoon. "Do you want any more of this noodly stuff?"

Groaning, Jessica pushed away from the table. "If I take another bite of anything I'll explode."

"Are you sure?"

"I've never been more sure of anything in my life." She stood, indulged in a luxurious stretch, and automatically began clearing the table.

Devon put down the carton and took the plates from her hands. "I'll do that. You go put your feet up."

She gave a quizzical laugh. "Is there anything in particular I should put them up on?"

He shrugged. "The sofa, the coffee table, the bed... anything that makes you comfortable."

"Ah. Well at the moment, I think I'll just leave them on the floor until the kitchen is cleaned up." She scooped the utensils off the table, along with the stemware and headed toward the dishwasher.

Devon followed, carrying the plates. "How's your headache?"

She smiled, still tingling from the afterglow of lovemaking. "What headache?"

"See? I told you. The Monroe remedy has never failed." He puffed his chest, looking exceptionally pleased with himself.

"Oh, really?" She stuffed the spoons in the dishwasher's silverware basket then straightened, propping her hands indignantly on her hips. "And just how many times have you used it?"

Avoiding her gaze, he busied himself by arranging the plates on the rack and murmured an unintelligible response.

Her fingernails impatiently tapped the tile counter. "I didn't quite catch that."

He cleared his throat and straightened. "Just once," he confessed. "But since it worked, that means it's never failed, right?"

His sheepish grin melted her heart. All she could do was shake her head and chuckle. "Remind me never to challenge you to a duel of semantics." The final word was barely out of her mouth before she was overcome by a yawn.

"Looks like you've about had it," Devon remarked.

"Umm." She yawned again, then rubbed her face with her hands. "I'd probably better turn in pretty soon. I have an early meeting tomorrow."

A peculiar expression clouded Devon's eyes. He closed the dishwasher, pursed his lips and stared blankly at the floor.

She frowned. "Is something wrong?"

"Hmm?" He glanced up, his gaze still clouded. "I was just thinking that since you've been working so hard, some time off would do you good."

After reminding him that she'd already taken over ten weeks off this year, she brightened and added, "But if you're in the mood for a weekend getaway, why don't we go back up the mountain and see if Bill will rent us another motorcycle? Maybe we could get two this time because I'd love to learn how to ride one by myself—"

"Good Lord, no! I mean..." He rubbed his eyelids, then dropped his hands to his side with an exaggerated sigh. "I was hoping for something longer than a weekend."

"A vacation? How wonderful!" Visions of Maui and Aspen floated through her mind. She wistfully imagined the two of them lounging on a sunny beach or swooshing down the slopes toward a cozy lodge fireplace. It would be glorious, the adventure of a lifetime. Unfortunately, it would have to wait. "It'll be months before I have more vacation time accrued."

He covered a nervous cough. "I wasn't exactly thinking about a vacation, either."

Something about his somber expression put her on guard. "So what, exactly, were you thinking about?"

He tried for a nonchalant shrug that didn't quite make it. "Something longer than a vacation."

"Are you talking about a sabbatical?"

"That's closer to what I had in mind."

She folded her arms, bewildered and increasingly concerned about the direction this conversation was taking. "Spit it out, Devon. Say what you mean."

He stuffed one hand in his slacks pocket and rubbed his chin with the other. Finally, he took a deep breath and blurted, "I think you should quit your job."

Obviously, she'd misheard. She blinked, rubbed her ear, and blinked again. "Would you repeat that?"

He did, this time adding a rushed sales pitch. "Imagine being able to sleep as late as you want, then spending the entire day reading or gardening or... or doing needlepoint. You could do anything you want, go anywhere you want, to the beach or the park or the shopping mall—"

"Where all my checks would bounce because I'd be stone-cold broke!" Jessica was so astounded by Devon's ludicrous suggestion that she couldn't believe he was actually serious. "Even if I could afford to be a lady of leisure—which I most certainly can't—my favorite reading is the Wall Street Journal, I hate needlepoint and as far as gardening goes, I'm probably the only person on earth who can kill a cactus."

Waving away her protests, Devon pressed on. "What about volunteer work? The point is that you'll finally have the time to do the things you enjoy."

"I *enjoy* my *work*. Oh, this is absurd. I don't even know why we're wasting time talking about it." Tossing up her hands, Jessica brushed by him and marched into the living room with Devon right on her heels.

"We're talking about it because it's important," he insisted. "Look at you. You're exhausted and you've got every right to be. You've been through hell." He took her shoulders, turning her to face him. "I want to help you."

"How? By telling me to sit on my lazy bottom until I go bankrupt?"

"That's not going to happen. I have enough money for both of us."

Jessica sucked in a sharp breath and went rigid.

"I've got it all figured out," Devon told her. "I can cover your condo mortgage and basic living expenses out of my salary. For the medical costs, I can draw down my deferred-compensation account— Why are you looking at me like that?"

Jessica pulled away, exhaling all at once. Her lungs ached. The room was spinning. She licked her lips, holding up a warning hand when he reached out. "How do you know what my mortgage payments are?"

He flexed his fingers and returned his extended hand to his side. "I made a few telephone calls."

"Using your journalistic credentials, no doubt." Jessica was too stunned to be angry. "Why didn't you just riffle through my bank statements, or even better, confiscate a copy of my federal tax forms? No... don't tell me. You've already done both of those things, right?"

"Of course not," he said miserably. "Look, I know I might have been out of line—"

"*Might* have been?"

"All right, I admit it. I violated your privacy and I apologize, but I had to make sure I could handle the payments."

"You're really serious," she murmured. "You actually want me to quit my job and take money from you."

"It makes sense, Jessica. You'll have time to recover, get your strength back."

"I see. And where will you be while I'm doing all this... recovering?" The truth in his eyes sliced her like a blade. "You don't know where you'll be, do you? Maybe Europe, maybe Africa, or maybe there will be a lovely little war somewhere in Asia. It doesn't really matter. The point is that you'll be off somewhere."

Unable to look at him, she turned away, rubbing her upper arms. Humiliation settled over her like an icy cloud, seeping into her bones, squeezing bitter tears from beneath her quivering eyelids. She felt like a fool.

Days ago when Devon had spoken of his travels, Jessica had caught the weariness in his voice and his unspoken distaste at being a neutral observer of other people's misery. She'd honestly believed that he was considering a career move and had allowed herself to hope they might actually have a future together. Despite the fact that he'd never spoken the words, Jessica had thought that Devon loved her. The realization that she'd evidently confused love with pity made her ill.

She stiffened her spine, determined to conceal her pain. "Have you given any thought as to whether this generous financial support would be tax deductible?" As he silently grappled with the curious question, she shot a quelling look over her shoulder. "I'm just wondering whether I'd be one of your legitimate charities or just a common mistress."

He went white. "You know better than that."

"Do I? Ah, well, no matter. The answer is no in either case." She made a production of glancing at her watch. "Now, if you'll excuse me, I have some figures to prepare for tomorrow's meeting."

As she turned, Devon pivoted to block her way. "Look, I don't know what to say except that I'm sorry. When the idea first occurred to me, I should have been up front with you right away. Okay, I blew it big-time but I just wanted to make things easier for you." When she didn't respond, he raked his hair in frustration. "I never meant to make you angry."

Unfortunately, Jessica wasn't angry. She wanted to be; in fact, she wanted to be furious that Devon considered her to be as needy as poor little Katrina. The problem was that she was too hurt to be mad and besides, she knew that Devon's intentions were as sincere now as they'd been with Gunda's disabled grandchild.

The last thing Jessica wanted, however, was sincere intentions. She wanted Devon's heart and that, apparently, was something with which he wasn't willing to part.

She faced him with as much dignity as she could muster. "Come to think of it, I'd like to make things easier for you, too. After all, you have more scars than I do and your job is a heck of a lot more dangerous. How about turning in your resignation and letting *me* take care of *you?*"

He sighed, shifted his hands to his hips and stared at the floor.

"I'm serious, Devon. And it wouldn't be charity, either. Heaven knows I could use a housekeeper and since you can load a dishwasher with the best of them, I figure you could earn your keep and then some." She aimed a soft punch at his bicep. "So whatdaya say, bud? Have we got a deal here or what?"

He absently rubbed the back of his neck. "Enough already. I get the message."

She let the phony smile fade away. "Good. Then we understand each other. Now, it really is quite late and as you've pointed out, I'm tired."

He looked up woefully. "You want me to leave?"

In response, she undraped his jacket from the arm of the chair and handed it to him. "Good night, Devon."

For a moment, he simply stared at the jacket, absently fingering the ribbed collar. Then flipped it over his shoulder and looked her square in the eye. "I'll see you tomorrow," he said. A moment later, he was gone.

Jessica was alone again. And she couldn't suppress the ominous feeling that tomorrow might never come.

Sunlight sprayed into the expansive parlor with blinding intensity. It should have been a cheerful sight; instead, it was a chilling reminder that the afternoon was waning. The day was nearly gone. The final day. A day without Jessica.

From what seemed a great distance Devon heard an intermittent beeping sound. It was annoying, rather like the frantic buzz of insects in a bottle. He vaguely realized that the raspy disconnect warning was emanating from the telephone receiver clutched in his hand. He hung up the phone. The sound stopped.

Devon slouched back in his chair, covered his face with his hands and replayed what had happened last night in his mind. He still couldn't figure out exactly what had gone wrong. He understood that because of his clumsiness, Jessica had misinterpreted his suggestion that she quit her job. He could understand her indignation. But he couldn't for the life of him understand the sudden distance in her eyes, the coolness in her voice.

Perhaps she'd recognized his peculiar desperation and been frightened by it. Of so, he couldn't begrudge that fear. His desperation scared him, too, because the woman he loved was being stalked by a hidden danger, an invisible foe that Devon had been helpless to challenge.

All of a sudden, he'd had the horrible sensation of cringing in bushes, of still being a powerless prisoner of his own indecision. Images and emotions had been all jumbled up in his mind. He'd been compelled to do *something*. So he'd come up with a grandiose scheme that made her feel like catalog merchandise and made him seem like an insensitive cad.

He groaned and pinched the bridge of his nose. Apparently he *did* know what had gone wrong. But now there was no way to fix it.

"I thought I heard the telephone."

Startled, Devon straightened and saw his father standing in the doorway. "Yes."

Crandall scrutinized his son's sober expression and apparently didn't like what he saw. The older man's complexion paled, his eyes dulled, his lips compressed into a thin line. "It's time, isn't it?"

Devon stared past the cheery sunbeams spilling through the window. "Yes," he whispered. "It's time."

With the television droning in the background, Jessica took her dinner—a bowl of soup and some buttered toast—to the kitchen table. She sat wearily, propped her elbows on the table and stared into the bowl, noticing its contents for the first time. It was tomato soup. She detested tomato soup.

But in her current mental fog, one can had looked pretty much like another, and besides, food was food. Since her only goal at this point was simply to keep the body fueled, she sipped a spoonful without paying attention to the flavor.

It had been such a long day, probably because she'd spent so much of it trying not to cry. She'd tried to tell herself that the disagreement she and Devon had last night wasn't the end of the world, and that a single argument didn't necessarily indicate the end of a relationship. Unfortunately, she hadn't believed herself.

For the past weeks, she'd been blinded by love; last night, those blinders had been forcefully removed. Devon had wanted to assist her, to support her, to do anything and everything to help her through this difficult time in her life— a life he'd said nothing about wanting to share. The only conclusion Jessica could draw was that he was a kind and generous man who wanted to be her friend—a close, intimate friend, to be sure, but a friend nonetheless. Jessica wanted so much more. As one moody ballad had so aptly described, she loved him too much to ever start liking him.

With a pained sigh, she wrinkled her nose at the red liquid on her spoon and pushed the bowl aside. As she nibbled her toast, she glanced at the television and noticed that the news anchor seemed unusually tense. In the corner of the screen was a superimposed map of the Baltic territory that had been in dispute for several years. It was also the country where Devon had last been assigned.

She reached for the remote and turned up the volume. For the next ten minutes she was riveted to the screen by the worst of all possible news. The cease-fire had been broken. United Nations troops had been ambushed and nearly two dozen soldiers had been killed, along with a German film crew. Fighting had broken out along the border with a previously neutral country. Several other European nations were blustering with threats of war. The United States Congress was in an emergency session. The President was expected to make a statement, the subject of which was speculated to have grave national consequence.

It was a disaster, a crisis of global proportion, the most awful thing that could possibly happen. Until she heard the knock on her door and knew without doubt that things had just gone from bad to worse.

## Chapter Fourteen

One look at Devon's grim face confirmed Jessica's deepest fear. She sagged against the open door. "They're sending you back."

"Yes." He stood silently for a moment, as if measuring the extent of her sadness. "Can we talk?"

"Of course." She stepped back, continuing to use the door as a crutch while he entered the room. After the strength returned to her knees, she closed the door and clasped her shaking hands. "When are you leaving?"

"In a couple of hours."

The room lurched. She swallowed a gasp of dismay. By the time Devon had turned back toward the foyer, she'd managed to compose herself. "I guess this is goodbye."

"I hope not." He studied her for a long moment, then stuffed his hands into the pockets of the same fatigues he'd been wearing when Jessica had picked him up at the airport.

That had been less than a month ago. It seemed like a lifetime. During those precious weeks, Jessica had peeled away his veneer of rumpled apathy and glimpsed the sensitive soul he'd taken such pains to conceal. She'd seen his vulnerability, been touched by his tender heart; already that image was fading.

This unfamiliar man, with his rigid stance and shuttered gaze, bore little resemblance to the gentle lover to whom she'd given her heart. Now the adventurer was back, the reckless vagabond cloaked in khaki. She knew that the man she loved was still in there, buried beneath layers of camouflage and pockets bulging with survival gear; but she couldn't help but wonder if she'd ever see him again.

"Jessica?"

She looked up and saw the fleeting softness in his eyes before he glanced away. When his gaze returned, it was flat and unreadable.

"This won't be forever," he said firmly. "I'll be back."

"When?"

"I don't know." His shadowed jaw tightened. "I can't ask you to wait."

He didn't have to. She had no choice. No one could ever take Devon's place in her heart. She loved him, plain and simple, yet it was a love she dared not express. He was, among other things, a man of honor. If she asked him to stay, he would. But at what cost? She'd be asking him to give up the career that was his life, an integral part of who he was. Even if Devon did love her—and she was acutely aware that he'd never uttered that word—how could she ask such a sacrifice? The answer was clear. She couldn't ask.

So she lifted her chin, silently vowing to endure this loss as she'd endured the other tragedies of her life—stoically, silently and alone. "Crandall knows, of course."

"Yes."

"How is he handling it?"

After careful consideration, Devon chose a cautious response. "We've talked. He understands."

Jessica doubted that. "Acceptance isn't the same as understanding."

"No." His hands emerged from his pockets, fingers flexing as he took a step forward. For a moment, she thought he would reach out but he didn't. Instead, he crossed his arms as if to ward off the temptation. "What about you, Jessica? Do you understand or merely accept?"

She started to say "both" but that wasn't true. Since he'd requested honesty, she offered it. "I don't understand your compulsive need for danger."

"It's my job."

"Reporting events is your job. We both know you go far beyond that. Your trademark is taking unnecessary risks, throwing yourself into the fray and gambling with your life as though it had no meaning to you." Her voice broke. She blinked away a blur of tears but not before she saw his stunned expression. She ducked her head, certain that if she looked at him, she'd never be able to choke out her final, poignant plea. "Dying is easy, Devon. It's living that's hard. Please, before you charge into a hail of bullets, think about the people who love you. Your life has meaning to them."

She stood there, crying quietly, wanting to be brave yet unable to stem the tide of silent tears. Seconds ticked by. The distance between them seemed an unbridgeable chasm. Jessica wanted to embrace him, to kiss his beloved face and beg him to stay with her forever. But when she felt his warm arms surround her, all she could do was press her wet cheek against his chest and sob.

He touched his chin to the top of her head. "I'll write."

"I'll write, too."

"You take care of yourself, okay? Eat right, get plenty of rest and don't forget to take your medicine."

Sniffing, she stepped back. "I'll be fine."

"I know." He stroked a knuckle under her chin, then tipped her head back and took her lips in a slow, sweet kiss.

He released her slowly, took a shuddering breath, then stepped away and went reluctantly to the front door. She spun and reached out. Their fingers touched. "Stay safe," she whispered.

"Stay well," he said softly. And then he was gone.

Hours later, Devon stared out the airplane window, lulled by the droning jet engine and the rhythmic sighs of his slumbering seat mate. Far below, the North Atlantic sea was shrouded in melancholy blackness. Inside, the cabin was dimly illuminated by reading lights above the few hardy souls who, like himself, were unable or unwilling to sleep.

Unlike those fellow passengers, however, Devon wasn't engrossed in a good book. He was preoccupied with a gut-wrenching search of his own tormented soul.

*Dying is easy. It's living that's hard.*

The simple statement exploded like a mortar in his mind. Jessica had practically accused him of being suicidal, which most certainly wasn't true. Devon had never wanted to die; he simply wanted others to live. He'd done foolish things, yes. He'd done dangerous things, but always in an attempt to save a life. Tommy's life.

Devon squeezed his eyes shut trying to shake off the haunting image of young Tommy Murdock. Because he'd done nothing, Tommy was gone. For twenty years Devon had been trying to atone for that paralysis of fear and indecision; he'd never been able to pass an accident without stopping to help, or view danger without attempting a rescue.

In retrospect, he realized that during such times, his own safety had never been a consideration. But then risking one's life was not a particularly courageous act when that life wasn't regarded in high esteem.

Devon's eyes sprang open as the unexpected thought sent a chill down his spine. Could it be true? Was there a dark place deep inside him that considered his own life as less worthy than that of others? Had he been subconsciously courting the final escape of death in some kind of vain attempt to resurrect his lost friend?

Man, that was heavy stuff. If any part of it was true, then Jessica's perception had been more accurate than he dared admit. That scared the spit out of him.

Jessica tossed her keys on the table, flipped on the television and spread the newspaper out on the coffee table. With one eye on the TV, she thumbed the remote until a news channel appeared, then zoomed up the volume and concentrated on scanning the front page of the paper.

The headlines were frightening. Cities under siege. Refugees streaming toward the borders. Hospitals overrun with wounded civilians. And while an entire country was gutted, politicians met on neutral ground congratulating themselves on having established bureaucratic rules for the carnage. Business as usual in a crazy, mixed-up world. For Jessica, it was the most terrifying time of her life. Somewhere in the midst of that deadly chaos was the man she loved.

With her heart in her throat she scanned each article searching for a name, a byline, a subtle hint of where Devon might be. She found mention of a hotel where some journalists were staying. The place had been bombed, but no one had been hurt. An airport had been closed by sniper fire. Again, no casualties.

Jessica's racing heart slowly returned to normal. Any extraordinary occurrence involving one of the Associated Press's Pulitzer prize reporters would have been big news. Since nothing had been mentioned, she convinced herself that as of this moment, Devon must certainly be all right.

She sighed, slouched down and draped her head over the back of the sofa. Two days. Devon had been away for only two days. They'd been the longest days of her life. She bitterly regretted not having asked him, begged him to stay. Eventually he would have resented that request—perhaps even despised her for having made it—but at least he would have been safe. Miserable, but safe.

But it was too late now. Devon had made his choice and Jessica had to live with it. She could only pray that it was a choice that he, too, could live with.

A glance at the dashboard clock confirmed that Jessica had less than fifteen minutes before the five p.m. news. She tapped the steering wheel, glaring at the red light as though impatience could rush the timed cycle, then pressed the accelerator the moment it flickered to green.

By the time she pulled into the parking garage, there was barely five minutes to spare. She was out of the car before the engine's final shudder. After dragging her dry cleaning out of the back, she tucked the afternoon newspapers under her arm and rushed to the stairs because she didn't want to wait for a poky elevator.

Puffing hard, she burst into her corridor and zipped down the hallway with the plastic-wrapped garments flapping over her shoulder like cellophane wings. The moment her key hit the lock, the door flopped open. She froze, wondering how she could have forgotten something as basic as locking her front door. Of course she'd been so emotionally distracted lately that nothing she did, or didn't do, would surprise her. Still, she was extra cautious.

With her wary gaze focused beyond the entry area into the living room, she took two steps and nearly tripped over a lumpy canvas duffel just inside the doorway. As she stared down at the familiar bag, her mind went numb. For a moment, she thought she was hallucinating.

The clinking sound in the kitchen, however, was definitely not her imagination. She stood there like a stupid statue as a man dressed in civilian clothes emerged carrying a jar of spaghetti sauce.

"You're home early," he said. "Do you think this stuff would be okay on macaroni? That's all I could find in the pantry."

She swayed, barely aware that her freshly cleaned clothes had slithered into a crumpled heap at her feet.

"I can tell by the look on your face that you're wondering what I'm doing here." Devon set the jar on the table, avoiding her stunned gaze by staring at the sauce as if expecting it to rise up and fly. "Well, the thing is, a funny thing happened on my way to the war. When I got to Germany, I realized that I'd forgotten to return your key. Now, I sure as hell wouldn't want the key to *my* place floating around Europe, so I figured I'd better return it so you wouldn't, you know, be worried."

Tears pricked her eyes but she was still rooted in place unable to move, barely able to breathe. He was alive. He was here. He was home. She wanted to scream her joy, to dash into his arms and run her fingertips over every inch of his body to make sure that this wasn't just a glorious dream. But she couldn't feel her feet and her tongue had glued itself to the roof of her mouth.

Evidently misreading her silence, Devon jammed his hands in his slacks pockets and angled a dejected glance in her direction. "Maybe I should have mailed the key. I mean, if you've made other plans or something—"

"Devon!" Jessica barely recognized the raspy croak as her own voice. Half blinded by tears, she managed to open her arms and sob his name again.

In a heartbeat he was there, embracing her, kissing her face, his breath warm against her moist cheek. He murmured her name as though it were a prayer, then explored her face with his fingertips, stroking every curve, every crease.

While his thumb tested the softness of her lips, she frantically returned the intense inspection, probing through the thin fabric of his shirt for the telltale bulge of bandages. "Have you been hurt? Is that why they sent you back?"

"No." He gently grasped her wrists, kissing each hand before pressing them to his chest. "I wasn't sent back, Jessica. I refused the assignment."

She searched his eyes. "But I thought that your job, your career was the most important thing in your life."

"I thought so, too. I was wrong."

"I don't understand."

He sighed. "I'm not sure I do, either. All I know is that I've spent my entire life searching for...something. When I was on the plane, I suddenly realized what that something was and I knew that I'd already found it."

"What was it that you'd found?"

"It'd take me half the night to find the words to describe it."

Jessica took his hand and led him to the sofa. "I have all the time in the world."

They settled onto the cushions, knees touching, fingers entwined. Devon stared at their tangled hands for a moment, then spoke softly. "Over these past weeks, my father and I have gotten to know each other. For the first time in our lives, we've really talked to each other and do you know what? We're so much alike it's frightening."

Jessica smiled. "What led you to that conclusion?"

"There were a lot of little things, I guess. For instance, we both like Hawaiian pizza."

She emitted a startled laugh. "Pizza?"

"*Hawaiian* pizza," he admonished. "There aren't that many people who can tolerate a marriage of pineapple and pepperoni smothered in pizza sauce."

"Yes, well, I can see how that would create a profound emotional bond."

"There were a few other things, too."

"I should hope so." She studied his wistful expression. "Tell me about them."

"Well, let's see. It's kind of unique that we both talk in circles to avoid betraying our feelings. But that wasn't what really got to me." He paused, drifting back in his mind to capture the memory. "When I was a kid, I always resented Dad's business because it was more important to him than I was. Then I grew up and found myself doing the same thing. It seems that we've both been using work to isolate ourselves, but I never used to understand why."

"And now you do?"

"Yes," he whispered. "Now I do."

When he fell silent, Jessica held back the urge to pressure him into revealing more details. Whatever he'd learned obviously had been pivotal in the decisions he'd made, decisions that had monumental consequence in the direction his life would now take. She swallowed her desperation, waiting, hoping he'd share that crucial information with her.

"Has my father ever told you about my mother?" he asked suddenly.

"No. As a matter of fact, I don't even recall him ever mentioning her."

That information didn't seem to surprise Devon. "He never mentioned her to me, either. At least, not until a couple of weeks ago." There was a faraway look in his eyes. "She was a champion skier. I never knew that. My father told me that they met on the slopes and fell madly in love."

The image of the staid and stoic Crandall Monroe being madly in love with anyone was startling, to say the least. Still, Jessica managed to maintain an even expression. "That sounds very romantic."

"Yeah, it does, doesn't it?" He smiled. "Dad tells me that I look like her."

"Then she must have been very beautiful." When he hiked a brow, she hastened to explain. "I wasn't implying that you're beautiful. I mean, you're very good-looking, of course, but—" Interrupted by his amused chuckle, Jessica decided on a judicious retreat. "So what else did you find out about your mother?"

"That she and my father were very happy until I came along."

An ominous tingling sensation slid along her nape. "What happened then?"

The amused twinkle faded from his eyes and his lips settled into a grim line. "I killed her."

Jessica gasped. *"What?"*

"My mother died in childbirth," he said quietly. "I knew about that because Aunt Emmaline took great glee in telling me and reminding me that my father blamed me for her death. Now I realize that wasn't true, that in fact he blamed himself because he'd been the one who'd wanted to start a family."

"Oh my God." Jessica could only imagine how that devastating loss must have shattered the fragile family. Every time Crandall had looked at his young son, he must have been torn apart by guilt and grief. And Devon had been just a child, unable to understand anything except the pain of his father's rejection.

Jessica had often wondered why Crandall never remarried, particularly since there'd always been a bevy of lurking women, each hoping for more than a disinterested glance. Most had been disappointed; others had found fleeting favor, although Jessica had never even known Crandall to have anything remotely resembling a meaningful relationship. Now she understood that he'd buried himself in work to insulate himself from another devastating emotional loss. And like a dutiful son, Devon had followed in his father's footsteps.

"After all these years, how did you finally discover that Crandall had blamed himself?" she asked.

"He told me." Shrugging off her astonished stare, Devon added, "I know that seems incomprehensible, but for the first time since I can remember, my father and I actually had an honest conversation about things that really mattered. And it was all because of you."

"Me?" She straightened. "What on earth did I have to do with it?"

"You're an incorrigible nag, that's what. You were always in my face, bombarding me with affirmations on the importance of family and reminding me that fathers aren't immortal. I'll admit I didn't come around all at once, but once you planted the idea, I was forced to rethink my priorities."

"Is that why you refused your assignment, because you wanted to reestablish a relationship with your father?"

"Partly, I suppose." He absently tapped the back of the sofa. "But you were the main reason."

Jessica's heart skipped a beat. She swallowed hard, moistened her lips and tried to speak without stammering. "M-me?"

He looked away, seeming torn by something she couldn't quite fathom. Before she could speak, he turned toward her, eyes glowing softly, and stroked his knuckles across her cheek. "I love you, Jessie. You have to know that by now."

"I..." She touched his palm, pressing the back of his hand against her face. "I thought you did. I prayed that you did but I wasn't sure."

"Be sure," he murmured. "Because I will never in my life love anyone the way that I love you."

The words settled like sweet honey in her heart. For a moment, she was struck mute by a surging rush of emotion. Surely no one had a right to experience such elation, such aching joy. She nuzzled the back of his hand, kissing each roughened knuckle, thrilled by the soft tickle of tiny hairs brushing her sensitive skin.

After a moment, she tested her voice. "I think that I fell in love with you at the creek, when you courageously risked your life to save a stranger, but it might have happened the night you told me about your childhood and I saw the pain in your eyes. The timing doesn't matter. What does matter is that you are one of the finest men that I've ever known. I love you, Devon Monroe. I will always love you."

He withdrew slowly, extracting his hand from her loving grasp. Turning away, he stared across the room with blank features and eyes filled with torment. "Nothing about me is courageous, Jessica."

"What are you talking about?"

The haunted look on his face scared her half to death. "I've spent a lifetime trying to prove that I'm not a coward. The truth is, that's exactly what I am."

It took a moment for her to catch her breath. "That's ridiculous."

"It's true. You don't know..." The words trailed off as he stared into space. After a moment, he spoke in a voice thick with emotion. "I told you that when I was young, I spent time in a juvenile detention facility."

"Yes, I remember. It was called Blackthorn Hall, wasn't it?"

"Hmm? Yes. Blackthorn Hall."

"That's where you met the friends you told me about...let's see, Roberto Arroya and Larkin McKay. They were your roommates, weren't they?"

"Yes. But we had another roommate, too. His name was Tommy Murdock." Devon pursed his lips and studied his own flexing fingers. "Tommy's not with us anymore. I think you need to know why."

A stifling hush fell over the room. Jessica was afraid to breathe. For several long minutes, Devon sat silently, jaw twitching, eyes riveted somewhere in the past. Then he started to speak, so quietly at first that she could barely hear. He described Tommy's quick grin and infectious laugh and how the gutty little guy had struggled to keep up with stronger, healthier boys. Devon spoke with such affection and undisguised admiration, that Jessica was instantly engrossed in the story.

So engrossed, in fact, that Tommy became real to her. Sh
listened in rapt fascination, feeling as if she actually knev
the brash, ponytailed youngster. In her mind, she saw hi
crooked smile and heard his squeaky little giggle. She coul
envision young Tommy and his boisterous cohorts huddle
in the Hall's damp basement, sharing their secret dreams
their hopes for the future.

Then the mood changed. Devon's eyes dulled. Jessica'
heart thudded with dread. Slowly, methodically, Devon de
scribed that final basement meeting where the angry room
mates had voted on a foolish act of retribution—an act tha
would forever change the course of their young lives.

From that fateful moment, events had spiraled toward :
tragic destiny. By the time Devon revealed the disastrou
result, Jessica was in tears.

The dull monotone couldn't disguise the depth of hi
sorrow. "I never should have let them take Tommy away,'
he said. "If I'd just stepped out of those damned bushes
he'd still be alive."

It took a moment for Jessica to catch her breath. He
heart went out to Devon and to the other boys, who mus
also have been traumatized by having witnessed the trag
edy. But with compassion came understanding. For the firs
time, Jessica truly understood the complex nuance of Dev
on's secret torment, the feelings of failure and guilt tha
drove him to prove his worth over and over and over again

She also recognized the Tommy Murdock incident as th
source of the overprotective anxiety that Devon had dis
played toward her illness. Everything made perfect sens
now. His nomadic lifestyle hadn't been motivated by a thirs
for adventure, as she'd first believed; instead, it had been a
affirmation of courage and an escape through which he'
sidestepped a very real fear of emotional loss.

She placed a compassionate hand on his arm. "You can'
blame yourself."

"Why not? I was in charge. Tommy was my responsibil
ity. I'm to blame for what happened to him."

"No, you're not," she insisted. "It was an accident, a horrible, tragic accident."

"Which never would have happened if I'd only stepped forward and given myself up like a man."

"But you weren't a man, Devon. You were a little boy." Since his narrowed gaze indicated that was an argument he wasn't ready to accept, Jessica lifted her chin and switched tactics. "All right, then. If we concede that each of us bears lifetime responsibility for childhood mistakes, then my father's blood is still on my hands."

His head snapped up. "That's not true and you know it."

"Do I?" She weighed her next words carefully. "The last thing my father heard before he died was an expression of his own daughter's shame. I'm responsible for what I said. I'm responsible for the pain I caused him. Am I also responsible for his death?"

"Of course not." As his own pain melted into compassion, Devon anxiously took her hands. "You were just a child, Jessica. You can't—" His eyes widened.

"That's right," she whispered. "I was a child who made a childish mistake. You urged me to absolve my own childhood guilt and I did. Listen to me, Devon. That scared little boy in the bushes did the very best he could in a very bad situation. He has suffered enough and so have you."

He stiffened slowly, absorbing her words along with the alien concept of bestowing mercy on oneself. He'd never considered that before, never thought of himself as being worthy of self-forgiveness. For everyone else in the world, mistakes were allowable, even inevitable. But not for him. That paradox had somehow embedded itself in his brain and the cost had been dear.

Somewhere along the line, he'd confused cowardice with courage but it was Jessica who'd had shown real bravery by confronting life's hardships with grit and determination. In the face of such strength and compassion, Devon could offer nothing less.

Jessica's sweet voice captured his attention. "What are you thinking?"

He regarded her somberly. "I was just wondering if your job offer was still good."

That was apparently not the response she'd expected. "You want to be my housekeeper?"

"No. I want to be your husband. Unfortunately, I find myself temporarily unemployed and until that situation can be remedied, I thought I'd take you up on your offer." He angled a wary glance and saw her chin sag in astonishment. "If that's all right with you, of course."

"Did you just ask me to marry you?"

"I think so." He cleared his throat. "But you don't have to answer now. I mean, it's a big step. I'm sure you'll want time to think abou—"

"Yes."

He blinked. "Excuse me?"

"I love you, Devon Monroe. I want to be your wife." As he eagerly reached out, Jessica held up a restraining hand. "But there are conditions."

He swallowed hard. "Name them."

"First, I know how much your work means to you. You're good at what you do and before the ink is dry on your resignation, every newspaper in the country is going to be pounding down the door." She paused, biting her lower lip to still its quivering. "I won't stand in the way of your career but I won't be left behind, either. I want to know that when major decisions about our lives are to be made, we'll make them together."

"Marriage is a partnership. Partners have equal votes." God, he wanted to hug her until she squeaked. "Are there any other conditions?"

"Just one." Her eyes filled with happy tears. "Promise me forever."

With a ragged cry, he succumbed to his need and swept her in his arms. As he did, the quagmire of past fears melted away.

By admitting that bravery lies not in the willingness to die but in the tenacity to live, Devon could finally accept love and forgive the frightened twelve-year-old who'd once cowered in the bushes. Now he could make that commitment to Jessica and to their future. He could promise forever.

For Devon Monroe, Blackthorn's dark legacy was over.

\* \* \* \* \*

*Watch for THE AVENGER, the next book in Diana Whitney's exciting Blackthorn Brotherhood miniseries—coming in the fall of 1995.*

Get Ready to be Swept Away by
Silhouette's Spring Collection

# Abduction
## *Seduction*

These passion-filled stories explore both the dangerous
desires of men and the seductive powers of women.
Written by three of our most celebrated authors, they are
sure to capture your hearts.

**Diana Palmer**
Brings us a spin-off of her Long, Tall Texans series

**Joan Johnston**
Crafts a beguiling Western romance

**Rebecca Brandewyne**
*New York Times* bestselling author
makes a smashing contemporary debut

Available in March at your favorite retail outlet.

ABSED

# Take 4 bestselling love stories FREE

## Plus get a FREE surprise gift!

## Special Limited-time Offer

**Mail to Silhouette Reader Service™**

3010 Walden Avenue
P.O. Box 1867
Buffalo, N.Y. 14269-1867

**YES!** Please send me 4 free Silhouette Special Edition® novels and my free surprise gift. Then send me 6 brand-new novels every month, which I will receive months before they appear in bookstores. Bill me at the low price of $2.89 each plus 25¢ delivery and applicable sales tax, if any.* That's the complete price and—compared to the cover prices of $3.50 each—quite a bargain! I understand that accepting the books and gift places me under no obligation ever to buy any books. I can always return a shipment and cancel at any time. Even if I never buy another book from Silhouette, the 4 free books and the surprise gift are mine to keep forever.

235 BPA ANRQ

| | | |
|---|---|---|
| Name | (PLEASE PRINT) | |
| Address | Apt. No. | |
| City | State | Zip |

This offer is limited to one order per household and not valid to present Silhouette Special Edition® subscribers. *Terms and prices are subject to change without notice. Sales tax applicable in N.Y.

USPED-94R                                    ©1990 Harlequin Enterprises Limited

## SAME TIME, NEXT YEAR
### Debbie Macomber
(SE #937, February)

Midnight, New Year's Eve...a magical night with
Summer Lawton that James Wilken knew could never
be enough. So he'd spontaneously asked her to meet
him again in exactly one year's time. Now that time
had come...and with it, a friendly reunion that was
quickly turning to love!

## Don't miss
**SAME TIME, NEXT YEAR,
by Debbie Macomber,
available in February!**

She's friend, wife, mother—she's you! And beside
each Special Woman stands a wonderfully
*special* man. It's a celebration of our heroines—
and the men who become part of their lives.

Don't miss **THAT SPECIAL WOMAN!** each month—
from some of your special authors! Only from
Silhouette Special Edition!

TSW295

*Silhouette*

SPECIAL EDITION ™®

# WHAT EVER HAPPENED TO...?

Have you been wondering when much-loved characters will finally get their own stories? Well, have we got a lineup for you! Silhouette Special Edition is proud to present a *Spin-off Spectacular!* Be sure to catch these exciting titles from some of your favorite authors:

*HUSBAND: SOME ASSEMBLY REQUIRED* (SE #931 January) Shawna Saunders has finally found Mr. Right in the dashing Murphy Pendleton, last seen in *Marie Ferrarella*'s BABY IN THE MIDDLE (SE #892).

*SAME TIME, NEXT YEAR* (SE #937 February) In this tie-in to *Debbie Macomber*'s popular series THOSE MANNING MEN and THOSE MANNING SISTERS, a yearly reunion between friends suddenly has them in the marrying mood!

*A FAMILY HOME* (SE #938 February) Adam Cutler discovers the best reason for staying home is the love he's found with sweet-natured and sexy Lainey Bates in *Celeste Hamilton*'s follow-up to WHICH WAY IS HOME? (SE #897).

*JAKE'S MOUNTAIN* (SE #945 March) Jake Harris never met anyone as stubborn—or as alluring—as Dr. Maggie Matthews in *Christine Flynn*'s latest, a spin-off to WHEN MORNING COMES (SE #922).

Don't miss these wonderful titles, only for our readers—only from Silhouette Special Edition!

SPIN7

## SILHOUETTE SPECIAL EDITION BOOKS ARE MOVING!

Your favorite Silhouette Special Edition books have been available at your local retail store in the last two weeks of every month. Special Edition is moving!

Starting with February 1995 publications, Silhouette Special Edition books will be available two weeks earlier at your local retailer.

Look for all Special Edition titles in the first two weeks of every month, and happy reading!

### SILHOUETTE BOOKS—WHERE PASSION LIVES!

SSE-CYC95